PRAISE FOR *Mark of*

The technical aspects of crime fiction stories are often inaccurate, if not just plain wrong, and the plots recurring, unreal or both. Lincoln Cooper's novel, Mark of the White Rabbit, *is no such disappointment. The author builds an engaging plot, taking the reader down a series of seemingly unrelated rabbit holes, while sprinkling hints along the trail of a ruthless killer inviting the reader to connect the dots. I simply could not put down the book.*

—**J. TERRANCE DILLON**, *criminal trial lawyer and former Assistant U.S. Attorney for the Western District of Michigan*

Lincoln Cooper wastes no time plunging readers into the bloody deeds of an elusive, extremely clever serial killer for whom the white rabbit mentioned in the title is intimately connected to the killer's motivation and actions... Mark of the White Rabbit is an engaging read, one you can get into quickly after a few short chapters introducing several key players. Once in, you don't want to put the book down. While the serial killer's identity and narcissistic cleverness are of greatest interest, the author sprinkles some romance and social issues into the novel to add realism to an otherwise gruesome story. Cooper uses lots of dialogue to keep the story moving at a pace just fast enough for those who don't have time for... literary flourishes but yet manages to make his characters real and likable. Does the killer get caught in the end? Read it and find out! Quite enjoyable to say the least.

—**VIGA BOLAND**, *5-star review by for Reader's Favorite*

Readers are encouraged to go to www.MissionPointPress.com to contact the author or to find information on how to buy this book in bulk at a discounted rate.

MISSION POINT PRESS

Mission Point Press
2554 Chandler Road
Traverse City, Michigan 49696
www.MissionPointPress.com

ISBN: 978-1-954786-42-4
Library of Congress Control Number: 2021914412

Printed in the United States of America.

LINCOLN COOPER

Mark of the White Rabbit

MISSION POINT PRESS

Dedicated to my wife, Carol, who struck me with the thunderbolt, and inspired me to write.

"Murderers are not monsters, they're men.
And that's the most frightening thing about them."
    — Alice Sebold, *The Lovely Bones*

PROLOGUE

July 4, 1977. Southern Illinois.

*H*and in hand ahead of him, the teenaged girl and boy stumbled with every step, their breathing rushed by the dread of not knowing what would happen when they got to wherever the man was taking them. The moonless night slowed their progress, confounding direction. The man turned to look behind but could no longer see the van he had left by the side of the dirt road trailing off the state highway. The three had covered only a hundred yards or so, the muck sucking at their shoes with every step.

When they started out, the night was alive with the deafening racket of tree frogs, which cut to an eerie silence once they invaded the marsh. The man brushed away the sweat dripping from his forehead with the back of his arm; his shirt was soaked, and it stuck to his back. Slapping constantly at the voracious mosquitoes buzzing around his ears and face, he pinched his shirt collar between his fingers and pulled it away from his body to fan in some air.

Suddenly the dense thicket of reeds broke to reveal a clearing, and they stopped to stare at the dim outline of a small building. The man looked up at the levee to the south. Nothing moved, and he shoved the teens forward. The rusted hinges of the door screeched as he yanked it open. He jerked his head around. Once inside, it only took moments before his eyes adjusted to the blackness. Stale odors of dust, oil, and rot permeated the air. A few empty boxes and cans littered the floor. He grunted and pushed the pair to sit down. They promptly obeyed, feeling their way to the floor. The boy started speaking, but the man ordered him quiet with a loud shush. Bending down on one knee close to the girl, the man wondered if it was the faint scent of her perfume, or merely fear, that he smelled.

The boy abruptly sat up with a rush of courage and grabbed the man's arm, but he quickly swiped his hand away and shot the boy twice point-blank with the .22 pistol he had been carrying. The teen fell back against a card-board box in the corner. His gaping mouth formed a black sphere in his face, which appeared chalky, almost ghost-like. In a moment, the annoying gurgling stopped. The man could hardly make out the two small holes in the boy's forehead and cheek.

The girl had screamed loudly, but the shots ringing in the small space muted the sound. Now she made a whimpering noise, shaking uncontrollably, fearing what was coming. Sitting back on his haunches, he could sense her staring at him. He had chosen her because she was the favorite. The boy was just collateral—wrong place, wrong time. He waited until her moans subsided to mere quivering. After a prolonged stillness, he raised up straight, slowly pulled the large hunting knife from his belt, and held it by his side where she couldn't see.

CHAPTER 1

Friday, October 31, 2008. Western Michigan lakeshore.

Mitchell Quinn's four-wheeled banker's chair squeaked as he leaned back and crossed his new Texas boots on the worn desktop in his office at the Lakeview Village police station. Licking his thumb, he rubbed a smudge from the detailing on the right toe, relieved it wasn't a gash in the leather. For months he had hedged spending so much, until he read somewhere that the company had made a pair for Tommy Lee Jones. Watching the character Jones played in that movie about the small-town, West Texas sheriff felt like looking in a mirror twenty years into the future. He wondered if he would come to a similar end-of-the-road but with no real bad guys to chase down.

It was early. No staff yet. He stared at the stack of paperwork he had come in to do but knew he wouldn't; not that it would matter. Swiveling his chair around, he peered through the cracked window at the empty street, resenting that things would soon become even more tedious. At least during summer and early fall the lakeside resort drew huge crowds of vacationers and with them welcome relief from the routine. Winter typically held no such diversions.

Mitch slid his feet onto the floor, sat up, and reached for the wood-framed photograph of a blonde woman and towheaded boy, which sat on the corner of the desk. He set it down flat and slowly ran his fingers over the surface. Looking up, he panned the room, his eyes coming to rest upon the Rockwell calendar hanging next to the door—his mother's gift subscription from a Christmas past. A large red, marked circle stood out over today's date, along with the handwritten reminder "four years." He recommitted to a cemetery visit after work, but not to stopping by the office Halloween party at the Battery Bar later. Too many tempting demons, hopefully conquered. Then he balked, thinking it only appropriate for the chief to make an appearance, and that he might go and leave early.

Returning the frame to its place, Mitch stood and walked across the room to the trophy-laden shelves he had been meaning to clear out ever since his dad passed away. He stared at the state title trophy and removed the MVP ribbon draped over it. Laying it in his palm, he wondered what entreaties by his father managed to persuade the school board to display the trophy at the station, instead of in the case at the high school—a supposedly temporary concession, never remedied.

He replaced the ribbon and dropped his gaze to the middle shelf holding his red beret, special agent badge, and the citation from the Army's Criminal Investigation Command. Removing the commendation from its tiny easel, he crossed back to his desk. He rested the casing on its edge, pushed his chair back with his feet, and regarded the citation for a long moment, arms folding across his chest.

"Seek diligently to discover the truth, deterred not by fear nor by prejudice," he said to no one, repeating aloud the inscribed creed. He jerked at the sudden, loud bang of the back-hall door slamming shut.

"Hey Chief, that you?"

Deputy Martin "Willy" Willoughby barged into the office, as was his habit, waving as he passed by the window-wall between Mitch's office and the adjacent open room full of deputies' desks. The station occupied what was once the Lakeview Savings and Loan, which moved away years before after merging with a national bank. Believing the building a good fit for the police station, the township converted it, even keeping the large vault in a back room, which served well for secured storage of confiscated evidence and police-issue weapons.

Mitch sat up. "Yep. Just me, Willy. Thought I'd get in early and clear some of this paper off my desk."

Willy hung his hat on the wall rack by his desk and sauntered over to the open galley in the rear corner of the room, snatching his cup from the rack. "Got a lot more time now, huh chief? No stream of teens cruisin' the streets every night, like in summer. Our DUI count's droppin' right off the charts."

Mitch rose and walked around to join Willy at the coffee station. Looking down at the deputy, he recalled the first time he had seen him—one of five teens arrested for vandalizing vacant summer cottages. Willy had struggled to appear defiant, trying to impress his companions, but something about him smacked of desperation. When no parent attended his preliminary exam, a call upon the Willoughbys' revealed a household broken by financial destitution and alcohol abuse. Subsequent efforts to salvage the boy often seemed like pulling a drowning puppy from the water, only to be bitten for the kindness, but Mitch was now gratified that his persistence had paid off.

"So, you're saying you'll miss your speed trap at the bottom of that old bridge?"

Willy pulled the coffeepot from the brewer and clumsily over-poured his cup onto the countertop. Shaking hot coffee from his hand, he grabbed a rag hanging by the sink. "Well, I sure as heck don't like it when I nab a drunk driver and his lawyer gets him off. And then blames it on me. Last week the jury let that college boy go, and he'd been drinkin' for sure. That lawyer of his twisted things around like I did something wrong."

"I'm thinking you'd be smart to keep better calibration records, deputy. If you did, that defense counsel wouldn't have had such an easy go of it. Do your homework next time."

"Yeah, okay. You're right, Chief. But it still pisses me off. I had him, and it should have stuck."

"Next time, Willy. We'll just have to find something else for you to do now that things are slowing down."

"Like what?"

"Ha! Word is they're looking for a new dogcatcher over in West Village. Maybe you should apply."

Willy took a sip as he returned to his seat. "Yeah, right. But if the township board doesn't give us a raise for next year, I may have to."

"What the heck would you do with more money, Willy? You've got no one to spend it on but yourself, and you don't do anything when you're off-duty but watch TV and play video games." Mitch knew he was being unfairly critical, but he worried that Willy seemed to have no social life outside of the station, and he couldn't recall him ever having had a date.

"I'd get a motorcycle; a Harley maybe."

"Shoot, you'd probably wreck it in a week, or worse. If I can somehow talk the board into hiking our pay, don't go buying a Harley-Davidson." Mitch walked back to his office.

"Hey Chief! Since it's Halloween, maybe we'll have some action tonight. Remember that buncha high school kids who made all the trouble last year?"

"Yeah. Too bad they didn't stick with toilet paper. They did quite a bit of damage. Reminds me of someone I used to know." Willy frowned. "I think we can do without that kind of excitement. For now, what else is going on in our fair village?"

"Nothin' much yet. But I did see sumthin' pretty weird a little while ago."

Mitch raised his boots back to the desktop as he reached to grab the morning paper he had brought from home. "Oh, yeah? What was that?"

"Well, I was walking back from breakfast over at the Satellite, and I see this big, black pickup parked by the drugstore. It was one of those stretch four-by-fours with a hard canopy cover in back. It caught my eye because the side and back windows were all tinted out. Anyway, I tried to look inside, and I could barely see this huge crate in the back. It looked sorta like a big, uh…well, like a casket I guess."

Mitch peeked over the top of his paper. "A casket?"

"Yeah. But wait. That's not all. As I started to walk on by the front, right there on the passenger seat there was two of the biggest rabbits you ever saw. White ones."

Mitch broke into a broad grin. "Big white rabbits, huh? What the heck did you have for breakfast, Willy?"

"Honest, Chief, that's for sure what I saw. There were two of 'em." Willy vigorously scratched his crew cut. "Somebody must have something pretty weird goin' on over the weekend. I mean, man, this is Halloween, not Easter."

"Who knows? It was probably a breeder, or maybe..." Mitch lowered his voice. "Maybe it was just a traveling magician." Both laughed.

"Whatever it was you saw, Willy, it won't come to anything. Nothing of any real consequence ever happens in Lakeview." Mitch sighed as he returned to his paper.

CHAPTER 2

Same Day. Detroit.

"You've got to get rid of her, Lance," Harlan Milbank whispered to the trim, white-haired man in the Armani suit seated next to him. "I don't mean that literally, of course." The two of them sat among other Democratic Party notables at a ten-top table in the main dining room of the Detroit Athletic Club, a historic venue for the elite "who's who" dating back over one hundred years.

"She's a liability that could destroy your candidacy. Why add this distraction to what will already be a political brawl without it?"

Harley, as he was affectionately called by colleagues and political foes alike, blew a near-perfect smoke ring from his protruding lips and set his Cuban in the table's ashtray. When initially asked to steer Lawrence "Lance" Atwood's campaign, he already knew of Lance's reputation as a womanizer, but now he was seriously concerned that any publicity of his proclivities would quickly derail their prospects for success. Such scandal was exactly what the media craved, especially in the middle of what promised to be a hotly contested election.

"The Republicans will run the present attorney general. He's a real straight shooter…a family man. Publication of an affair would be blood in the water." Harley's chair moaned beneath his growing corpulence as he turned to his protégé and whispered, "Also…imagine how that would play out with Anne and the kids."

Atwood winced. His eyes focused on the attractive brunette sitting a few tables over. He knew she was an aide for the state congressman seated across from her, and he was contemplating how to maneuver an introduction.

"Are you even listening to what I'm saying, Lance?" Harley's pudgy fingers brushed back a few strands of his comb-over as he leaned closer.

Turning to Harley, Lance answered with a *tsk*. "Stop worrying, Harley. I've got it under control. I'll take care of things this weekend."

"I'm just saying that your likely opponent is formidable, and you shouldn't add any handicaps."

"You may be the best campaign manager in the country, but you don't know Rob Patterson like I do. We go all the way back to high school, and we went to the same college. He couldn't beat me at anything then, and he sure as hell won't now."

"And you may be the best trial lawyer in the country, but your experience in politics is nil. I've run national campaigns, not to mention numerous state elections, and keeping my candidates' press exposure positive is a big part of the job. If we're going to get you in the governor's mansion, we've got to eliminate any, um, indiscretions."

"Settle down, Harley."

Harley grinned salaciously and replied, "What are you going to do, my boy? Screw her to death? If so, better make sure to cover your, uh…tracks." He coughed with laughter as he reached for his wineglass.

"I said I'll take care of her. By Monday, she'll be nothing but a pleasant memory."

CHAPTER 3

Same day. Grand Rapids.

Prudence Wheatley sat stiffly upright over her steno machine, as was her habit when transcribing depositions. She was typically a person of habit and usually capable of keeping up with the quick back-and-forth of questions and responses... but not today. Though she tried hard to concentrate, her mind kept wandering to thoughts of the upcoming weekend, the first time they would be together in weeks.

The plaintiff's lawyer, who had been grilling Alan's expert witness for over four hours, dropped his pencil on the yellow notepad in front of him. "That's all I have."

"You're done then?" asked defense counsel Alan Redmond.

"For now. But I may have more follow-up, depending upon what you have."

Redmond smirked. He knew from years of taking and defending depositions that you almost never examine your own witness in a deposition. Doing so only gave the opportunity for more questions from opposing counsel, either those they had forgotten to ask directly, or new ones raised by your examination. Exceptions included the possibility that the witness might not be available to testify at trial or if the testimony needed rehabilitation. Today, neither applied. Turning to Pru, he nodded and announced, "Let's call it a day then."

The witness jumped up, briskly shook Redmond's hand, and scurried away, scowling at the opposing counsel. "Guess he wanted to make sure there'd be no more questions," said the other attorney.

"You gave him a pretty hard time, but I thought he held up well. We'll see how your guy does the next go-round."

Pru glanced at her watch, saw it was already after 3:30, and quickly gathered the exhibits scattered on the table. She then started packing up her steno machine.

The other attorney leaned in toward Redmond, whispering, "Tell me about our court reporter. She's Black Irish gorgeous, but she seems a bit slow on the uptake in the reporting department."

Redmond turned and glanced at Pru, smiled, and whispered back, "That…is Prudence Wheatley. Don't mistake her good looks for lack of ability. And don't judge her by whatever was going on today. She's meticulous, smart; in my opinion, she's the best."

"That's quite a testimonial. Beauty and intelligence—a combination that can't hurt her business prospects."

"She's my go-to reporter. I'll rearrange my schedule to get her if I have to. She's that good. You'll see when you get the transcripts."

Alan's compliment was no exaggeration. Prudence Wheatley was an exceptional reporter, and her abilities did not go unrecognized by attorneys across the state. She was among the busiest and most successful in her profession.

"Either you're her business agent, or you've got something more on your mind."

"I have for a long time." The lawyer looked over Alan's shoulder at Pru, who was still packing up.

"I'll admit, it's a challenge," Alan said. "She got divorced a few years ago, not long after mine. I've been trying to make it something more than work ever since, but she tells me that she doesn't mix business and social life. Not a bad policy...admirable."

The other lawyer shook his head. "That'll change. The way she looks, it's only a matter of time."

"Let's just hope it's me that changes her."

"Well, good luck with that." The lawyer picked up his briefcase, stopping to say goodbye to Pru as he left.

Redmond followed, leaned over Pru, and asked, "Grab a drink?"

"No thanks, Alan. Much appreciated, but not today. Gotta go."

He frowned. "Hot date tonight?"

Tilting her head, Pru replied through a smile, "That's none of your business, Mr. Redmond."

"You sure I can't talk you into just a short aperitif, pretty lady?"

"You're a smooth talker, Alan, but I can't."

"Okay Pru, but can I at least get a rain check—and soon?"

"Maybe next Thursday, after the Benton Company depositions. We'll see how it goes."

"Great. You've got them set for here again, right?"

Pru quickly pulled on her jacket and grabbed her

equipment. "You know I do. Have I ever disappointed you?" Winking a sly grin, she twirled around and walked toward the door.

Alan gawked after her as she left, muttering to himself, "Every day."

CHAPTER 4

Same day. Michigan lakeshore.

The man sat behind the steering wheel of the pickup with arms crossed, staring straight ahead with the motor running. Any passersby might have thought him asleep, but he was just going over the details. Like always, it had taken months of research, following the parties, tracking their patterns and habits. He had been down this very road dozens of times, repeatedly scouting what he now believed was the perfect location. Not his first choice, but fate intervened a few weeks ago when he overheard their discussion at their restaurant rendezvous. He listened from the next booth as they hatched the plan for this weekend. That made up his mind, and now it was finally all coming together. All that remained was the execution.

After a long while he turned off the ignition, opened the door, and stepped down onto the road. His boots crunched on gravel as he moved behind the vehicle and raised the rear hatch. Grabbing the jack assembly, he hefted the spare tire, slammed the hatch shut, and dropped his load next to the vehicle with a loud clank. Looking up, he froze when he saw a car approaching from the opposite direction. He quickly pulled his coat collar up around his face.

The sedan slowed and stopped beside him. The jowly face of a middle-aged man in a hunting cap appeared as the window lowered. "Looks like you could use some help."

He shook his head, forcing a smile. "No, thanks."

The driver cracked open his car door to get out. "No trouble. Glad to lend a hand."

The man held up his hand. "Much appreciated, but I've got it."

"You live around here?"

"Nope. Just out for a drive."

"Well then, the least I can do is give a good impression of the neighborhood. It's getting colder and...."

As he started to get out, the man grasped the window frame firmly. "Sir, I'm okay. Really."

Seeing the expression on the man's face, the samaritan quickly sat back down and closed his door. "Well, all right then. I guess I can tell when I'm not needed."

The man raised his palms upward. His voice was apologetic. "Thanks for asking. I've had a bad day."

"I've got to get back to town, anyway. I just came out to close things up. Good luck with that." He raised the window as he drove away.

The man waved as the car disappeared in the distance, finally turning at the end of the road. Relieved, he leaned back against the side of the pickup. After a few moments, he walked behind the vehicle and observed the scene. A spattering of snowflakes drifted in the growing darkness. The few cottages across the road were barely visible through the dim half-light of dusk. The only sounds were the rustling of leaves in the wind and the waves dying along the nearby lakeshore.

Walking out to the middle of the two-lane blacktop, he scanned the horizon in both directions. He then stood there motionless, concentrating on the spot where the car had disappeared earlier. Suddenly he jerked to the faint, guttural moan of an engine in the distance, and watched as headlights flashed from a car starting to turn onto the road a half-mile away. He hesitated just long enough to confirm it was the right vehicle, then he sprang into action.

The man hurried to the passenger side of the truck, jerked open the door, and retrieved the camel-colored day coat and short-brimmed plaid cap inside. Quickly donning the hat, he slipped on the jacket while plucking a briar pipe and horn-rimmed glasses from his hip pocket. He jabbed on the spectacles, lit the pipe, and blew a cloud of smoke as the classic red Mustang pulled to a stop. Pointing at the tire and jack lying by the wheel well, he drew a relaxing breath and began shaking his head dejectedly as he walked toward the car.

CHAPTER 5

Same day. Earlier.

Pru sped up the entrance ramp to the highway, heading west toward Lakeview Village and the big lake. She was leaving Grand Rapids later than she had hoped. Settling in for the hour-long drive, she flipped open her cell to call Atwood and alert him that she was on her way. When the rings turned to voicemail, she closed the phone and turned on the radio, squealing loudly to the sound of *Sex on Fire* by Kings of Leon. Gyrating in her seat, she began singing along with the recording. A man spied her from his passing car and waved, smiling and wide-eyed. When her cell rang, she muted the music and picked up.

"Pru, I told you never to call me on that other number!" Lance barked into the phone.

Pru squeezed her eyes shut. "Damn," she whispered to herself. "I'm sorry, Lance. I was just so excited about the weekend I must have hit the wrong number on my cell."

"It's okay for your office to connect for business only. But not you personally. Got it? You know how important it is right now that we're careful, discreet. It can't happen again, Pru."

"I know. It won't. I promise."

"It better not. Now, why did you call?"

"I just wanted to let you know I'm on my way to the lake, sweetheart. I'll be there in less than an hour and can't wait to see you. It's been over a month, and I ..."

"Pru, I'm at an event and I can't talk. I'll be there as soon as I can tonight, all right?"

"Yes, Lance, I'll call when..." The line went dead. She dropped the phone on the passenger seat, banged the steering wheel with her fist, and shook her head. "Stupid me."

Pru strained to refocus her thoughts on the coming weekend. She was good at compartmentalizing negatives, a knack that at times caused her more problems than it solved. Smiling to herself, she thought about how she could assuage Lance's disappointment. "Alright!" she yelled aloud as she unmuted the radio. *Rise Above This* by Seether blared out, and she started tapping her fingers on the dashboard in sync. "Yes, I will," she sang.

Less than an hour later, Pru broke from her daydream, realizing that she was only minutes from the beach house. She grabbed her cell to call Lance. Steering with her forearms, she balanced her phone on the steering wheel and punched in the numbers to his private line. As the phone began to ring, she looked up to see a man leaning against a large black pickup parked on the side of the road ahead.

"This is not what I need right now," she muttered as she cut the call, set her phone on the passenger seat, and pulled over slowly. Pru lowered her window. "What happened?"

"Good afternoon, young lady." The man smiled broadly and nodded over his shoulder. "Flat tire. I went to run some errands and, dumb me, I left my cell phone back at our cottage. We're just up the road a little way. I was about to start walking, so I'm glad you came along."

She looked him over and relaxed as he peered back from behind his glasses. "How can I help?"

"I hate to bother you, but it would be great if you could give me a ride." He drew closer and extended his hand, reaching through the open window. "I'm so pleased to meet you, Ms. Wheatley."

Pru's mouth opened wide at the sound of her name as he gripped her hand tightly, jerking her toward him.

CHAPTER 6

Same day. Late afternoon, Lansing.

"He's unethical ... and a chronic philanderer to boot, Rob." Cynthia Worthey seethed at the thought of their emerging nemesis as she argued to the attorney general. They were meeting in his state capitol office to discuss his likely opponent in the next gubernatorial race, now just two years away. Cynthia's boss, Robert Patterson, was the chief legal officer in the state.

Patterson had prosecuted cases for almost sixteen years, the last six as the attorney general. He had an unsurpassed conviction record and little left to accomplish. The party elite had repeatedly encouraged him to run for higher office, but the timing had never seemed right—not until now. The current governor's term limit would expire with the next election, and the only thing standing in his way was Lance Atwood.

"Atwood's got to be the biggest ambulance chaser of all time. The man's a blemish on our profession."

Patterson grinned and leaned back in his desk chair, gazing at his zealous protégé. Cynthia had been Rob's go-to assistant for the past three years, and she was proving to be every bit as good a trial lawyer as her mentor. She was tough as nails and relentless, often to the extent of vindictiveness toward her adversaries, especially men. He knew she bitterly resented what she perceived as the glass ceiling for women in the legal profession.

Worthey continued her harangue. "How can anyone with half an ounce of integrity possibly consider voting for him?"

Soon after she was hired, Cynthia emerged as the best and brightest among the various up-and-coming prosecutors in the office. Standing almost six feet tall in heels, she was a formidable figure in the courtroom—dignified, articulate, and always adorned in sharply tailored suits accompanied by designer shoes, which she affectionately called her "fashion passion." Patterson particularly appreciated that she was African American, born and raised in Wayne County, and graduated magna cum laude from the University of Michigan to boot—all of which would bode well in his run for governor. He expected she would accompany him on the campaign trail but knew she still had a lot to learn about the peculiarities of politics. Curbing her adversarial zeal would be a priority and a challenge. The fact that she was a member of his political party was a bonus.

"Think about it, Cynthia. Atwood's got more name recognition than any state political candidate in memory. His 24/7 television ads have him in every living room in the state, boasting about all those million-dollar verdicts."

Patterson rose and turned to the window behind his desk, bending a blind to expose the view of the evening traffic departing downtown.

He pivoted back to Worthey, speaking as he sat. "Hell, if you ask any cab driver in Detroit, Lansing, or any city in the state for that matter, who they'd want to represent them if they had a personal injury lawsuit, guess whose name you'll hear? That's a big advantage in the voting booth."

"Okay, I'll give you that." Worthey adjusted the oversized frames on the bridge of her nose. "The wrongful discharge award he got for that teacher against the city school district was all over the nightly news for days. But word is that Atwood had an affair with his client in that case. That's my point, he …"

"No. You're missing the point. That affair was never proven, he still got a blockbuster verdict at trial, and they reinstated her to boot. It was a brilliant bit of lawyering. I think we'll see the same tenacity from him when he's running for office."

Slumping into the tufted wingback across from her boss, Worthey crossed her Jimmy Choo heels. "Rob, I've got to think the womanizing makes him vulnerable. That teacher is supposedly only one of many, and she was his client. That's an ethics violation. If we could expose that during the campaign, he'd lose his law license, and I doubt the public would be eager to put him in the state driver's seat after that. We should meet with her and try to convince her to come out with it."

"Come on, Cynthia. Even if she would cooperate, and I can't imagine why she would, that won't make any difference for two reasons. First, his party doesn't give a damn about their members' sexual indiscretions. Secondly, the press will spin whatever narrative helps their party. They're in the tank for the Dems. You know that."

"I still think it's worth a shot, boss. You've heard that old saying, 'Hell hath no fury like a woman scorned.' Plus, he's got a family. How can anyone support a guy who cheats on his family like that?"

"Look, we'll keep it in the hopper and see what develops. I just hate to go there if we don't have to. One thing is certain: In every big election, there's always some information or event which comes out of nowhere. It ends up driving the press narrative and often even decides the winner. This one will be no different. Whatever the surprise may be, let's just hope it'll help us."

CHAPTER 7

Saturday. Early morning.

After he left the car as planned, the man made the long walk back through the woods to the beach house. When he finally arrived, he waited in the trees for another forty-five minutes, assuring that all was clear, and Atwood had come and gone. Then he used the keys he had taken earlier from a wall rack to open both the rear garage door and the entrance from the garage into the house. He placed his shoes by the doorstep and removed the now-muddied pair of topsiders he had taken earlier, setting them beside his own. Then he put on a thick hairnet, latex gloves, and disposable booties.

Once inside, he took out a small penlight and shined the beam ahead of him as he made his way through the hallway to the kitchen. He stopped momentarily, scanning the beam slowly from left to right, then retraced his steps down the opposite hall, pausing at a utility closet. He dragged out the vacuum, along with a plastic bucket filled with cleaning supplies. Moving on to the master bedroom and bath, he began cleaning every surface he might have touched.

Twenty minutes later, he entered the large walk-in closet, circled the center island, and grabbed the tie he had used before from the rack. He walked over to the king bed and pulled back the edge of the covers, again knotting the tie to a headboard post. Then he quickly returned the cleaning equipment to the closet, removed the waste bag from the vacuum, and placed it on the floor by the back door. Bounding up the stairway to the second floor, he unlocked a window latch in a side bedroom above the first-floor roof overhang. On his way out, he stopped and slowly scanned around before he picked up the bag and returned to the garage. After locking the door, he removed the booties and put on his shoes, leaving the mud-covered topsiders by the step. Walking out onto the patio, he paused to scrutinize the large firepit, then checked his watch before disappearing back into the woods.

CHAPTER 8

Early November. Indianapolis, Indiana.

"I was sorry to hear about your dad, Dani. We worked together pretty closely a while back." FBI agent Peter Brimley stood by his metal desk in the Federal Building in Indianapolis, welcoming the daughter of his old colleague and fellow agent, John Sparro. She had called the day before to set up a meeting, saying she had something very important to show him.

Danielle Sparro gazed intently at the eyes behind the horn-rimmed glasses of the slender figure standing in front of her. Brimley straightened the knot of his knit tie and tugged at the sleeves of his dull brown suit as he reached out to greet her. The clammy touch of his hand left her rubbing her fingers across her palm. She thought him a perfect caricature of Ichabod Crane, without the nineteenth-century garb.

"Thank you, Mr. Brimley. I appreciate your seeing me on such short notice. Dad always told me that if I ever needed agency assistance, you were the person I should call."

Brimley waved her to the adjacent faded wooden chair. "Well, I hope that I can be of help, Dani. What can I do for you?"

She sat, her stare never leaving his eyes. "Before dad died, he was working on a cold case file originating in Colorado. That's where he retired, you know."

The agent shifted uncomfortably in his seat, his ankle on his knee, and picked a piece of lint from his pant leg.

"It's probably best to start where dad did. There was a gruesome murder several years ago near where he lived—an older couple. Supposedly it started as an identity scam. A local man was charged and convicted; but based on his review of the evidence, dad realized the verdict was a mistake."

"A mistake?"

Dani sat back in her chair and inhaled. "Yes. The real killer planted incriminating evidence, and the local authorities fell for it. But dad found proof that the real murderer was a serial killer. I retrieved his file when I inventoried his effects after the funeral. I brought it, hoping you'd look it over."

Brimley leaned forward, peering curiously at the large accordion folder she held in her lap.

"It's a pattern the killer has repeated many times over many years."

"Hmm. That's quite a…story, Dani." He stared blankly with his hand over his mouth, slowly shaking his head. She couldn't tell if he was faking interest.

"Now let me get this straight. Your father started

investigating an old double murder case in which they already accused a man, and that man was then tried and convicted?"

She pursed her lips and nodded affirmatively.

"Okay. But then your dad, uh, 'concluded' that another person, a serial killer, was the one who actually committed the crime?"

"Yes, Mr. Brimley. I know it sounds far-fetched when you say it like that, but it's true, and that's why I'm here in Indy."

"Well Dani, I'm at a loss. You're right about how all of this sounds, but regardless, this is a state matter. There being no federal crime, the FBI would have no authority to get involved. That being the case, how can I possibly be of help to you?"

"Please…just bear with me."

Brimley folded his hands on the desk in front of him and tilted his head.

"Do you remember that girl killed up in Wisconsin, almost two years ago? You know—the one whose remains they found in a burn pit in that trailer park. She had gone there to look at one of the mobile homes being sold and then disappeared. They later found her car on the property, and they charged the owner and his cousin with raping and killing her."

"Yes, I recall that. Are you going to tell me the serial killer your dad was chasing really did it?"

"That's right. He did. Those two men are innocent."

"But Dani, weren't those two men also convicted by a jury after a thorough investigation—and a highly publicized trial?"

"Yes, that's true. But there were serious questions

about the motives of the local authorities and about planted evidence. Also, he showed up at the trial."

"Wait. You saw him? You attended the trial?" Brimley asked.

"No. But my dad did. It's in his notes. In here." She patted the folder.

"All this and no one ever caught him, or even suspected him, except your dad?"

"Yes. But believe me, Mr. Brimley, he's very, very good at what he does."

"Apparently, he was good enough to fool many different law enforcement agencies, repeatedly?"

She twisted in her seat and reached into the folder. "Let me show you what dad found, Mr. Brimley. There's so much evidence pointing to him, and you'll see the similarities in the other cases. If you'll just—"

Brimley interrupted. "Look, Dani, I very much appreciate you coming here to see me. That aside, as much as I respected your father, as you yourself said, this is all very, um, unreal."

Dani raised the folder. "He didn't imagine all of this."

"And I'm not saying that. But it's not uncommon for retired agents to get wrapped up in, well, they just want to go on trying to solve crimes, especially cold cases. With some, it can become an obsession."

"My dad was not obsessed. He was just committed to stopping a terrible man from hurting any more people."

"I'm certain he did an excellent investigation, and he believed what he found supported his conclusions." Brimley opened a side drawer, pulled out a file folder and laid it on the desktop.

"Truth be told, I read the report of his death before

you came here. I got it from a fellow agent in the Denver office. I'm told that your father was apparently having some personal difficulties before he died."

"Dad was fine. He wasn't sick, or depressed, or anything like that." She paused, remembering what she had been told afterward. The investigators discovered his body on the floor of the entry hall of his home, with a rope around his neck. The rope was wrapped around a light fixture lying next to him, the other end tied to a second-floor balcony railing. The investigators concluded that he had strung the rope from the fixture in the ceiling and then swung out from the balcony. His weight must have brought the fixture down at some point. That explained his broken neck and the gash on his head.

She jerked up to the edge of her chair. "There's no way he did that to himself...absolutely no way!"

"I appreciate your reservations, Dani. But there was no evidence of foul play, nothing."

"There was absolutely no reason for him to kill himself. It was the man he was after. I'm sure he did it."

"So, you think this serial killer murdered John too, and made it look like suicide?"

She nodded vigorously.

Brimley swiveled his chair around, paused, and stared out the window. After a few moments, he turned back. "Okay. The least I can do for the daughter of an old friend is see if we can find this serial killer in our files. So, what's the man's name?"

Just then the phone on his desk rang. Brimley raised his hand and looked at the name displayed on the phone. "Please excuse me. I have to take this call, Dani. It's important."

He picked up the phone and held his hand over the receiver, saying, "Why don't you leave that file, or just send me a copy? Whenever you can." Brimley then put the phone to his ear. "Brimley here…"

Dani sighed and nodded. Her shoulders slumped as she stood and slowly left the room.

CHAPTER 9

November 6. Lakeview.

Willy passed by the station receptionist Rita Howard as he left for his afternoon rounds in the Village. She was on the main phone line.

"Yes, ma'am, I know the place. Yes, just off the highway there. Alright. I'll get someone on this right away. I expect we'll be in touch very soon. Let me just take down your number." Rita penciled down the number and a name on the pad lying in front of her. "Thank you for calling this in, ma'am."

She hung up the phone and looked at Willy with serious concern. "That lady on the phone just told me her kid and his friends found an abandoned car out at the old strip mall. You know, the one just off State 31?"

"An abandoned car? So? Wouldn't be the first."

"Yeah, maybe, but this one has blood in it, she said. Said those kids were pretty shook up."

"Phooey! I'll bet this is just another prank."

"Well, we gotta check it out, you know, just in case.

You're probably right, but the chief would have your ass if you didn't, and it turned out to be true."

"I know. I'm on it. I'll call in after I check it out." Willy grabbed his Stetson and left.

Twenty-five minutes later, Willie parked after having driven twice around the perimeter of the deserted strip mall, located a quarter mile or so off the highway exit ramp north of the village. He stared through his rain-splattered windshield at the car parked inside the largest of four connected store units giving the building its name, Four Fronts Mall. Little of the overall structure was intact, only a dilapidated shell with most of the windows broken, roof leaking, and the parking lot and grounds heavily weeded. Two large garage-type doors hung open on one end of the unit, and just inside the now-gaping opening sat a shiny red '67 Mustang.

Willy's steps echoed through the vacant space as he walked toward the car. He bent over, stuck his head through the open passenger door, and shone his flashlight inside the car. The beam reflected off the chrome stick shift between the front bucket seats as he panned the dash and floor. He stood up and reached in to grab the back of the passenger seat, pulling it forward with a loud squeak. As he pointed his light into the back seat, dark stains spilled over the red leather seat and onto the floor. Leaning in, he reached down and ran his fingertips across the crusty carpet. After checking from the driver's side, he opened the glove compartment and removed the contents. Returning to his squad car, he called in to the station. Rita answered.

"Hi Willy. So, what did you find?"

"The car is out here all right, and it looks just like the kids said. Is the chief back yet?"

"Yeah, he just walked in. I'll transfer you."

Mitch picked up. "What's up, Willy? Rita told me about the kids finding that car at Four Fronts."

"Yep. I found it alright; and there's blood in it, just like they said. At least it sure looks like blood…in the back. It's an older-model Mustang, late sixties, I'd say; red; with no plates; and I found no proof of insurance or registration. Just the owner's manual, ladies' sunglasses, and makeup stuff."

Mitch grimaced, recalling a missing person complaint received days before. The owner had been driving a red Mustang when last seen.

"Can you give me the V-I-N? I'll call it in right away."

Willy read the ID from the dashboard back to him.

"You stay there and run some yellow tape around the area. Close it off. I'm thinking this is that missing woman's car. The one we got the MP bulletin about. So be careful not to touch anything. That includes the car. Okay?"

Willy looked down and closed his eyes, shaking his head. "Sorry chief. I already did. The passenger side door was open, and I had to grab the back seat headrest to look in. Also, I opened the driver's door and glove compartment. I just wasn't thinking."

"Not to worry, Willy. You did what you had to do. Next time wear latex. Now, just do like I say. I'm going to run down the VIN and get some more info on the owner. I'll call for CSI."

Willy pulled a small notepad from his jacket pocket. "I'll make a list and be ready when they get here."

"Okay. When they do, describe everything. Then go interview the kids who found the car and their parents. Find out everything they saw, did, touched, messed with, or even smelled. Now I'm signing off. I'll get back to you later." Mitch cut the call and walked over to the counter where he had last seen the report of the missing woman. He remembered something about court reporting.

CHAPTER 10

As Willy hung up his phone, a large black pickup passed along the road in front of the mall. Willy had no way of knowing this had been the driver's routine for several days. The man slowed when he spotted the police vehicle through the missing front window, passed the mall, then sped up down the road half a mile and turned around. Stopping about a hundred yards from the mall, he parked in a small roadside clearing. The man then left the car, entered the woods, and walked back toward the site, staying parallel to the road while hidden by trees and underbrush. As he drew nearer, he began scanning the ground, looking for any trace of the trail he had made the night he returned to Atwood's beach house. It had not rained again since, and he looked for the traces of his footprints.

When he reached a point providing a clear view of the mall storefronts, he knelt on one knee and waited. In minutes, a police van drove up and proceeded to the rear of the mall. He watched as two men and a uniformed officer gathered around the area where he had left the Mustang. Unable to see the car or anything the men were doing, he walked deeper into the woods to search for his earlier tracks. It didn't take too long before his search paid off. Not far into the woods and directly across from the mall, the topsiders had left a clear trail leading south toward the beach house. The ground had since hardened, boosting his confidence that he would leave no new signs along the way. He followed the footprints for about a hundred yards or so, assuring that there would be no mistaking their direction when the police eventually found them.

Satisfied, he headed back to his truck, reasoning along the way that the time required for the police to check out the Mustang would give him an opportunity to make the show in Lapeer. He was anxious to see how his entries would fare. Having already won two Legs with one of his bucks, he relished the thought of finally achieving a national champion. He reasoned some time away would be refreshing, and he also looked forward to spending a few days at his ranch.

CHAPTER 11

Days later.

"**A**lan, I hate like hell to say it, but right now we don't have a clue where she is or what the hell might have happened to her. But we're making progress."

Alan Redmond gaped at the county prosecutor, Dave Bartlett. He was seeking an update on the search for Prudence Wheatley. Save for news they had found her car in a deserted strip mall, there had been no helpful information despite his repeated calls to local police. Frustrated, he finally called his former law school classmate and begged a meeting. The two graduated a year apart, and although not close friends, they had maintained an amicable, professional relationship ever since.

Bartlett's huge frame spilled over his desk chair, which creaked as he raised up. His hand engulfed a coffee cup, one pudgy finger jutting in Alan's direction. He was the oldest of nine children in a Catholic family from Grand Rapids, a city thirty-five miles or so east of Lakeview.

Dave was a heralded football lineman, an accomplished student, and a finalist Rhodes Scholar, a recognition he often boasted of sharing with Kris Kristofferson. He had graduated third in his law class out of 175, and he was the moot court champion.

By comparison, Redmond was a silver spoon and had only one estranged sibling. He was a gentleman C student, and a survivor of two failed marriages with a gift for gab, which—together with his affable nature—he had parlayed into a marginally successful insurance defense practice. Besides a penchant for top-level vodka, his most notable shortcoming was his credulity. He was trusting to a fault, a ruinous flaw for trial lawyers, whose stock-in-trade requires persistent skepticism. Most of those who knew him thought him to be chronically naïve, a trait which had placed him on the losing end of more than a few transactions, both business and personal.

"Look, we're busting our humps day and night trying to find her. I already told you that the police officers in the surrounding communities have been checking out every bar, restaurant, shop, gas station, and even grocery stores, questioning everyone they can. They've distributed dozens of flyers with her photo and directions on how to contact us anonymously."

"Christ, Dave!" Redmond replied. "That just sounds like a bunch of activity with no results. None. It's been over a week since Pru disappeared. From everything I've heard about these kinds of situations, the longer a person's gone, the more likely something bad has happened. Usually something really bad."

Bartlett had asked Mitch Quinn to join the meeting.

He sat next to Redmond and put a hand on the lawyer's forearm. "As a matter of fact, Mr. Redmond, we have some very encouraging prospects."

Redmond stiffened attentively. "I'm all ears."

Mitch looked at Bartlett, who waved him on.

"After they found the car, we called for tracking dogs. They picked up two scent traces. One was clearly connected to the kids who found the car. We questioned them extensively that same day, and they really had nothing more to add.

"The other was curious. The dogs followed the scent away from the car, lost it, but then picked it up directly across the road."

"So? What does that mean?"

"We're not sure. It looks like someone probably left the car and crossed the road. Whether it was the person who drove it there or merely a curiosity seeker, it's impossible to tell at this point. We don't even know if it was the same person because we had no clothing or other object with the scent to start with," Bartlett said.

Mitch resumed, "But oddly, the scent on the other side of the road crisscrossed. That confused the dogs for a bit, because it ended up leading in two directions—one back to a small roadside clearing west of the mall. The other headed south along some footprints we found a little deeper into the woods. The dogs lost the scent pretty quickly, but we were able to follow the prints for some distance. They eventually played out about three quarters of a mile or so from the mall."

"How do you explain that?"

"I'm not sure we can. Any scent left on the night Prudence Wheatley disappeared could just have dissipated with time. There's disagreement on how long tracking dogs can pick up a scent. Some say two weeks at most, others say months. A lot apparently depends on the dogs and how they're trained."

"So, you're telling me yours were the two-week variety? C'mon chief. You've got to do better than that. Pru could be being held somewhere right now, and in danger, hurt or worse."

"I wish I had more. The fact that the dogs picked up the scent across the road soon after we found the car could indicate someone may have been there more recently. We found the tracks because they were in the deep woods. There was lots of cover from the heavy rain we had that night, but it would still have been muddy to walk in. When we got further south, the forest opened to a clearing. The ground there is much harder, rockier, and the footprints ended."

"So, are you thinking the same person who left the scent made the footprints?"

"It's possible."

"Well, is there anything in that area to give us a clue where he went?"

"The only thing in that general direction is a cottage association along the lake, but that's well over a mile further south. Just in case, we're trying to contact local property owners, but no one lives in that neighborhood full-time. They're all seasonal; some even live out of state. So, we've had to track them down where they live, and that's very time consuming."

"You said some prospects. What else have you got?"

Mitch reached for a stack of papers on the edge of Bartlett's desk. Pulling one from the pile, he continued,

"We got her call records from her cell phone provider just yesterday. We've also been working with their subsidiary company, which owns the cell towers in the area. They're cooperating, but we had to get a subpoena."

Bartlett ambled over to a coffee cart next to Mitch. Lifting the pot, he winked. "We were able to get it pretty quickly though." After he poured himself a cup, he held up the pot to the two men. Both shook their heads and he returned to his seat.

"Anyway, the records show some calls to and from her phone that Friday afternoon. Aside from one to her office, there were six calls. Three from her cell were to two different numbers, the second two of which were unlisted. The first call from that one came right after she had called the other one."

"Wait, you said one unlisted number. Does that mean you identified the other one?"

"Yes, we did." Bartlett raised one of the call sheets. "It's a cell number for an attorney named Lawrence Atwood. You may have heard of him, Alan. He's a big-time litigator."

"That's no surprise, Dave. I know Atwood. He's a client of Pru's. She does a lot of work for him, just like she does for me. Probably calling about our deposition. We had one scheduled together for the week after she disappeared."

"Well, we tried to contact him, but his office told us he's out of town. We asked them to have him get back to us as soon as he returns."

"So, what happened when she called Atwood's number?" Alan asked.

"He never answered. It went to voicemail," said Bartlett.

Mitch reached over to the cart and poured a glass of water. "It seems curious that the call from the unidentified number came into Ms. Wheatley's phone almost immediately after her call to Atwood. Almost like he called her back on a different phone."

"Probably just coincidence. It happens. Pru's in high demand."

Mitch nibbled his lip. "Maybe. Anyway, we're still waiting for more ping records to see if we can somehow trace her exact location. I mean, the location of her phone. They've told us it can be difficult if her phone is shut off, or if it's destroyed; but we also …"

"And they can trace her?" Redmond interrupted.

"There's a way you can track where the caller is, or was, when a call was made or received. But you need ping records."

"What's a ping?" asked Redmond.

"Cell phones automatically send out signals, or pings, to local cell towers in the area where they're being used. For example, if someone is traveling with a cell phone, the phone will ping nearby towers it passes along the way. By tracking the pings through the cell tower grids, you can get a kind of map of the area where the cell user was."

"Or is, if she's staying in one place," said Dave.

Mitch continued, "When there's more than one cell tower in the area, you're able to get a decent location by using what's called triangulation."

"What's that?"

"Cell towers are typically configured with three sets of

triangular, uh, wedges, let's call them," Bartlett answered. "Each wedge covers roughly a third of the service area and picks up the cell phone signals in that wedge. The towers measure the phone's location by the strength of the signal and the round-trip time to and from each tower. The triangulation process can close in more tightly on the phone's location."

"How many towers are in the area where her car was found? Wouldn't that be where you should start... logically?"

Bartlett and Mitch exchanged smiles. "The good news is, there are several towers in that area, which should help considerably," said Bartlett. "Once we get the tracking results, we should get a good idea of where the phone is now."

CHAPTER 12

November 11. Lapeer, Michigan.

"That's a good-lookin' bunch o' Americans ya got there, mister."

The man looked up, twisting to his right in his folding lawn chair. Standing over him was an obese geezer wearing a straw hat and sporting a few days' worth of white whiskers, his thumbs tucked in the bib of his dark blue overalls. He turned momentarily to his left, gazing at the cages full of large white rabbits arranged on the large cart next to his folding chair. He then swiveled back to the commentator.

"I breed Californians myself. Those're my cages over there, at table forty-six, behind ya." He nodded, but the man didn't move. "I'm Herman Wheeler. Our farm's over near Grant." The farmer's hand protruded from his checkered flannel shirt. "Just Herm is fine. Pleased to meet ya, Mr....?"

The man inspected the affable neighbor, then slowly rose, and grabbed his hand. "James."

"Ya got a first name, Mr. James?"

"Stewart. Stewart James."

"Well, Stew. Okay if I call you Stew?

The man shrugged.

"You ain't from around this part o' the state, are ya, Stew?"

"Why do you ask?"

"I don't mean ta be nosy. Just tryin' ta be friendly. But we've never met. I been watchin' ya all morning, and you ain't moved from your chair since ya first sat down—except for groomin' your rabbits, that is. Figured you must not know many o' the folks here. Lots o' regulars. Ya do many shows here in Michigan?"

The man's eyes narrowed. "No."

"I just happened to notice ya. Can't help lookin' around, seein' who's here and all. It was my wife who first said sumthin'." He again nodded in the other direction.

The man turned to see a rotund woman in multicolored spandex leggings and a gray sweatshirt, sitting next to a table full of cages containing numerous white rabbits with black ears. She gave a friendly wave, but he turned back without response.

"We're pure Michiganders ourselves. We only show our herd here in the state, but there's enough shows in-state to keep us busy. Anyway, you'll soon learn ya won't do well around here if ya don't gussy up to the judges. It's gettin' awful these days; not much fun in it anymore. Used to be only the best rabbits won. Lately it seems like whoever kisses the most ass gets Best in Show."

"How does that happen?" The man stepped back, folding his arms across his chest.

"Well, when you get a minute, go on over to table one fifty-six. You'll see a buncha Jersey Woolys. They're a good enough breed, but these days they've been winnin' a lotta top spots…at least the ones you'll see at table one fifty-six."

"Why is that?"

"If ya ask me, it's that little gal breedin' 'em. Evelyn Newsom's her name. If ya get over there, take a good, close look at her. She's a clever one. A real schemer if ya ask me. And she ain't hard on the eyes, neither." He smirked. "Then, pay attention to the judge who hangs around her spot. Lord's his name. Byron Lord, if ya can believe that. He's like a bee ta honey. And ya can tell she sure eats it up."

The man twirled slowly around, surveying the enormous rectangle of carts laden with rabbit-filled cages lining the perimeter of the auditorium. The Lapeer Rabbit Club was hosting this month's contest for the American Rabbit Breeders Association. Seeing the thousands of caged contenders on display, he was reminded that rabbit shows were as widely attended around the country as dog shows, yet the hounds got all the attention.

"They're cheating?"

"Well, I won't say that, but sumthin' sure smells funny, if ya know what I mean."

"I may just have to pay that judge and the Jersey breeder a visit." He had come close to best in show a few times, having taken the top spot in his breed more than once, but someone else always seemed to win out in the final vote for the top prize. It galled him that the results might be corruptively preordained.

"If ya do and ya find sumthin', let us know, will ya? If there's a fix in, I'd be all about puttin' a stop to it. There's enough game playin' in these shows without somebody guaranteein' the top prize ahead o' time. Anyway, are you gonna be at the Coldwater show comin' up, Stew?"

"No. I have other business."

"Oh? What's that?"

The man ignored his question as he looked back into the auditorium. After a quick scan, he spotted a couple engaged in flirtatious conversation by a cart at the opposite corner of the hall. His instincts told him those two were the alleged offenders. He lifted a camel jacket from the chair back, picked up the plaid hat laying on the top of the cage next to him, then began to walk away. Turning slightly as he passed Wheeler, he said. "Watch my rabbits."

The man skirted the long perimeter of carts, rounded the last corner, then slowed to a stop barely within earshot of the man and woman, who were still intently conversing. He inched closer, trying to make out what they were saying. When he caught the eye of the woman, she nodded his presence to her companion who turned abruptly. "Can I help you?"

The man stepped in close, staring intently into the eyes of his questioner who appeared to be at least mid-fifties, with a slender build and narrow shoulders. Thin fenders of white streaked his temples, offsetting an otherwise full crown of obviously dyed, jet black hair, and a beak-like nose protruded from between his closely set eyes. The man imagined a crow.

"Yes, Mr." Dropping his eyes to the name tag on the man's lapel, he finished. "Lord."

"This is my first show in Michigan. Can you tell me … are the judges fair?"

The couple exchanged quizzical looks and Lord pivoted to face the man. "I'm sorry? What are you saying?"

"I'm asking if the people judging this event are fair."

"Why would you ask such a thing?"

"Word is there may be some favoritism."

"Just who did you hear that from? I can assu—"

The man switched his gaze to the woman. "What do you say about that, Ms.?"

Lord interjected. "Ms. Newsom is an experienced breeder whose Woolys, especially her does…" she lowered her eyes as he smiled in her direction, "have won in numerous categories, including Best in Show, and I'm sure she'll attest to the integrity of the judging."

Straightening her shoulders, she replied. "Yes, I can at…"

The man cut her off. "I'm sure she will. But you're a judge, aren't you?"

"Yes, I am and …"

"Well then, Mr. Lord, we'll see how you do when the time comes." He turned and walked away.

The two stared after him. "Sir? What's your name?" Lord called to him.

The man turned his head. "We'll meet soon enough."

"Well, I never…" said Lord. "How impertinent! Do you know who he is? Have you seen him at any other shows?"

"I never saw him before. What do you think he's up to?"

"Sounds like he's fishing for a favor himself. But in any event, maybe we'd better keep an eye on him. I'll check in on his entries later."

Newsom put her hand on Lord's arm. "We'll be fine. Are we still on for tonight?"

The man grinned as he turned back from a second

look at the couple, huddled again in earnest conversation. His breed was not scheduled until later, so he decided to wait and watch, picking up as much information as he could. The farmer and his acquaintances would be helpful sources. Later he would make an excuse of illness or some emergency and withdraw his entry before they called for the Americans. No use risking more exposure, but he committed to following up on Byron Lord as soon as his business in Lakeview was completed.

CHAPTER 13

The next week.

The wind was picking up along the lakeshore, dark gray clouds moving in quickly from the north, portending snow. Mitch stared southward at the mix of dark blue and khaki uniforms spread out along the dunes. Nineteen officers had been scouring the area since daybreak, moving awkwardly through beach grass clinging to the steep sand wall cutting up from the shoreline. Along this mile-long stretch of lakeshore, most of the homes were built at least thirty vertical feet above the beach.

Mitch had received Prudence Wheatley's phone records late the day before, the data showing pings had been recorded on October 31 in an area somewhere north of Lakeview, potentially including the neighborhood they'd begun investigating since finding her car. The pings were being picked up by three cell towers a few miles apart, providing a much smaller area to search, but it was still almost a thousand acres. As the two groups closed in on one another from opposite directions, Mitch repeatedly called Prudence Wheatley's cell number, everyone listening for a ring response. Both groups were now only twenty yards or so apart.

Mitch gazed up and down the otherwise deserted beach as the searchers approached. Looking to the left-hand group, then the right, he yelled, "Anything? Anyone?" One by one the men silently shook their heads.

"Well, our next move is up. The houses in that neighborhood are all that's left on the ping grid."

Willy pointed at a wooden stairway ascending the dune some thirty yards away. "We can start over there."

An officer standing near the stairs suddenly yelled out, "Hey Chief! I think I hear something."

All the men scrambled over to the deck at the bottom of the steps and stood listening. Mitch heard a faint ringing, and Willy vaulted up the steps two at a time. He stopped near the top and jumped into the dune grass covering the slope. Mitch watched as he reached down into the grass and yanked up a ringing cell phone, shouting, "Got it!"

Mitch ran up the stairs as Willy offered the phone to him. "You've got to put it back, Willy. Right where you found it."

"What? Why? It's what we're after, isn't it Chief?"

"I'm sure this is private property, Willy." Mitch couldn't remember exactly how it worked. His memory told him state courts had ruled that a landowner on the lakeshore owned the property to the established highwater mark, but he had no idea where that might be.

"If whoever owns that house up there owns this dune, we'll probably need a search warrant to take this phone."

One of the assisting officers from the adjacent county spoke up. "But don't we have probable cause, Chief?"

"Maybe. But I don't want to take a chance and end up losing this as evidence if we're wrong. I'll call Dave Bartlett, and we'll see how quickly we can get a warrant." He reached into his jacket for his cell. "Go ahead and put it back, Willy."

Another of the deputies said, "I wonder who lives up there?" The others followed his gaze. All they could see was the edge of a second story rooftop rising above the crest of the dune.

"Hey Chief!" one policeman called out from the back of the group. "I'm pretty sure that's the last house on the association road." Mitch turned to see who had shouted, recognizing one of his own deputies, Willard Kennedy.

"So ... what about it, Will?" he shouted back.

"Well, after you found that car, you remember how you assigned me to contact the property owners?"

Mitch stepped back down the stairway to the deck where Will was standing. "Uh, huh. And ...?"

"Well, the neighborhood up there has a long road lined with summer cottages. If that's the end one, it's owned by some big trial lawyer. You know—that guy with all the TV commercials. The ones that say, 'Don't take a chance, win with Lance?' I think his name is Lawrence Atwood."

"Well, isn't that the coincidence." Mitch muttered aloud. "Did you talk to him?"

The deputy shook his head. "Nope. I left a message at his office, but I never got a call back. If we hadn't started searching for the phone, I'd planned to try again to contact him today."

Mitch looked back up at the home. "Well, we'll just have to see if Mr. Lance Atwood can help us out." He turned and called out, "Come here, Willy. I've got a job for you."

CHAPTER 14

The man sat on a stool in the barroom, his back to the bar as he gazed intently out a bank of windows facing the lake, which disappeared into the horizon against a dull gray sky. A half-full mug of beer and an empty shot glass rested on the bar behind him. He had held onto the phone purposefully at first, waiting to see what the police could find without it. Once it became clear they were stumped, he decided to turn it back on and leave it someplace obvious—but not too obvious. He knew it was only a matter of time before they found it, and once they did, they would eventually have to search Atwood's beach house.

"You want another, mister?" the bartender asked hopefully. Typical for late fall weekdays at mid-afternoon, there was little after-lunch activity in this or any other of the almost two dozen restaurants in or near the downtown area.

The man swiveled around, peered down at the empty shot glass, looked up and shook his head.

The server shrugged and said, "If you want anything else, let me know. I'll be in the back."

As he started to leave, the man spoke. "You work here long?"

The server put his hands on the bar. "Almost four years. But I've lived here all my life."

"I'm curious about your town."

"What about it?"

"Is it safe?"

"Safe? What do you mean?"

"I mean, is this a safe, secure community?"

"Why do you ask?"

"I might just rent a spot."

"Safer than most, I guess. Not much crime, except for summers. Lots of tourists. The population swells five-fold, they say. And the traffic. It's bumper-to-bumper on weekends. But this time of year, it dies down to nothing. You won't have trouble finding a place to rent; and the prices will drop."

"What's wrong with tourists? Don't they bring money?"

"Well, sure. I guess it's not so much the tourists themselves. Although the boating crowd likes to drink...a lot. But they mostly party at the marinas. Then there're the teenagers." He stuck his thumb over his shoulder. "That's the main drag right out front. It runs all along the channel. Every Friday and Saturday night they troll the strip in their cars."

"That doesn't sound like such a big deal."

"No. But we also get a lot of bikers, especially in summer; and they can bring trouble. You know, drinking, drugs, fights."

"Must keep your police busy."

"Oh, we're just fine as far as that goes. Our chief is ex-military police."

"Military, eh? He's pretty good then?"

"You bet. The best."

"Hmm. Good to know."

The server rubbed his hands together. "Well, I should get back to work. You sure I can't get you anything else?"

"No. I think I'll just take a look around."

The server spun around and walked back to the kitchen, leaving the man to himself. After a few silent minutes he stood up, laid a twenty-dollar bill on the bar, and strolled out. He knew the police had been searching that morning and decided to drive over to see if they had found any of the clues he had left for them.

CHAPTER 15

East Grand Rapids.

"Lance darling, what's gotten into you lately? You seem to be so ... preoccupied." Anne Atwood sat under the brightly lit makeup vanity of her master bathroom, meticulously tweezing an eyebrow.

Hearing no answer, she began teasing her almost-shoulder-length natural blonde hair with one of a set of ivory-handled combs arranged on the vanity surface. "I mean, the election cycle is just barely warming up, and they adjourned your trial for what, a month?"

Perched in the seat of the large bay window in the adjacent sitting room, Atwood had been watching three teenage boys carrying skates and hockey sticks carefully testing the ice at the edge of the Atwood's property, the shoreline of which bordered Reeds Lake, a centerpiece of their small community. He turned from the window at the sound of Anne's high heels clicking across the hardwood floor.

"I'm sorry?" he said as he broke from his thoughts.

As always, his wife appeared flawless. Not a single thing about her was out of place as she stood in the doorway, cloaked in a sheer dressing gown, busily attaching an earring. She wore her accustomed expression, which suggested she knew something about you that you wished she didn't. Anne Atwood exuded a combined air of superiority and cunning. In a word, she was intimidating, and Lance loved it.

"I said…what's going on with you lately? You're somewhere else all the time these days. Are you … are we in some kind of trouble?"

"Not at all." He stood up and sauntered across the room to slip his arms around Anne's tiny waist, pulling her closer. "You've got to understand. This political game is not like trying lawsuits, which I've done scores of times. There's a lot of nuance and gamesmanship to this business and, if I'm going to get it right, I've got to study it—to think about the best way to prepare for the campaign."

Anne put her hands on his chest and firmly pushed him back. "I'll go along with finding the best way to win, darling. But since when have nuance and gamesmanship worried you at all? Those are your stock-in-trade, Lance. So give me a break. What's happening?"

Lance stared back silently. In her stiletto heels, they stood eye to eye. He pulled his arms away, turned, and walked back to the window. Anne followed quickly behind him.

"You have that guilty puppy look, Lance. Tell me you haven't gotten yourself into another situation … have you?"

"It's not like that. But it's complicated. I've got a lot on my mind."

"It had better not be like that teacher you were screwing. That could have cost us everything. Of all the stupid… for God's sake. She was your client!"

"I thought we put that behind us, Anne. Over and done—you agreed."

"We agreed that it wouldn't happen again! That's what you said."

Lance approached her and took her hands in his. "When was the last time we had sex, Anne?"

"What? What does that have to do with this?"

"That has everything to do with this, with us. Why the hell do you think I looked elsewhere? You just…"

Anne yanked her hands from his. "I just what? I've gone along, Lance. From the very beginning. You've got to give me that."

"Hah! You always want to ignore the elephant in the room, don't you! But I've got to give you your due in manipulating the argument. Three years on Wellesley's debate team taught you well."

"I will not go over the same old ground again. This is a tired discussion. But what I do want now is your commitment … and I mean a promise you will keep, to do everything you can to become the next governor. From there, the sky's the limit. My father will pave the way. He…"

"Ah yes! Your father—the great senator, Charles Henry Harrington. Good old Charlie. He'll fix everything."

"Damn it, Lance. He's always been there for us—for you. We live in his house, in his community. You can't say you haven't taken advantage of that."

"Okay. Okay. I'll admit that much, but you're still circling the issue." Lance began untying the knot to her dressing gown sash. She grabbed his wrists, but he didn't stop. With her hands still holding on, he pushed his own up to the collar of the dressing gown and pulled it down over her bare shoulders, pinning her arms against her sides. Her lips parted, and she began trembling.

"Don't. Please, Lance."

He looked down at her breasts, cupped in a black lace push-up bra. "You know what I want, Anne. If you'd just..."

"Not now." Glancing at the clock on the bed stand, she pried away his grip. "The Taylors' cocktail party is in less than an hour."

"Screw it! If I'm going to run this damned political gauntlet for you and Daddy, then I need consideration."

"What kind of consideration are you talking about? All you have to do is what you do best, persuade people to your side."

"You mean your side, don't you? And what I'm talking about is between you and me."

"You will never change, Lance, so don't expect me to. We are who we are. Live with it."

"Damn it Anne, I've been living with it, just as much as you have. I'm just not as...cold."

She walked over to the window. Outside, dusk was turning into dark. The light in the room was dimming.

Lance grabbed one of the crystal glasses from the rolling bar, poured a half-full glass of Jameson, and chugged it down.

Anne turned to face him. "I'll make you a deal. If you win, I'll do everything you want of me. Is that a good enough incentive for you?"

"For now, that'll have to do. Not that I have any reason to think you'll abide by your own terms. But know this. I'll win the damned election all right; I'll be the next governor, and then I'll collect what's mine. First, though, I've got something else to deal with." Lance started to place his glass on the bar when his cell phone rang.

Anne watched his expression change from recognition to concern as he answered. "Who is it, Lance?" she asked.

CHAPTER 16

Atwood Beach House.

M itch and Willy had left the others by the beach and made their way up the stairs to the top, where they stood facing the back side of a sprawling, two-story log home.

"This sure as heck isn't what I'd call a cottage. It's more like a friggin' log castle," Willy said.

"Here's what I need you to do," Mitch said, leveling a finger toward the house. "I want you to walk along that side over there by the garage and look for anything unusual. Any disturbance of the building; any sign of a break-in. Check the windows. See if you can spot anything at all suspicious. Okay?"

"Yes sir." Willy nodded and walked off.

Mitch called after him, "I'll take the other side, and we'll meet in front."

Minutes later they convened at the front door. "Anything?" Quinn asked.

"Not a thing, Chief. Everything looks normal—if

you can call this place normal. You want me to go get the phone now?"

"No. Not yet, Willy. We know that's the phone we're after. It's not going anywhere. I want to check with Dave Bartlett first. Just in case though, let's see if anyone's at home."

Mitch walked up to the front door and knocked loudly. Both listened for any sound. Hearing none, he banged again and peered through the narrow glass framing the double entrance doors. As he did, Willy looked down at the mat on the stoop and leaned over to pick up what appeared to be a key ring and fob.

"Somebody must have dropped this, chief."

Mitch looked closer at the object Willy held in his palm. "Let me see that."

Willy dropped it onto Mitch's gloved hand, and he twisted the piece of plastic attached to the fob. It had a logo printed on one side of what he realized was a plastic bottle opener.

"Well, well, what have we here?" They both read the inscription. "I think our Mr. Atwood is going to have some explaining to do." Mitch handed the fob back to Willy. "For now, put it back exactly as you found it. We can decide what to do with it later. Understood?"

"Got it, chief. But aren't we gonna see if she's here? She might be inside, right?"

"No. At least, not yet. I've got to think about this."

They walked back around the house and stood by a railing at the edge of the patio. Mitch knew breaking in without a warrant could jeopardize any evidence they might find; however, a delay could prove fatal if Prudence Wheatley were inside and physically hurt. Looking at the men below staring back up at him, he pulled out his phone and called Dave Bartlett.

"Dave, it's Mitch Quinn. I need your advice. We've located the cell phone, out here on North Shore beach. We found it in the backyard of an attorney named Lawrence Atwood."

"Jesus! You found it in his backyard?"

"Well, not exactly his backyard. It was on the dune behind his, uh, house." Mitch turned back to the expansive building rising behind him. He then described their search, what else they had found and how, explaining his dilemma of choosing between breaking into the house or awaiting a warrant.

"Under the circumstances, I think we should go in, Dave. If she's in there and alive, we need to get her out."

"You started on public land, right? And then found the phone?"

"Yeah, but I'm guessing the dune is on his land. If it is his, it was on private property. I just don't want to screw things up if it's needed at a trial."

"I think you've got probable cause."

They decided that Mitch and Willy would find a way inside, but only to look for Prudence Wheatley. If they found her, a warrant would be irrelevant. Bartlett said he would try to get the judge to sign a warrant that afternoon if they came up empty-handed. Mitch told the group to sit tight on the beach, and he and Willy looked around for the easiest point of entry. Willy carried a small set of tools, which they used to pick the lock on the rear door. Once inside, they moved quickly through the house, but found no sign of Prudence Wheatley.

After returning outside, Mitch called Bartlett right

away, dismissed the searchers, and told Willy to remain on guard. He then headed back to the village. As he drove past the public beach by the entrance to the association, he didn't notice the man parked in a far corner of the deserted lot.

By the time Mitch reached Bartlett's office, the search warrant was ready to go, and they left for the court, hoping they could still catch Judge Avery at the courthouse. When they entered the district courtroom a few minutes later, the judge was engaged in the last motion of the day. Seeing them, he quickly called for a recess, led them back to his chambers, and listened intently as Quinn pleaded their cause. After hearing what they had found, he waved for him to stop and removed a pen from beneath his robe.

"I'm going to sign this, but I want you to know that you're on thin ice. Because we have a missing person, I'll go along. But understand, Mr. Atwood may try to quash this, and he could succeed if he does."

"We appreciate the support, Judge. Finding that key fob at his front door goes a long way to putting her on the property. Chances are she was there, and maybe Atwood will know where she is."

He handed Bartlett the signed warrant. "Well, then you go get her, and bring her home."

After leaving the judge's chambers, they stopped briefly in the courthouse hallway. A few citizens stood in lines at a window counter a few feet away. One man was taking a particularly long time completing some papers, but the two paid him no mind.

Dave held up the warrant. "I'll give Atwood a call and let him know. We don't have to, but I want to see what he'll do. I'll invite him to join us."

"You think Atwood might try to prevent the search? Or maybe he'll even go out to the house tonight to remove any incriminating evidence?"

"It's possible. But if he's going to fight it, we might as well know it now. You can have someone there waiting for him if he goes out tonight. Otherwise, I'll tell him we'll meet him there first thing tomorrow morning."

"Isn't this kind of risky? I mean, if he fights it and he wins, won't we lose our chance to get whatever may be in there?"

"We could. But think about it. She's not there. Maybe she was but only maybe. There could be a logical explanation for everything, and I'm not one of those prosecutors who'll do anything for a conviction. He's innocent until we prove him guilty, and we're a far cry from there. I'm willing to give him a fair chance to cooperate with us."

Quinn shrugged. "Your call Dave, but the cop in me says we should just go in without him, and let the cards fall where they may."

"Well, let's just see what we find tomorrow when we get to search the place."

"You mean, *if* we get to search it."

CHAPTER 17

"Okay. Tell me again, Lance. Can you remember anything even remotely suspicious you saw while you were there?" Harlan Milbank stood looking down at his protégé, who sat at the end of a sofa in his home study. Lance was still worked up from the discussion on the phone when Dave Bartlett called to tell him they had a warrant to search his beach house. He contacted Harley right after they hung up. He and Anne had skipped the cocktail party, and she had already left to attend their dinner party alone. Now the two men were gauging the prospects of what might be found in a search.

"Hell, Harley, the whole damned thing was suspicious. I can't think of a damn thing I didn't already tell you that night." Atwood sat with his elbows on his knees and his fingers against his forehead, his tie askew beneath his open collar.

"Then there's nothing for them to find, unless you overlooked something. Now concentrate. When you searched the house that night, was there anything to suggest that she was ever there?"

Lance stared back indignantly. "No. And I went through all the rooms she might have gone into before I got there."

"So, you didn't check every room, then?"

"There was no reason to, Harley. The only rooms I didn't look in were the kids' rooms on the second floor. Why the hell would she go upstairs? She couldn't have been there very long before I arrived."

"All right. Now, what about the cell calls? Remind me about those."

Lance grabbed his cell phone from a side table. "She called once on this line. I called her back on my other cell." He looked at the recent call record.

"The first call was at 4:07 p.m. I was pissed off because we had agreed she would never call that number. Not even for an emergency. You know I always keep another prepaid cell for personal calls. Anyway, all the other calls were made to or from that other cell number. It's not listed. We talked once when I called her back, and then she called about an hour later."

"Well, we know they'll get your number on her cell records, if they don't have them already. Never admit to anything about those other calls. We can explain the first as just business. Are we clear on that?"

"That's not a problem. We've done a lot of legal business together the past few years. There'll be plenty of evidence to prove that. In fact, we had a deposition scheduled for the week after she disappeared."

"Did they tell you what they found that got a judge to sign a search warrant?"

"He didn't give me a clue. He just said they had probable cause, and the local judge agreed. I doubt a judge anywhere outside of that Podunk village would have granted it, but it is what it is."

"I'm still surprised they allowed you to meet them tomorrow. Don't the authorities usually just search the place right after they get a warrant?"

"That's what this Bartlett told me. He said he was just giving me a courtesy call, that they would either go in tonight or no later than tomorrow morning, and if I wanted to join them I could. I'm sure as hell going to. I said I'd meet them first thing in the morning."

"Why don't you get counsel and try to get the warrant quashed? Or you could at least maybe get a delay. Wouldn't it be better for you to go in first and have another look around?"

"He said the place was being guarded, and that they wouldn't do anything until I got there. No one's allowed inside in the meantime. Since this is a missing person case, and it's been three weeks since she disappeared, I don't think there's a chance in hell of getting that warrant quashed."

"Well, it's for sure going to be an interesting day tomorrow. There's a lot on the line, Lance—your entire future." Harley walked over to the bar and poured himself a scotch.

CHAPTER 18

Next morning.

The man sat huddled amid a stand of pine trees topping a dune overlooking the Atwood beach house. Snow had fallen sparse but steady since he had arrived at daybreak. He followed Mitch when he left Atwood's beach house the day before, trailing him back to Lakeview. He watched as Mitch entered the prosecutor's office, then leave a short while later accompanied by a large man in a suit. When they walked to the court building, he concluded they must be seeking a search warrant. He then decided to stake out the beach house, wanting to make sure they found all that he had left for them.

He hunched down further into the dune, arms wrapped around his shoulders, his feet propped against the trunk of a small pine. A single squad car remained in the driveway below. He was getting drowsy and fought to stay awake. Just then his chin jerked up from his chest at the sound of a car pulling in. The big man he had seen with Mitch the day before stepped out of a tan Buick, his footsteps crunching on the snow as he crossed to the sentry's car. Exhaust clouds billowed from each of the vehicles. After a brief conversation, he paced slowly to the front door of the house, holding his hands to the sides of his face as he peeked through a narrow glass window. Stepping away, he bent down to stare at something on the stoop, then returned to his car.

A short time later another squad car drove up and parked, Mitch exiting as soon as it came to a stop. A smaller policeman stepped out and joined him. After a sign from Mitch, the first car drove away. The men spoke briefly, stomping their feet against the chill. Then they all walked over to the front door. He watched contentedly as Quinn removed a clear bag from his pocket and stooped to pick something up from the porch with a pen, dropping it in the bag. Then they all walked to the rear of the house, disappearing around a corner. A few minutes passed before the group re-emerged, all three quickly getting into the prosecutor's car, each stamping and huffing.

CHAPTER 19

Mitch sat in the passenger side of Bartlett's car and held up two small plastic bags, one in each hand, staring at the contents. Bartlett cocked his head closer, peering at the bags. "It will be interesting to hear Atwood explain these. Now I've got to wonder what else we may find once we get inside."

"You think he'll bring his lawyer?" Willy sat in the back, leaning forward with his arms against the front seats of the car, head stuck between Dave and Mitch.

"Hard to say, Willy," Bartlett answered. "Atwood was calm when I called him yesterday. At least while we were on the phone. He didn't act surprised like I thought he would. But there was something else, right when I first told him we had a search warrant. A pause. Almost like he expected it."

Mitch dropped the bags in his lap. "You think he knows something then?"

"Not sure. I wish I could've seen his face. That would

reveal a lot. It's kind of like questioning a witness on the stand, insofar as it's much better when you can watch their expressions and observe body language. It can tip whether they're being truthful or hiding something."

Mitch looked over Bartlett's shoulder out the window. "Well, looks like you'll get your chance shortly."

"He's a cool cust…" Dave swiveled around as a Lincoln Navigator turned into the circular drive. "Well now, here we go."

The vehicle came to a stop and Lance Atwood stepped out alone, pulling on a hip-length black leather coat to cover his gray cashmere turtleneck and slacks. He stood still, waiting for them to come to him. Dave reached him first, and Atwood gazed at him suspiciously. "I'm Lance Atwood. And you are?"

"I'm Dave Bartlett, Mr. Atwood. I'm the Lake County prosecutor. We talked on the phone." Turning to the others, he said, "This is our chief of police Mitchell Quinn, and—"

Atwood's eyes narrowed as he interrupted. "Oh, yes. You're the high school football star. I had a little research run on you, Quinn. They said that you once ran down a prisoner who bolted from the courtroom during an arraignment. Apparently, you tackled him on the courthouse lawn. True story?"

Willy pushed forward between the two. "That's true, sir. I was there." Atwood briefly glanced at him, then returned his stare to Quinn.

"I'm Lakeview Deputy Martin Willoughby, Mr. Atwood. You can call me Willy. Everybody does." Willy looked at Mitch, then back at Atwood, neither of whose eyes moved from the other.

"And I hear you're running for governor," Mitch said.

"I don't think we're here to talk politics, I just—" Dave tried to break in, but Atwood interjected.

"So, this all has to do with that missing court reporter, Prudence Wheatley?"

"That's right, Mr. Atwood. She's been missing for weeks now."

"I don't know how I can help you, Dave." Lance paused, smiled at Bartlett, and said, "Okay if I call you Dave?" He didn't wait for an answer, looking back to Mitch. "But know that I've got my lawyer on call. If I want, I can have this search shut down in short order."

"We found Prudence Wheatley's phone on your property, Mr. Atwood, during our search of the area," Mitch began. "We tracked it to the dune behind your, uh, house, and—"

Holding up his palm, Atwood said, "I'm not just going to let you tear up my house because you found a phone on my property, no matter who it may belong to. There is a public beach nearby. Anyone could have put that phone there."

Mitch continued, "Well, Mr. Atwood, it's possible someone left it there. In fact, finding the telephone on your property raises plenty of different possibilities and lots of conclusions to match. What we need to know is how did her phone end up here and why?"

"Bottom line, Quinn, is that I have no idea how it got there and clearly neither do you. Otherwise, we wouldn't be doing this now."

"Maybe not, but we also have Ms. Wheatley's phone records, which show that someone made a call to your number on the afternoon of the last day anyone saw her, so—"

Atwood cut him off again. "So, that means nothing. She worked as a court reporter for me, many times. And yes, I got a call from her that afternoon, but we never spoke. I was busy and couldn't talk."

"Any particular reason she would be calling you then, Mr. Atwood?" said Bartlett.

Atwood's lips clenched. "As a matter of fact, there was. We had depositions scheduled for the following week. She had offered to drop off some transcripts from depositions taken in the same case a couple of weeks before. I assumed at the time, and I do now, that she was calling about that."

Mitch and Bartlett exchanged glances. "She was going to drop off those transcripts out here, at this address?"

"She had offered to, but to my knowledge, she never did."

"So, how did you confirm that? Did you come out here to check?"

"No. Uh, I've not been out here since, well, I, let me think. It was early fall when my wife and I came out to close up."

"Then how do you know she didn't deliver them?"

"I never got a call. Pru, uh, Ms. Wheatley, was very thorough. If she had dropped them off, she would have called me. She didn't, and then she disappeared."

"Okay, but there's something else." Mitch pulled a small plastic bag from his coat pocket.

Atwood stepped closer, peering at the object in the bag. "What is that? A key ring? Where did you get it?"

"We found it this morning, on your front doorstep."

Mitch noticed Atwood flinch slightly. "So what? Whose is it?"

"Look a little closer at the inscription, Mr. Atwood. It's actually a sort of keepsake, you might say."

He took a quick look and shrugged.

"It's the logo from the State Court Reporters' Organization. They were included in the attendees' packets at their convention held last spring. Prudence Wheatley attended that event." Bartlett had checked with the organization the afternoon before, confirming the information.

"Look gentlemen, I came all the way out here out of civic duty, to help you guys in your investigation. If this is going to turn into an interrogation, maybe I had better call my lawyer after all." He looked over at Bartlett. "Did you come here to charge me with something, Dave?"

"We're not accusing you of anything, Mr. Atwood. We only have a search warrant for your property. Maybe something happened out here, while you were away, and we just want to figure out what that might have been. Finding Ms. Wheatley's phone out in back of your property suggests, at the very least, that she may have been there."

"Okay. I'll go along with that."

"Unless you're going to call your lawyer to stop us from entering your house, why don't we all go inside and get warm?" Mitch said.

Atwood stood silent, then stepped past the others. "What the hell? I have nothing to hide. Let's get this over with."

CHAPTER 20

Once inside, Atwood shut the door and faced Mitch. "I was going to say that maybe she just came to the door to see if I was at home, accidentally dropped her key ring, and then she decided not to leave the transcripts outside until she could confirm I'd be coming."

"I suppose that's possible, but weren't you at least curious?" asked Bartlett.

"Curious about what?"

"Weren't you the least bit curious about what happened to the transcripts?"

"I never made it out that weekend like I'd planned. Then I learned she'd disappeared. What can I say? I didn't hear from her, so I assumed she didn't come out."

"Well, when we found her car there were no transcripts in it. So, if she didn't leave them here, and they weren't in her car, any idea what could have happened to them?"

"None."

"Did you ever follow up to find out where they ended up?"

"Eventually I got copies from her office, after she went missing. I guess it's possible she forgot them and figured that out when she got here."

"So, we're at least in agreement that she was here?"

"Look Quinn, if she was here, I don't know what may have happened to her."

Mitch let the conversation drop and walked into the adjacent kitchen. "Can you describe the floor plan so we can look around?" Atwood complied, then Mitch said to Willy, "You start upstairs, I'll begin down here on the first floor. Dave, why don't you take the office?" He moved down the hall toward the master bedroom. Willy plodded up the spiral stairway.

Bartlett followed Atwood back into the living room. He stopped to stare out a wall-to-wall, ceiling-high bank of windows overlooking an expanse of patio across the back of the home, the lake spreading out to the horizon beyond. He whistled. "Wow! Spectacular view!"

Lance beamed. "Thanks. The architect is from New York. He's damn good. By the way, the office is through that door to the right."

"Why don't you sit while I take a look?" Dave said. Atwood pulled out his cell phone and started to leave the room.

"Please do not leave this room while they're searching, Mr. Atwood. It wouldn't be good for you to disturb them."

Atwood stopped. "Worried about me, are you, Dave? Well, don't be. I was just going into the kitchen to make a few calls." Bartlett started to speak, but he was interrupted by a loud knock at the front door.

"I can't imagine who that could be," Atwood said.

"It's probably the crime unit. They're going to join us."

The lawyer held his palms upward and hunched his shoulders. "I sure hate to see our public servants wasting so much of the taxpayers' money on this kind of boondoggle. But then, it's your party, isn't it, Dave?" Atwood left to answer the door.

Bartlett could hear the exchange of introductions in the next room. Atwood returned, leading two men behind him. Bartlett recognized CSIs Chuck McNulty and Gil Strong. "Hey guys. Welcome to the party." Pointing behind them, he said, "The chief is down that hallway next to the front door. Willy's upstairs." They headed in opposite directions.

"I'm going into your office, Mr. Atwood. I'd prefer it if you stayed right here to make your calls."

Blowing out a long sigh, Atwood plopped onto the couch.

CHAPTER 21

After an interminable thirty minutes, Atwood looked up from his cell phone as Bartlett hustled past him, veering toward the hallway. He barked over his shoulder, "Stay put, Mr. Atwood. I'll be back shortly."

"Not to worry, Dave. I won't move a muscle."

As Bartlett entered the master bedroom, Mitch turned and asked, "Isn't Atwood's wife blonde haired?"

Bartlett shrugged. "Not sure. I've never met her, but I think that's the case from the pictures I've seen."

"Gil and I found several long, dark hairs on the bed and on the floor."

Bartlett folded his arms across his chest. "And Prudence Wheatley had dark hair."

"We also found this." Quinn moved to the head of the bed, pulled back the pile of pillows, and pointed to a necktie knotted around the post. He lifted the loose end with his pen.

Bartlett leaned in and grinned. "Nice tie. Must have left in a hurry, huh?"

"The Atwoods could be into some bedroom antics, but we'll have it tested for DNA just in case. If that was used as a restraint, it might still have some cells left on it. If they're Mrs. Atwood's, he can have it back."

Just then Willy leaned through the slider to the patio. "Hey Chief! You better come look at what Chuck found out back."

The two men followed him outside, where they saw the CSI agent standing next to a firepit holding an object with a large set of tongs. As they approached, he said, "Willy and I finished upstairs, so we took a look around out here. When I looked in the firepit, I saw this and pulled it out. Looks like there's more down there."

Bartlett shrugged. "So? You found some burnt wood in a firepit? Quite a discovery, Chuck."

"Look closer. Doesn't that look like a piece of bone?"

Mitch grabbed the object, turned it in his latex glove and motioned into the pit. "You need to get samples of whatever's down there, Chuck. I want this bagged, and especially any other large pieces. Get all that you can."

As the technician turned to retrieve more equipment, he almost ran into Atwood standing behind him. "Whoa! Mr. Atwood." The others pivoted.

"I saw you all running over here. What's all the commotion about?" He looked back and forth from the chief to Bartlett.

"That's what we're looking to find out," said Bartlett.

"Okay if I stay?"

"For now," Bartlett replied.

Chuck quickly returned to the patio carrying a large metal case, set it down, and opened it. Inside was an assortment of vials, packages, and tools. He pulled out a large piece of plastic, spread it out next to the short stone wall around the pit, and reached for the long set of tongs lying next to him.

Gil soon joined them, and Quinn pointed at the camera slung from his shoulder. "Take lots of pics of the material removed from this pit. Chuck, make sure you bag each item and record everything for the chain of custody."

Over the next twenty minutes, the group stood by silently and watched as the agents removed an assortment of fragments and placed them on the plastic sheet on the patio, Gil dutifully photographing each step of the process.

Atwood drew up beside him and stared at the display on the ground. "So? What the hell is the big deal about burnt wood in a firepit?"

Turning to Atwood, Mitch answered, "Chuck says it looks like bones." He watched for Atwood's reaction.

"What the …? If those are bones, I'd sure like to know who in the hell put them there."

"And just how do you think that might have happened, Mr. Atwood?"

"For all I know the local townies burned an animal—a dead dog or something they got out of the woods." He swiveled to Bartlett. "Dave, you know that those crazy teens do all kinds of shit out here, especially after things close down for winter."

"Um-hmm. I don't disagree. They do from time to time," Bartlett admitted.

"Okay. But just the same, we'll take the samples and see what we've got," said Mitch.

"Do what you want. Like I said to Dave, it's your party." Atwood whirled around and stomped back to the house.

Mitch then pulled Bartlett away from the others, toward the end of the patio, whispering to him as they walked. "If that stuff turns out to be what Chuck thinks it is, don't we have enough for an arrest warrant?"

"Let's not get ahead of ourselves. What if the DNA test of the hair from the bedroom doesn't pan out? Or what if the material in the pit isn't human? We're left with a key fob and a phone."

"And some muddy shoes."

"Shoes?" Bartlett stopped and looked at him quizzically. "What shoes?"

Mitch walked back toward the house, with Bartlett in step, leaning over him. "You remember it rained like hell the night Prudence Wheatley disappeared, right?"

"Um-hmm."

"And we tracked all those footprints across from where the car was found, leading in this direction?"

"Yeah. So?"

"Well, Willy spotted a pair of old topsiders sitting next to the steps by the garage entrance to the house. They had mud all over them. Assuming the weather hasn't washed them out, we'll make plaster casts of those footprints we found leading away from the Four Fronts Mall. If they match, we've got Atwood near where we found the car—unless somebody stole the shoes and put them back, or one of his kids wears a size eleven."

Bartlett burst out with a laugh. "Mr. Atwood will indeed have some 'splainin' to do. I think now we've at least got a murder suspect. Let's see what he has to say, and then we'll talk about what to do next."

CHAPTER 22

Later that day.

"I t was the county prosecutor; Dave Bartlett is his name. There was a local hero police chief, some dimwit deputy, and two CSIs. They tried to interview me after, but I told them I was done for the day." Right after the investigators left, Atwood had called his mentor, who was now probing for details.

"Did they tell you what they took away?" As they spoke, Harley made notes on a small pad as he sat in his office. He jotted *Evidence? Charges? and Lawyer?*

"I don't know all of what they've got, Harley, but I do know they have her phone. They said they found it on the dune behind the house. The only other thing they showed me was a keychain with the court reporters' association logo on it, which they think is hers. They said it was lying on the front doorstep. I mean, what the hell was she doing there? The garage door has a keypad, and she had the numbers. The interior door was open for her. All she had to do was park and go inside."

"What did you tell them? How did you explain those things being there?"

"I told them she was going to drop off some deposition transcripts."

"Damn. That puts her out at the beach house for sure."

"For God's sake, Harley, they had the phone and key fob. I had to come up with something—some reasonable explanation for why she would've been out there."

"I guess you're right. Is that all?"

"No. They also found some kind of crap in the firepit out back."

"What kind of crap?"

"I don't know. One of the CSI guys claimed it was bones, but to me it looked mostly just like burnt wood. Christ! I'm not sure we even used that pit at all last summer. Whatever the hell it was, they took a bunch of it."

"But why would they take burnt wood from a patio firepit? Unless …" Milbank dropped his pen on the pad, sitting up in his chair. "Lance, you didn't…?"

"What the fuck, Harley! What are you asking…did I burn her up? For crying out loud, I don't need that from you!"

"Cool down, Lance. I was just…"

"If that's what you're thinking, you can go the hell back to one of your has-been congressmen, and I'll get a different campaign manager."

Harley squirmed. "I'm sorry. I just remembered the comment you made back at the charity event that afternoon at the Athletic Club. Of course, I knew you were kidding, but your remark just jumped into my head."

Lance exhaled into the phone. "I just said I would take care of things. That's all! I was going to break it off like

I've done with all the others. Whatever happened to Pru that night, I had nothing to do with it."

"Forgive me, Lance. It was just a knee-jerk reaction. But if anything remotely suggesting…well, you can bet the press would make hay out of it. We need to get ahead of this."

"That's your job, Harley. Do it."

After a long pause, Harley spoke. "Why not bring in someone like, say, a Jules Goldman?" He wrote *Goldman?* on his pad.

"Nah! The minute I get a high-profile criminal lawyer like Goldman, the assumption is that I'm guilty. That's not the impression I want to give." Lance was aware that Goldman was the top criminal lawyer in Michigan, a worthy counterpart to Lance himself, except he specialized in criminal law as opposed to civil cases. He had represented notorious criminals and organized crime figures in numerous high-profile cases over the years; more than one alleged murderer had been freed because of his considerable trial skills.

"I'm just saying maybe you should bring Jules on board. Get his input so there are no missteps. You can have him on call behind the scenes. We cannot let this get out of hand."

"Look, if worse comes to worst, the only thing that I have to hide is an affair, and if that's the most they can prove, so what?"

"Good-hearted court reporters don't go missing while visiting a client's home every day, Lance."

"I'm going to meet with Bartlett, but without Jules Goldman. You won't talk me out of it."

"But that's so risky!"

"Damn it, I'm innocent! I think it'll go worse for me if I just lawyer up and don't talk to them. They'll think I'm hiding something."

"Well, aren't you?"

Atwood hesitated.

"Lance, I do believe that you're innocent. But that's not the question. It's what the police think that matters right now. And later, it's what a jury will think if, God forbid, you're charged with something. So, take the advice you'd give to a client. Get a good lawyer now, when he can help you fend off worse problems, and not later—when the shit has already hit the fan."

Another pause. "Okay, okay. Just to satisfy you, I'll give Goldman a call. But that's all. If I can't handle a small-town county prosecutor, I might as well hang it up."

CHAPTER 23

Mitch returned to town with Bartlett, leaving Willy to take their cruiser. "Some party we had, eh?" He removed his hat as he stepped into the car, tossing it in the back seat. "I'll say one thing, that guy is smooth."

Bartlett twisted to look behind as he started to back out. "I've always said that a good trial lawyer has to be a good actor, and Atwood's supposed to be one of the best. His explanations were plausible."

Mitch stared out the window as they pulled away. "Maybe so, but somebody tossing her phone behind his house from down on the beach is a stretch. That key fob gets her to the front door. And if some stranger took her, why would he toss the phone out there where it could be found?"

"He could have panicked. Maybe they struggled; she tried to call for help, and the attacker just threw the phone away. Afterward, maybe he couldn't find it in the dark. That dune grass is pretty thick," Bartlett said.

"Okay. But if she was there just to deliver those transcripts, where'd they go? An attacker would not have given those a second thought. They would either still be on the doorstep, in her car, or maybe even somewhere around the yard. But they aren't."

"If Atwood had something to do with her disappearance, wouldn't he have just taken them himself, and gotten rid them?"

Mitch rubbed his eyes. "Good point."

"And why would he toss the phone in his own backyard? Wouldn't he destroy that too?"

"Touché. But what if they had an argument? Say it happened out back. It got heated; he grabbed the phone and pitched it. In all the excitement, he either forgot about it or couldn't find it later."

"C'mon, he had plenty of time before yesterday to find it. All he would have had to do is what you did—call it and listen. He wouldn't have to look all over, just stand on his patio."

"I suppose it could have been an argument—a lovers' quarrel, and things got heated. Atwood strikes me as someone with a temper. So, he killed her. Then he panicked, burning her body in that pit to cover up the murder."

"But what about all that blood in her car? There wasn't a trace in the house. And that still doesn't explain the phone." Mitch sighed in frustration.

"Hopefully, the DNA results will help tell the story. I expect it's going to take a while to get them back, but without them, we don't have a body, no murder weapon, and still no clear motive."

"I'll give you this, counselor—there's a hell of a lot that doesn't add up."

Shortly after they arrived at Bartlett's office back in Lakeview, his secretary announced Lawrence Atwood was calling. To their surprise, he asked to meet with them Monday morning, and they agreed upon 10:00 a.m. He stressed that he wasn't bringing a lawyer. Bartlett then prevailed upon Mitch to handle the interview alone.

"You can do it, Mitch. Plus, since I'll be prosecuting the case, I don't want to be a witness to whatever is said."

"That's a bad idea, Dave. Isn't there somebody else in your office who can do it? I don't have much experience with interrogating lawyers, certainly not ones as shrewd as Atwood."

"Nobody else here does either. You've got more capital murder case background than anyone in this office. Maybe in the state."

"That was a long time ago. I haven't handled one like this for years."

"Well, bone up on it, Chief. You da man. There's nobody else, and I won't take no for an answer. Now, let's talk about what you're gonna do on Monday."

CHAPTER 24

Before arriving early for his Monday appointment, Atwood spent almost an hour on the phone with Jules Goldman, who gratuitously briefed him on what to expect from his impending interview. Since Atwood had not yet hired him, Goldman admonished him not to disclose any sensitive facts, as they would not be subject to attorney-client privilege. He also advised Atwood to cancel the meeting, or at least have him go along. Atwood thanked him and rejected the advice.

As he entered Bartlett's office, Atwood stopped at the door, seeing Mitch seated alone at a conference table.

"Good morning, Mr. Atwood. Come on in and have a seat."

Atwood eyed him suspiciously as he slowly came forward and took off his camel overcoat, folding it over the chair before sitting down. Looking around the room, he said, "Where's Dave Bartlett? I thought he would be here."

"Sorry. He can't make it. I'll be conducting this interview. Is that a problem?"

"Not at all, Quinn. But didn't you mean to say interrogation?"

"You volunteered for this meeting, Mr. Atwood."

"True." He looked tentatively at the recording equipment sitting in front of him. "But I didn't agree to a recording. This was just supposed to be a friendly sit-down. If you want to continue, you can forget recording our little talk."

"Why? Is there something you don't want on the record?"

"I have nothing to hide, Quinn. Let's just say I'm skeptical. I had that associate of mine dig up a little more background info on you last night. You're just full of surprises."

"You seem to have your people working overtime. I hope it was worth the expense?"

Atwood tapped the recorder. "As long as that's off, you can fire away. Ask me anything you want."

"All right, no recording." Mitch pushed the recorder aside and placed a pad in front of him. "Why don't you tell me about your relationship with Ms. Wheatley?"

"Again? I thought we already went over all of that yesterday."

"Just humor me, please."

Atwood reiterated the facts exactly as he had the day before. He impressed Mitch with the detail, not to mention his confidence.

"I'm still confused why you didn't try to contact her and find out what happened to those transcripts. Why didn't you just call her back?"

"Look, I probably thought about it at some point. I don't recall. But, as I told you yesterday, I didn't get back out there again before I met with you."

"Why not?"

"My plans changed."

"But at that point you couldn't have known she had disappeared. It wasn't reported until after she failed to show up for work on Monday. Weren't you concerned to know if she had made it?"

"I've had a hell of a lot going on, what with my practice and campaign preparations. Once I heard about her disappearance, sure, it concerned me."

"But didn't you need those transcripts for depositions the following week?"

"We canceled those when we learned that she hadn't shown up for work. That's when I asked about getting the transcripts from her office."

"You didn't call her back on a different phone, did you, sir?"

Atwood paused. "Different phone? What do you mean?"

"Her phone records show calls to her cell from an unlisted number right after she called you, and sporadically after that. All from the same number. Do you have another phone you use, say, for business, or...?"

"Why would I use another phone right after she called me?" Atwood hesitated. "Probably just another client. Mere coincidence."

"Possibly. Odd it was unlisted. And that client kept calling back. Not like you."

Atwood surveyed the room. "Can I have a drink of water?"

Mitch pointed to a decanter and glasses on a credenza behind Atwood, who reached over and filled a glass.

"What did you do that night, Mr. Atwood? October 31, that is. Where were you for the rest of the evening?"

"As I mentioned, I'd been at an event at the Athletic Club in the city. I attended with my campaign manager, Harlan Milbank. You can ask him."

"You were with him until when?"

"I don't remember exactly when I left."

"And after that?"

"Then I just went home."

"Assuming that Mr. Milbank supports your story as you said, can anyone else verify your whereabouts for the rest of the evening?"

"I suspect not, Quinn. I was alone."

"Then you tell me. Why aren't you the number one suspect in the disappearance of Prudence Wheatley?"

Atwood sat up in his chair, glaring contemptuously. "In any other setting, I wouldn't dignify that question with an answer. But I've come here today, voluntarily, to get this whole matter straightened out. So, the reason is quite simple—because I'm not guilty of anything. I had absolutely no reason to harm Ms. Wheatley, and I didn't. And you have nothing but pure speculation to prove otherwise."

Mitch paused, considering how best to proceed. "You have to admit, Mr. Atwood, the facts do raise a lot of suspicion."

"Oh yeah? How is that, Quinn?"

"That's some strange material our CSI found in your firepit."

"You've been trying to imply I had something to do with that since you met me at my front door. All this drama about bones. You must really be desperate to concoct such a ridiculous theory. Only some kind of wacko would burn a person's body in a firepit, and you can bet your badge I don't qualify."

Mitch frowned as he tapped his pen, deciding it was time to throw out some bigger bait. "One last question for you, Mr. Atwood. Do you and Mrs. Atwood ever engage in what some would call sex games?"

"What the hell kind of question is that?" Lance jerked to attention, his face contorted. Mitch thought he looked confused.

"We found one of your neckties, at least we assume it was yours, tied to your bedpost. Can you tell me how it got there?"

"What kind of trick are you trying to pull, Quinn? If there was a tie on our bedpost, then you must have planted it there. You and Bartlett are trying to set me up just because you can't find whoever it was who killed Pru Wheatley."

"Who said she was killed, Mr. Atwood?"

"We both know that when people disappear and the authorities don't find them right away, chances go up that they're dead." Atwood cocked his head, grinning smugly.

"They're running DNA testing on the tie. Results should be back soon."

"DNA on a necktie? They can do that?" Atwood said quizzically.

"Oh yeah. It's called touch DNA. Most folks outside of law enforcement know nothing about it."

Mitch explained the identification process requires only a very few cells for testing. In the early development of DNA testing, roughly quarter-sized amounts of body fluids such as blood, saliva, or semen were essential for competent testing. As the process was refined over the years, smaller sample sizes were necessary; now, DNA could be retrieved from cells on virtually any surface.

"So, DNA can be recovered from any skin cells found on the tie. That will tell us whoever it was that knotted the tie to the bedpost."

"That will prove nothing, Quinn. If it was my tie, and it has any DNA on it, it would be mine."

"Maybe. But they're also testing some other items we took."

"What other items?"

Mitch let the question hang in the air. "Thanks for your time, Mr. Atwood," he said as he tucked away his pen and notepad and rose to leave. "There's a lot to sort through here. These things take time. I'm sure Dave Bartlett will be in touch as soon as we complete our investigation." Mitch left Atwood sitting on the edge of his chair.

CHAPTER 25

December. Lansing.

Cynthia Worthey sat in a booth across from her boss in the State Capitol Building dining room, downstairs from the attorney general's office. A source alerted them that morning of the warrant to search Atwood's beach house, but, as yet, they had no clue what the police might have turned up. They mulled over the prospects of a connection with the disappearance of Prudence Wheatley, speaking in low voices.

"You know Rob, if Atwood's involved in this, it would be enormous. The biggest, maybe ... ever. Think of the headlines." She put her thumbs and forefingers together in front of her face and slowly spread her arms apart. "'Famous Trial Lawyer Indicted for Murder of Court Reporter.' Or better, 'Gubernatorial Candidate Charged in Murder of Paramour.'" Slumping back into her seat, Worthey chortled, wide-eyed.

Patterson looked out across the room. "Settle down, Cynthia. There's been nothing concrete to connect him to the disappearance of that woman, let alone any charges filed. But if they are and I were to get involved, it could look like I'm just grabbing headlines to pad my own run for governor. Plus, if my history with Lance Atwood, or I should say Mrs. Atwood, were to go public, it would be hard to argue I don't have at least the appearance of a conflict of interest."

"So, you dated his wife what, a hundred years ago? So what?"

"It was more than just dating. We were together for a few years, starting out our freshman year in college. Atwood came along and ended our plans. You think for one second the press wouldn't dig that up and make a big deal out of it? Hell, I'm a Republican."

Worthey tapped her decoratively painted nails on the tabletop. "Well, then why couldn't I take it on? I don't have a conflict. Think of it this way: If we put the great Lance Atwood out of business, the path will be clear for you to waltz right into the governor's mansion."

Patterson leaned in and spoke in a lowered voice. "And then you could waltz right into my job, right Cynthia?"

"Come on, Rob. You know it's not like that." Worthey's lower lip stuck out in a pout. "Okay. Sure, I hope to be the head honcho someday. But you know that I know I'm the *assistant* prosecutor for now. And I'm a loyal one."

"You're my right hand for sure; but understand, we'd have to be very careful going in and taking things over in a local prosecutor's backyard."

"If Atwood is somehow implicated, the AG's office has got to take over the case, Rob. I mean, maybe Bartlett's a pretty good lawyer, maybe not, but pretty good won't cut it if Atwood's charged. He'll bring everything they've got to bear, absolutely burying Dave Bartlett and Lake County."

Patterson knew he had the authority to take over a capital case from a county prosecutor. Although rare under any circumstances, it would be more typical for a local prosecutor to ask the state to intervene, especially in a high-profile prosecution requiring more resources than the county could afford. Bartlett's jurisdiction comprised mostly small burgs and villages, with only two moderately sized towns for tax subsidy. He expected Dave's township board would welcome the AG's office taking over the case, as they could ill afford a lengthy and expensive trial replete with exorbitantly priced expert witnesses.

Worthey kept pushing. "If we were to take it over, we could curry local favor by keeping Dave in the loop, maybe even have him involved as local counsel at the trial. He could be a good addition to the strategy team."

Patterson began sliding out of the booth. "Regardless, unless something changes, this is all a lot of rank speculation. We'll just have to wait and see what the investigation turns up. If they find something concrete, things will get very interesting, very fast."

CHAPTER 26

January. Saturday night.

Charlie Rafferty stood behind the bar of Rafferty's Saloon, a locals' watering hole on the outskirts of Lakeview Village, watching two bikers who had been drinking heavily and playing pool for the past hour. They'd moved into the dining area, and a heated discussion was brewing with a man sitting alone in the corner. Rafferty grabbed the arm of a passing waitress who had served that table earlier. "Gina, what's up at table ten?"

The young woman looked back at the table, shrugged, and said, "I think those guys want his table and he's not givin' it up."

"Tell Bobby to come out here. Now!"

Gina disappeared through the swinging doors leading to the kitchen. Moments later, a bearish figure filled the same doorway and lumbered over to the bar, asking, "What's up, Uncle Charlie?"

Rafferty looked up at his nephew, standing beside him in a grease-covered chef's apron. Stubble pocked his chubby cheeks, head resting upon a massive neck and bulging shoulders that strained against a too-tight Army Football T-shirt.

"I think we've got some trouble brewing over there in the corner." He nodded toward the men, and Bobby's eyes followed.

"So, what do you want me to do?"

"Keep an eye out and be ready. I'm thinking this could turn into something real quick; if so, I'll need you to break up any ruckus." Bobby nodded, moving closer to the open end of the bar.

As they watched the group in the corner, one biker placed his hands on the tabletop and leaned down close to the sitting man's face. The man stood up slowly, speaking calmly to the biker, whose voice grew louder as they faced one another. Rafferty noticed that a number of patrons had started paying attention.

Bobby hurried around the bar's end to the table, stepping between the two men. "We won't be havin' any trouble in here, guys. If you need to settle somethin', do it outside. Otherwise, I call the cops."

The biker staggered and stuck his chin out, looking back at Bobby through bloodshot eyes. "We just want a damned table. This dude is done; he should move." He stepped forward, bumping hard into the huge bouncer.

Bobby grabbed the biker's shoulder, spun him around, and jerked his thumb in the air. "That's it, buddy. You're outta here."

"I ain't goin' anywhere. Not unless he does." The biker pointed at the other man, who hadn't moved.

"C'mon mister. Maybe you'd better go too." The man returned a slight grin, picked up his jacket and slowly started toward the door. Bobby motioned both bikers in the same direction. They exchanged glances and followed.

Bobby watched them leave, breathing a sigh of relief. He walked over to his uncle, who had watched from his spot at the end of the bar. "Good job, boy. Glad to see you stopped all the fuss."

"I don't know, Uncle Charlie. I don't think it's over."

Rafferty walked over to the windows lining the front wall. He squinted over the curtains and grabbed Bobby's arm. "Maybe you'd better go check on those guys. Looks like they may be goin' at it out front. I don't want 'em scaring anyone away, and we don't want no cops."

Minutes later Bobby came back in, shaking his head. "You may wanna take a look at this, Uncle Charlie."

Rafferty followed him back outside, stopping three steps into the front lot. The two bikers lay sprawled on the ground. He walked over for a closer look. They were breathing but bloodied and barely conscious.

"Why don't you see if you can get these guys up? I don't want to call 911 until I find out if they want us to."

Bobby looked around, but the other man was nowhere to be seen. "Geez! They were only out here a few minutes. How'd that guy pull off all this damage?"

Rafferty put a hand on his nephew's shoulder. "I'm just glad you didn't have to find out."

CHAPTER 27

Later that month.

The initial DNA results on samples retrieved from the Atwood beach house and the Mustang had finally come back from the lab. The hairs recovered in the Atwood bedroom matched samples obtained at Prudence Wheatley's apartment, and the blood recovered from her car matched as well. The materials salvaged from the firepit were still being analyzed along with the tie they took from the bedroom.

Mitch and Bartlett sat huddled this Wednesday morning with Dr. Wilhelm Jacoby in his office at Michigan State University, where he was a tenured professor. Jacoby was also a board-certified forensic anthropologist, often the primary expert relied upon by the state in certain complex murder cases. They had sent the results to him for analysis and as a precursor to retaining him for expert testimony at trial.

The diminutive professor sat low in his chair across from his visitors, arms spread around the stack of papers in front of him. His pinkish scalp shone above fenders of curly white hair lining the sides of his head, contrasting with a dark Van Dyke beard; the many lawyers who relied upon his trial testimony appreciated his learned appearance. Peering over the wire rim lenses of his reading glasses at the two men, he expounded on a favorite topic.

"Deoxyribonucleic acid—that's DNA to most—is a molecule encoding the genetic framework of all living organisms." Jacoby went on with a prideful recitation, explaining that every human has a unique set of DNA, although over 99 percent of human DNA sequences are virtually identical. Despite this contradiction, there is sufficient difference between individuals' DNA to distinguish one from another via comparison. Although the DNA of related people is quite similar, unrelated humans have sufficiently different genetic material so that a specific person can be identified by DNA extracted from blood, saliva, bodily fluids, hair, and even bone marrow.

He noticed the disinterested expressions as he took a breath. "Forgive me, gentlemen. I so often lecture on the subject that I just can't help myself. I forgot that you're way ahead of most people I speak to on this subject."

"Doctor, with all due respect," Bartlett said as he sat up, glancing at Mitch, "we have DNA linking the deceased to the home of the accused. Problem is, without a confession—or some evidence showing that the suspect was there with her—everything is circumstantial. There's no body, no murder weapon, and frankly no clear motive. We need something to link the material recovered from the suspect's firepit to the missing woman."

"You probably already know that burned bones present a substantial challenge to identification, as compared to other media. Caveat aside, I can say what you retrieved from that pit comprises bones, which we've verified are most likely human."

"'Most likely' won't help us, Doctor," Dave lamented. "The standard is 'beyond a reasonable doubt.'"

"I understand that, Mr. Bartlett, but even if I were to confirm it as unquestionably human bone, that doesn't get you where you want to be. We need the DNA match and retrieving sufficient DNA results from burned bone is a very complicated process. You need to salvage enough tissue to perform the required testing. That is what we've been attempting to do. We've retrieved some minimal tissue, but it may not be enough to verify a match."

"Our question, Dr. Jacoby, is can you get enough to prove that the bones removed from that firepit were those of Prudence Wheatley?"

"To be honest, Chief Quinn, I'm not sure yet. Generally, provided we can salvage enough bone fragments or teeth from the remains, we are able to make an eventual identification. But various factors can complicate the process. These include the method used to burn the body, whether accelerants were used, and how much time has passed since the burning, to name a few."

Dr. Jacoby let the two men consider this for a moment. "In your case, gentlemen, we have several, shall we say, problematic factors at play. The remains were exposed to the elements for an extended period. As a result, much of what you gave the lab was corrupted. Additionally, there were no teeth, which are frequently the primary means used to identify decomposed human remains."

"Yes, but ultimately, can't you still make an ID with what you have, Doctor?"

"Again, I can't say at this point. The most intriguing aspect of your case is the fact that some larger fragments showed signs of being cut or sawed. Also, many appear almost as if they were subjected to, I know it may sound strange, but to some kind of... well, an explosion."

"An explosion?" Quinn recalled the scene at the beach house. "There were no signs of an explosion at the location, Doctor. The firepit was perfectly intact. Nothing around the grounds looked like anything exploded there, and we combed every inch of that place in a hundred-yard radius."

"Well, that level of destruction just wouldn't happen from a fire alone. If not at the site where you found them, apparently it occurred elsewhere, which means the remains were brought to the site afterward."

"Why the hell would..." Bartlett looked over at Mitch. "You think he had time to do all of that in one night?"

"I don't know. She was missing for a while. Maybe he didn't do it that night."

"But, blowing up her remains? Why? And where did he do it?" Mitch asked. "I've never heard of such a thing, Doctor. Have you?"

"Yes, I have. Historically, blowing up bodies after a crime is sometimes employed to make it more difficult to identify the remains—to confound the police if you will. Most cases of this sort occurred before modern DNA testing. With one exception, I can't recall any recent cases where the perpetrator gathered the fragments after deconstruction, then deposited them at another location."

"What was the one exception?" asked Bartlett.

"Yes. Well, it was just over two years ago. The

authorities discovered the remains of a young woman at the site of a burn pit at a trailer park in Wisconsin. It was owned by one of two murder suspects. The condition of the bones led some to conjecture that after they killed her, they blew up her body, then burned her remains and scattered them. I'm sure I can find the details if need be."

"I'd appreciate that, Doctor. But for now, let's focus on our killer. Humor me for a minute. Let's say he is particularly clever and wants us to think that no one would do such a thing, especially at his own home. Geez, I'm not even sure that I can believe it. Isn't it conceivable that's exactly why he did it? After all, if I can't believe it, why would a jury?"

The doctor folded his arms across his chest, raising his right index finger to his mouth. "Such a person would have to be exceptionally cunning. It's imaginable this individual might believe his own backyard is the last place someone would expect to find the victim's remains."

"That's why we've got to identify the bones from the pit. Without those, we can't prove Prudence Wheatley was killed," Mitch insisted.

"As you already know, our local labs are not equipped to perform this level of testing, so they had to send the samples out of state. Given the backlog of requests for DNA testing, the process often takes months—potentially longer in this instance, considering the complexities of the case. Even then we can't ensure they'll be able to tell if the bones belong to the victim."

Jacoby assured them he would try to expedite the testing, and after a round of goodbyes they left his office, heading down the hall toward the elevators. Bartlett spoke first. "Looks like we'll have to use what we already have to go for the indictment, and just hope we can get the DNA test results on the bones before trial."

The elevator doors opened. They both entered, and Mitch leaned back against the wall, folding his arms. "I can see coming up with the idea to get rid of the body in the firepit, but the rest is off the charts."

Dave punched the button for the first floor. "Maybe he thought the body wouldn't burn up, so he decided to blow it up?"

"But where could he do that? And how would he get it back to the pit? That's a lot of moving around for one night's work."

"Why did it have to be all in one night? He could have left the body in the car, or hidden it someplace, and come back later. It was a couple of weeks before you found the car. Plenty of time."

"It would be hard for Atwood to do all of that alone. What about an accomplice?"

Dave looked down at him. "That would make more sense, all things considered. Either way, it would have taken some planning. But who would help him?"

"How about that campaign manager of his? I'll bet winning the governor's mansion would mean a lot of prestige, and money, to someone like him."

"Is that enough of a motive to help someone blow up a body?"

"I've seen people do some pretty bad shit for a lot less."

"Well, right now it's all about the bones—that is, if we want to prove murder. Meanwhile, let's charge Lance Atwood and see what happens."

CHAPTER 28

February.

Lance Atwood sat in front of a shiny-topped mahogany desk opposite Jules Goldman, who leaned back in a leather Radcliffe desk chair pretending to listen. His offices occupied half of the thirty-sixth floor of the prestigious GMRenCen in the state's largest city. The huge wall of windows behind him offered a panoramic view of the shoreline across the river.

Goldman was trying to concentrate on Atwood's story, but he couldn't stop his thoughts from wandering. It was obvious that an indictment of Atwood was inevitable, and he kept imagining the press coverage once he got formally hired. There would be a trial of the century, keeping his name in the public eye for months. The fees alone would be enormous, not to mention the eventual book-and-movie rights.

His daydream was suddenly interrupted by Atwood's rebuke: "Are you listening to me, Jules?" Goldman looked up at the irritated expression of his prospective client.

"I can call you Jules, right? After all, if I'm going to pay you a very large retainer, I should have that privilege."

"Of course, Mr. Atwood. And I am listening. I'm just planning out exactly how to approach your defense in the event you're charged."

Atwood settled in his chair as Goldman continued. "Let's talk about Ms. Wheatley. Tell me about your relationship with her. And be completely candid. That will be critical moving forward."

"What do you want to know? I already told you I was fu... I was involved with her, sexually. We got together off and on for the last year or so. Nothing serious. At least not for me. Anyway, I never saw her that night, and I sure as hell did not harm her in any way. You've got to believe me."

"It doesn't matter if I believe you. It's the jury we must convince."

"Isn't that the prosecution's problem? We both know they must prove my guilt beyond a reasonable doubt. And their whole case is circumstantial. Hell, they can't even prove that she's dead. I'd say there's a hell of a lot of doubt here, wouldn't you agree?"

"Perhaps that's so. But we do have one other rather large problem. You've lied about your relationship with the missing woman and about your whereabouts on that night."

"I've thought about that, Jules. But picture this. What if I come clean? They can't prove a damn thing beyond that."

"If you do, they'll use it against you. A jury can be persuaded to convict, even in the face of reasonable doubt, if they are convinced you had both motive and opportunity. By coming clean, you'll be giving them both."

"But that's still all speculation. Won't the court instruct the jury that they can't speculate?"

"Yes, but the prosecution can argue any plausible theory, provided there is some evidence to support it—even circumstantial evidence. The court will instruct the jury that they can draw reasonable inferences. In other words, they can put two and two together."

"But isn't it better to just get it out now, rather than take a chance it may come out later? Wouldn't that be much worse?"

"How will you explain why you didn't tell them that before?"

"That's easy. I didn't because I was afraid of the consequences. That's the truth."

"The truth doesn't mean much to a prosecutor hell-bent on a guilty verdict. Prosecutors love to catch the accused telling a lie. You're talking about handing that to them on a platter."

"Whatever. I did nothing to Pru Wheatley, and I'll try to convince them of that now. Even if they don't believe me, maybe it will at least create some doubt in their minds. That could make them worry about what a jury might do."

"That's only relevant if you're looking to cut a plea bargain. I assume that's not something you're interested in?"

"Hell no. I'm not guilty of anything, and I'm surely not going to lie and say I am."

"The way things stand now, and considering the meager evidence they have, you likely wouldn't even have to take the stand. The cell phone and the key fob are explainable. She went to your house to deliver the transcripts—not enough to convict. Our defense is that you were home in bed. If the jury is convinced you weren't there, then none of the rest matters, anyway."

"I'd rather go with the truth, Jules. If I have to testify, so be it. I've won a hell of a lot of closing arguments before."

"There's a hell of a lot more riding on this argument than money."

"I expect any lawyer I'm paying to follow my directions, Jules."

"Have it your way, Mr. Atwood. I take it that you're hiring me to represent you?"

"Was there ever any doubt?"

Goldman grinned. "All right then, Lance. Since we're lawyer and client, it's okay for me to call you Lance, right? I'll have my secretary prepare the retainer agreement. Now, let's figure out how best to control this. Tell me again exactly what happened the night Prudence Wheatley disappeared. Start from the very beginning. When you left Detroit."

Atwood settled back and began recounting the events of that evening.

CHAPTER 29

Having received no contact from Pru following their abrupt disconnection earlier that afternoon, Atwood hurriedly left the city and drove across the state through a downpour. On the way, he called a state police contact, who confirmed no reports of accidents on the route she would have taken. He had tried her phone more than once, but the calls went to voice mail.

By the time he reached his beach house, the rain had dwindled to a fine mist. He pulled into the driveway and slowed at the sight of an open but empty garage. After parking, he entered through the unlocked door to the back hall, stopping in the kitchen at the sight of grocery bags on the counter. Curious that the lights in the room were on, he began calling Pru's name as he checked the main floor. Finding no one and seeing no light emanating above the stairs to the second floor, he crossed through the living room to the patio slider. When he slid open the door, his eyes snapped shut at the sudden rush of wind, and the drapes fluttered wildly. His steps clapped against the stone patio as he trotted over to a short rock wall lining the edge of the sand bluff descending to the beach. Other than his shouts of Pru's name into the darkness, the only sound was the breaking of waves below.

Returning inside, he snatched a decanter of scotch and a glass from the built-in bar, poured three fingers of Macallan 25 and settled into the plush cushions of the curved sofa in the center of the room. After downing a deep swig, followed by a few moments of contemplation, Lance rose and returned to the kitchen, scotch and glass in hand. He pulled out one of the island stools, sat, and gulped the remains of his drink. Refilling the empty glass, he reached for his phone and hit the speaker button when the desired number appeared. A familiar voice echoed in the kitchen. "Milbank here."

"Harley, I need your advice."

"Lance, surely you don't need my advice on affairs of romance? You could write a book."

"This is serious! Pru's not here." Lance then detailed his movements since he had arrived, leaving out one notable detail.

After a brief pause, Harley replied, "Well, did you find any of her things, maybe a suitcase? I mean, surely she'd have brought clothes for the weekend."

"Not a thing. The place is exactly as we left it the last time Anne and I were here, except for what I said. That's it."

"There's got to be a reasonable explanation. If something bad happened, you'd expect there would have to be some sign of it."

"It's weird—like she dropped off groceries and then

left in a hurry. When I got here, the lights were still on and the place was wide open."

Harley continued, "Well, she must have planned to come right back then. Didn't she ever call you?"

"That's the thing, Harley. She called once on the way out this afternoon, and we spoke briefly. Then she called back later, but when I picked up, there was no one there."

"Look Lance, regardless of what may have happened, you've got only two choices at this point. Either wait there for her to return, or you can go back home and see what unfolds. My advice is that you leave, and right now."

"But what if she comes back and everything's locked up?"

"Chances are she's not coming back tonight, or she'd be there by now. If you leave immediately, you can get back before daybreak. If all is well and good, then you'll hear from her. If it's not, you can say you were home in bed and no one's the wiser."

After a long pause, Lance replied, "Okay, okay. But I've got a bad feeling about this, Harley." He abruptly cut the call, closed the house, and left, having failed to report the uncanny image he had seen in the woods by his patio.

Atwood straightened, staring intently at Goldman. "And that's the truth!"

CHAPTER 30

Days later. Near Lakeview.

S itting alone at the hotel bar, the man wasn't drunk, but he was getting there. He jolted at the boisterous commotion as three women entered the room. They had clearly been drinking and were obviously unconcerned about other patrons, of which there were few remaining. It was after eleven on a weeknight, and the only waitress had left.

Seating themselves at one of the many empty tables, and after a few minutes of impatient waiting, one of them strode her way to the bar. She called out for service, and a bartender appeared from a doorway at the end of the bar. Slurring slightly, she said, "Three Stoli martinis. Very, very dry. And make them heavy pours." She propped her elbow on the bar and pivoted to look the man over.

"Well handsome, can I get you something?" Her voice had a husky rasp, accentuated by a hearty laugh. "I'm on an expense account, so it's free."

He returned a similar once-over. Her obviously dyed, dark auburn hair was pulled back in a bun. Mildly overweight, she appeared to be in her late forties, her skin creased by too much sun or smoking, or both, but subdued by ample makeup. A brassy swagger and unwavering gaze distracted attention from any physical imperfections.

"Single malt."

"Well, you sure know how to take advantage of a girl's generosity, don't you? No matter." She turned back to the man behind the bar. "Whatever he's drinking, he'll have another—on me." The bartender nodded.

"You care to join us?" The man looked over at the two females sitting across the room.

"Alright."

He rose from the bar stool, caught the eye of the server, and pointed to a tray on the bar. "I'll take that." The bartender shrugged and loaded the drinks on the tray.

When they sat down, she said, "So who am I talking to, sweetie?"

He hesitated, looking from her to her friends. "I'm … Roy."

Turning to her friends, she said, "Roy, this is Betsy and Leanne, and I'm Sheila. We work for that company over there." She pointed to the well-known slogan on the neon sign hanging behind the bar. "We had a sales meeting here in Lakeview the last couple of days. And what do you do, Roy?"

"I'm a … repairman."

"A repairman? What kind of things do you fix, Roy?" Betsy asked sarcastically, giggling at her friends.

"It's complicated."

"You mean like, technical? Like computers and programming? That sort of thing?"

"Sometimes."

"That's what I do, Roy; I'm in our IT department," Betsy boasted.

"Well, that sounds kind of sinister to me, Roy." Leanne's eyes widened kiddingly. "What are you, some kind of ... oh, I know. Maybe an industrial spy?" All three laughed.

Turning a hardened stare, he answered, "I only deal with people."

"Enough with the questions, girls. Let's leave Roy a little mysterious. I think that's kinda sexy." She reached over, her fingers playing with the hair at the base of his neck.

The small talk continued for two more rounds of drinks, the women doing all the talking. Sheila became more aggressive. Her friends eventually caught on, and they got up to leave. "We've got a forty-five-minute drive back to the city, and we have to work tomorrow, so this is good night," said Leanne. Both hugged Sheila and walked out.

"Well, it looks like it's just you and me, Roy." She eyed him coyly. "Are you staying here in the hotel?"

"No. Just over the bridge."

"Well, my room's pretty much within staggering distance. How about a nightcap?"

He looked around the empty room. "All right."

"I'll get the tab, and we can go upstairs."

Minutes later they entered her room. As soon as the door closed, she turned and slipped her arms around his neck. "Why waste time with another drink? I've already had enough, and I don't think you want my window to close. You okay with that?"

"Sure."

Pulling his head down to her, she kissed him hungrily. Then she reached around, unzipped her dress and pulled it from her shoulders. She let it fall to the floor, unbuckled his belt, unzipped his pants, and reached inside.

He yanked his turtleneck over his head and tossed it on the nearby chair. Taking hold of her arms, he began moving her backward toward the bed.

Sheila gawked at the markings on his forearm. "Wow! That's some wicked tat you've got there. What is that?"

The man held up his arm, staring at the garish tattoo.

Sheila shook her head. "Looks like some kind of animal... a pretty ugly one. Is that a...?"

"Are we just going to talk?"

"Sorry, Roy. It just kinda surprised me. That's all." She backed up and sat down on the edge of the bed. "Come here, lover."

He moved close to her, and she tugged his trousers and boxers to his knees. Pushing her back onto the bed, he reached down behind her waist and pulled her black thong panties up from her bottom as she raised her legs. She unfastened her bra and threw it aside. Propping herself on her elbows, she rested her heels on the edge of the bed frame.

The man leaned over her, placed the fingers of one hand around her neck and held her arm against the bed with his other hand. Her eyes widened as he began squeezing her throat. She grabbed his wrist. Growing frantic at the look in his eyes, she writhed, kicking her legs and trying to speak, her voice croaking. "Roy, what are you doing? Stop! Please, stop now!"

He raised up and loosened his grip, the tension in his body relaxing.

"Jesus, Roy. What the hell?" She scowled, rubbing at her neck. "I like fun sex, but not rough sex."

Looking down at her, he exhaled. "You got me worked up."

"I guess so." She laid back on the bed, looking up at him. After a few moments, she raised her arms toward him. "Alright, let's try again, Roy. But this time, go gently."

A few hours later the man rolled over in bed to the sound of deep breathing. His eyes adjusted to a band of light cutting across the ceiling overhead, the glare from the parking lot lights shining through slightly parted drapes into the blackened room. He could just see her long dark hair falling over the whiteness of her bare back.

Propping himself on his elbow, he slowly reached toward her, his fingers almost on her shoulder—then pulled back. He eased up from the bed, quietly dressed, and tiptoed across the room, holding his shoes. Sheila was snoring as he gently closed the door behind him.

CHAPTER 31

Late February.

"Attorney General Patterson. This is quite a surprise. What brings you to Lakeview?" Dave Bartlett broke into an artificial smile as he rose to greet his visitors. He had met Rob Patterson during various events over the years, but their relationship was strictly a professional acquaintance. He had no idea who the striking Black woman was.

"Sorry to barge in on you like this, Dave. I was in the area on other business and just thought I'd drop in and catch up." He turned to the woman next to him. "This is Assistant Attorney General Cynthia Worthey."

After shaking hands, Bartlett motioned toward the large conference table to one side of the room, and they all sat. "I don't buy for a minute that this is merely a social call. Why are you really just...dropping in on me?"

"Hah, you're one step ahead, Dave." Patterson straightened his tie knot. "All right. I confess. I do have an ulterior motive for coming here today."

"Now you've piqued my interest. Should I be worried

that you've brought along reinforcements?" He shot a sideways glance at Worthey. "No offense."

"None taken. I'm just along for moral support, Mr. Bartlett," Worthey answered.

"Moral support? For what?"

"Truth is Dave, I understand you've got a real ball-buster of a case cooking over here in Lake County." Patterson hesitated. "Word is that you're going to charge Lawrence Atwood with murder—or am I misinformed?"

Bartlett straightened, dumbfounded. "Well, I've got to congratulate whoever it is doing your intelligence. Atwood will be coming in with his counsel for the booking and then he'll be arraigned. Bail will be set, and he'll be released on his own recognizance."

"You mean he won't be jailed without bail?" Worthey was incredulous.

Bartlett remained erect, the look of unease and surprise stayed on his face. "No. We made a deal with his lawyer. He offered to bring Atwood in, and we agreed to an expedited arraignment and release pending trial."

"But this is a capital murder case!" Worthey almost shouted. "Who's to say he won't hightail it, even leave the country?"

"Look, Ms. Worthey, is it? He'll show, and he'll be booked and arraigned. I expect the judge will require house arrest."

Patterson watched silently. Although unusual in murder cases, he understood that Atwood was not a flight risk. "So, who's his attorney, Dave?"

"His name is Jules Goldman. I assume you've heard of him?"

"Arguably the best criminal attorney in the state. You're really in deep now, Mr. Bartlett," Worthey chortled.

"I'll admit he seemed pretty confident, but I think I can handle the case just the same."

"That's what I want to talk to you about, Dave." Patterson sat up, leaning in. "Atwood can afford a war, and that's what he'll bring. You can't. Or rather, your county can't. This damned recession, coupled with the lack of business taxpayers, surely must have been a drain on the county coffers. You'll need all the help you can get to underwrite a trial that could easily last for weeks, if not months."

"Lake County's financial condition is a nonissue if Atwood cuts a plea deal."

Patterson pouted his lips. "Dave, we both know that Lawrence Atwood will never accept a plea bargain. Atwood wouldn't hire Goldman if he had any notion of maneuvering for a plea bargain. They're gearing up, and Goldman has a huge staff of experienced attorneys."

Bartlett's expression soured. "I think I can manage."

"Come on, Dave. Face facts. You need money, and a lot, to win this case. Lawrence Atwood has it, and he'll bring the bank right through the front door with him." He watched for Bartlett's reaction.

"I understand you know your way around a courtroom, but you can't help what you can't control. That's why I'm here. The AG's office can take over the case for the county, and the state will pick up the tab."

"You can't just...," Bartlett caught himself, lowering his voice "You can't just come into Lake County and usurp my authority."

"Oh, but I can, Dave. It's the law. Look for yourself." He nodded to Worthey, who pulled some documents from the folder on her lap and slid them across the table. Bartlett picked them up and began reading.

After a few moments, Cynthia Worthey leaned her elbows on the table, folding her hands. "As you can plainly see, the attorney general's office has full statutory authority to assume the prosecution of a capital murder case. And it will always be the people of the state, not the people of Lake County, prosecuting Lawrence Atwood."

Bartlett shoved the papers aside. "I've been the county prosecutor here longer than you've been AG, Rob. The voters will wonder why I'm not handling the case, and it could surely come back to bite me in my next election."

"And I do not want that to happen, Dave. That's why I want you with us at counsel's table throughout the trial."

"I get to be your batboy, is that it, Rob?"

"Not at all. I can assure you that you will have a key role at the trial. You can even do some of the examinations." Bartlett turned to stare out the window.

"I need you with us, Dave. You're held in high regard here."

Worthey took the cue. "Given his reputation, you've got to agree that Lawrence Atwood isn't going to raise much support around here. After all, isn't Lakewood regarded as a religious community? That should provide us with a sympathetic jury pool to choose from—for the victim, that is."

Bartlett got up and moved around behind his chair. Looking down at them, he said, "Damn it! I hate that you're actually making sense." After a long moment's silence, he continued, "Okay, I'll go along, but only on the condition that I get second chair at trial. And I get to weigh in on all material strategy decisions going forward."

"Done!" Patterson exclaimed as he pounded his palm on the table. "Excellent decision, Dave. Effectively, we are all equals in a common cause. Now, exactly when and where will all of this go down?"

"He'll be booked at the police station first thing on Monday."

"Well, isn't that convenient?" chortled Worthey.

Bartlett winced. "Then he'll be arraigned that afternoon at the District Court. They asked for it be done quickly, to try to preclude press. And another thing—unlike any accused murderer I've ever seen—the man almost seems anxious to go to trial."

"That is pure Lawrence Atwood, Mr. Bartlett. He's not like any murderer any of us have ever seen," Worthey said.

Patterson raised a hand to quiet his assistant, asking, "Are you going to handle the booking, Dave?"

"No. Police Chief Mitch Quinn will do it.

"Looks like we came here none too soon. But tell me Dave, is this Quinn any good? I mean, Atwood's no penny-ante car thief, if you take my meaning."

"Don't be fooled by the fact that he's not a big city cop. Believe me, Mitch Quinn is as good as the best you've got in the city."

Worthey leaned in. "If this guy's so good, why the hell is he stuck here in this little burg?" She spread her arms. "I checked him out. The word I heard is he hit the sauce so hard he had to be laid off for almost a year."

Bartlett bit his lip, inching closer to Worthey. "I'll try not to be offended, Ms. Worthey. I've known Mitch Quinn almost my whole life; we're close friends. He's only in Lakeview because of family circumstances. His dad was the previous chief of police—and, yes, he had an issue a while back. But that's over, and now he's as good as can be."

"That's not very reassuring, and hardly qualifies him as a great detective."

Bartlett folded his arms across his chest and looked past Worthey at Patterson. "Mitch Quinn spent years with the U.S. Army Military Police. He graduated the CID Special Agent course, then took more training in advanced crime and investigative techniques. He investigated criminal cases for the military, everything from murder to drug smuggling and human trafficking. I'd say that qualifies him."

"Sounds like you're quite a fan of Chief Quinn, Dave," said Patterson.

"He's no pushover."

"Okay, I'll take your word that he's up to the task. But I want to see Atwood first. Arrange for him to meet us here before he's booked."

CHAPTER 32

Monday.

The footsteps of Lance Atwood and Jules Goldman echoed throughout the tiled, high-ceilinged hallway of the century-old building housing both county offices and courtrooms. Situated on four square blocks of land only a ten-minute walk from the lake, the three-story stone structure stood as a centerpiece amid the older section of Lakeview Village. Atwood was a step ahead of his lawyer and stopped in mid-stride.

"Why the hell are we wasting time meeting with Bartlett, Jules? What's this all about?"

"No idea, Lance. He called me and asked that we stop by his office beforehand. He confirmed that they're going to charge you today. Out of professional courtesy, to both of us, he said I could come in with you for the booking, provided I assured him that you would show. All he said about this meeting was that he has a matter he'd like to discuss in advance."

Atwood waited a moment before pivoting toward the stairs, saying over his shoulder, "Let's hurry up and get this over with, then. I want to see Quinn ASAP."

The two proceeded up the stairwell, opened the door marked County Prosecutor, and introduced themselves. The receptionist announced them by phone, nodded, and looked up. "You can go right in."

Entering Bartlett's office, they halted upon seeing the group convened around the large conference table. Atwood broke into a smile, nodding his head as he glared first at Patterson, then at Worthey. "Well, well, if it isn't the state's number one lawyer, Mr. Attorney General himself. Come here to gloat, Rob?"

"I have what I think you'll find to be some surprising news, Lance." Patterson stood and offered his hand. "My office is taking over your case."

Atwood ignored his outstretched hand and looked at Bartlett. "Well Dave, you certainly brought in the cavalry, didn't you? I'll bet it will thrill the taxpayers when they find out just how much of their money you're wasting. Especially once they realize you have no damned case against me."

He turned back and stared intently at Patterson. "You see, Mr. AG sir, I'm innocent, and at the end of the day, you will not get a verdict against an innocent man."

Jules Goldman had remained quiet, content to watch the interplay between his client and the newly organized opposing counsel team. At last he spoke up, saying, "Excuse me, Mr. Patterson, but will you yourself be trying the case? And if not, who will?"

Patterson appreciated that Goldman, a veteran of many criminal trials over the years, would want to learn who his trial adversary was. "I'm sorry, Mr. Goldman. I've not made that decision yet. But we'll be sure to let you know as soon as I do."

"Was there anything else on the agenda for this meeting, Mr. Bartlett?" said Goldman. "If not, we'd like to get the rest of today's formalities out of the way, so we can all go to work on our little controversy."

"Nothing more. We're done here." Everyone stood up.

"I guess I'll see you in court, Rob." Atwood turned to the other attorneys, focusing on the tall black woman. "And you are...?"

"I'm Cynthia Worthey, assistant attorney general."

"Well, you have my condolences, Miss Assistant AG. Maybe I'll see you in court too."

He and Jules turned to leave, but Atwood reversed direction and strode back to face Patterson. "You know Rob, all things considered, I didn't figure you would stoop so low. But that's what this is all about, isn't it? Grandstanding to try and beat me at ... something? Anything? All to save yourself from losing to me in the election. Pathetic."

Patterson grimaced. "I'm just doing my job, Lance. Nothing personal."

"That's bullshit, and we both know it! Anne and I ...." He let the words trail off.

"When you lose this time—and you will lose—you will regret this, Rob. I'll come back to bury you in the election! The voters won't support an AG who tried an innocent man for a crime he didn't commit."

"Lance, we're finished here. Let's go meet with Chief Quinn and get this over with." Goldman took his client by the arm and led him out.

CHAPTER 33

The man sat up in his truck, watching as the attorney general trailed several others out the door. The group stopped briefly to speak, crossed the parking lot, and separated to their cars. Bartlett and a tall Black woman pulled away toward the police station; Patterson headed in the opposite direction. After a minute's wait, the man started his vehicle and followed Bartlett to the station, parking on a side street and walking to the entrance at a leisurely pace.

Stepping inside, he stopped to stare at Mitch Quinn, who stood only a few feet away on the opposite side of a thigh-high gated railing. The chief was speaking to a middle-aged woman seated at one of many desks scattered around the room.

The woman leaned around Mitch, who had just picked up the mail from her desk. "Can I help you, sir?"

"Uh, yes ma'am...that is, maybe? I'm looking to get new license tabs."

"That's at the secretary of state's office, sir. They're

located out by the highway on State Street. It's on the way out of town. This is the police station."

"Oh. I'm sorry. I'm, uh, new in the area, and thought I had to check in here." As the man spoke, Mitch gave a quick look over his shoulder, nodded a greeting, and returned to the mail.

The man started toward the door, then turned back. "By the way, was that the famous trial lawyer I saw coming in here earlier? Lawrence Atwood, I think his name is."

Mitch set the papers down. "How do you know Mr. Atwood?"

"Oh, I don't know him. I've just seen him on TV. You know, on the news, and those talk shows. When he's been working on those big cases. Is there one going on here in town?"

"No sir. Nothing like that. Just another day at the office."

"Darn. Thought I might see something exciting first-hand. Sorry to have bothered you."

Mitch watched the man's back as the door closed behind him. He shrugged off the odd feeling he had. Something about the man's eyes.

CHAPTER 34

M inutes later, Mitch walked down the back hall of the police station toward a two-way mirror looking in on the interrogation room. Willy and Bartlett were standing in the hall next to a tall, very striking Black woman in a gray pantsuit. As he drew near, Mitch glanced through the observation window, seeing Atwood and his lawyer just seating themselves. He then looked to the woman, asking, "And who are you, Ms.?"

"I'm Cynthia Worthey, assistant attorney general for Mr. Patterson. He asked me to fill in for him."

Mitch shot Bartlett a confused look, saying, "Well, welcome, Ms. Worthey. So, let's get this show on the road then."

Mitch walked into the interrogation room, taking a seat opposite the two lawyers. The windowless room was barren except for the mirror behind him, a painted-but-peeling wooden table, and four battered steel chairs. The light green plaster walls appeared gray under a single overhead tube light.

"I'm Jules Goldman, Chief Quinn, Mr. Atwood's lawyer."

Mitch saw an expression of impertinence and superiority flash over Goldman's face. "Uh-huh. I've heard of you, Mr. Goldman."

"That's very flattering." He poked his chin at the mirror over Mitch's shoulder. "So, who have you got out there watching the show?"

"No one special, Mr. Goldman. No need to worry." He placed a recorder on the table in front of him. "Standard procedure. Any objection?"

"We hadn't expected our conversation to be recorded, Chief Quinn. We're only here in this meeting at my client's request. He simply has something to tell you before he's processed."

"Then presumably Mr. Atwood won't mind if what he has to tell me is recorded." His eyes moved to Atwood's anxious stare. "After all, you're going to tell me the truth, right Mr. Atwood?"

"You can count on that, Quinn."

"My client is in charge, Chief Quinn. Tape away."

"All right then." Mitch switched on the recorder, administered the Miranda warning, and began the interview. "You've asked to come here today in connection with our investigation into the disappearance of Ms. Prudence Wheatley, is that correct?"

Atwood nodded.

"I'm afraid you must answer verbally, Mr. Atwood."

"Sorry. I know that. The answer is yes."

"You indicated that you have something to tell me about this case, is that correct?"

"Yes."

"And what is that Mr. Atwood?"

Bartlett and Worthey watching outside glanced at one another as they both drew closer to the window.

"I want you to know I told you the truth when I said I didn't harm Prudence Wheatley, not in any way."

"You asked for a meeting just to tell me that again?"

"No. What I didn't tell you is that we were…more to each other than just a lawyer and a court reporter." He paused and glanced at Goldman, who was watching Mitch closely. "We were having an affair. And…" Atwood looked away.

"And what, Mr. Atwood?"

"And…I did go to meet her at our cottage that night, but she never showed. I mean, she had been there, but she was already gone when I arrived. I never saw her."

Mitch sat quietly, contemplating the impact of his confession. "So, why didn't you tell us this in the first place, Mr. Atwood?"

"I never imagined that I would be a suspect in anything. I figured you would find Pru, and this would all blow over. Opening up about us would only complicate things, or so I thought—make you and everyone else jump to conclusions, like I'm sure you are right now."

"Why the sudden change of heart?"

"It's simple. I know that I did nothing wrong, except maybe sleep with the wrong person."

Mitch thought he perceived a slight display of disapproval from Goldman.

"That's not a crime—not between two consenting

adults. But this has gone way too far. It's time you started looking for the real bad guy."

"What else didn't you tell us, Mr. Atwood?"

Goldman put his hand on Atwood's arm. "I think we'll stop there, Chief Quinn," he said. "I can assure you my client is telling you the same story today that he told me when we first met. I naturally had misgivings about his clarification of his activities on the night in question, but…"

"Clarification? You're mistaken if you think this changes anything, Mr. Goldman. We're still going ahead with the booking."

"For God's sake, Quinn!" Atwood spouted. "I suppose the next thing you'll be claiming is that, after I killed her, I put her body in the firepit and burned her up? On my own patio? Not even the attorney general could get a jury to buy that."

"Let's not argue our case here, Lance," Goldman cautioned.

"What I do know is there's no evidence of any intruder, and now you've admitted you were there when she disappeared," said Mitch.

"I never saw her, damn it! Just because I was there doesn't mean I killed her. There are lots of weird things about that night."

Goldman could see his client was getting agitated and rose.

"Lance, let's go."

Then Atwood blurted out, "Like that huge, white rabbit I saw out in the woods that night."

Goldman jerked his head toward his client. "White rabbit?"

Mitch pushed his chair back from the table. "Are you screwing with me, Atwood?"

"Not at all. I know it sounds crazy, but it really happened." Atwood then proceeded to tell part of the story he hadn't confessed to either Harley or Goldman.

"I was running around calling for Pru behind the house, and the damnedest thing you ever saw was out there in the woods, next to my patio. I'd just turned to go back inside but froze. Sitting out in the thick stand of pine trees, I saw a huge white rabbit. I mean big. I hurried over to the open slider, reached in, and switched on the floodlights. When I looked back, it had disappeared."

Mitch looked at Goldman, whose mouth now hung open. "Possibly you're angling for an insanity defense, counselor?"

"Understand this, Quinn; I'm not insane, and there's no way in hell I'd ever agree to that," Atwood answered.

"I'll say this much for you, Mr. Atwood, you've got one hell of an imagination."

"Do you honestly think for one second I would say something like that if it wasn't true?"

"Well, if that's your story, you can tell it to the court at your arraignment. Is there anything else you want to add before we close this interview?"

The two lawyers shook their heads simultaneously, then followed Mitch as he led them out. They passed by Bartlett and Worthey on their way, both looking on wide-eyed.

"Go on down the hall and take the last door on the left. I'll be right along," Mitch said to them. As he turned away, Bartlett grasped his shoulder.

"What the heck was that about a white rabbit?" he whispered.

"I'm not sure. It reminded me of something. I'll tell you later, after we book him."

"I'm heading back to the office, but I can hardly wait."

Sitting in a jail cell for just over an hour after being processed, Atwood then appeared in the district courtroom and pled not guilty to all charges, which Bartlett presented to the court. The judge set a date for a preliminary exam, levied bail of a million dollars, and ordered Atwood to wear an ankle monitor. The bondsman Atwood had called paid the required ten percent on the spot. The judge released him on his own recognizance but restricted him to house arrest.

As they were filing out of the courtroom, Mitch glimpsed a man sitting alone in the last row of benches, recognizing the stranger he had spoken to earlier at the station. His attention was distracted as he proceeded through the courtroom doors, coming face-to-face with a familiar Lakeview reporter. The hall was filled with reporters who had been excluded from the proceedings by the judge in response to a last-minute motion by Jules Goldman.

"Chief Quinn, you arrested the best-known lawyer in the state. He has just been charged with the murder of a woman who has been missing for months, but we understand you haven't found a body. What evidence do you have to prove he's the killer?"

Eking out a smile, Mitch's stomach turned as he thought of how much he hated press interviews. "No comment, Jason."

He looked over his shoulder for the stranger, but the

man had disappeared into the crowd exiting the courtroom. The rest of the onlookers moved with Mitch down the hall and outside, where a large group of reporters, television crews, vans, and equipment were assembled. Goldman walked down the courthouse steps to a bank of microphones, Atwood right behind, and made an introductory statement as the crowd surrounded them. Mitch left as Atwood started to deliver his denials.

CHAPTER 35

Early April. Lansing.

"It was a truly pleasant surprise to hear from you, Anne." Rob Patterson rose to greet Anne Atwood, pulling out a dining chair for her to sit. Not having spoken to her for years, he was stunned to receive a call from his old flame the day before, asking to meet for lunch. It had been several weeks since Lance Atwood's arraignment; press attention being at a peak, he had chosen this neighborhood Italian restaurant for its anonymity. Arriving almost half an hour early, he sat at a secluded table in a back corner.

Anne Atwood sat and broke into a warm smile. "I'm sorry to be late, Rob. I can't seem to stick to a schedule these days with all that's going on. Yes, it has been a long time—too long. Thank you for agreeing to meet with me, especially considering the circumstances."

He sensed an underlying tension, concluding the fallout was taking a toll. As he sat down across from her, he felt a wave of nostalgia. She had grown even more beautiful with age.

The waiter approached for their drink order. Before he could ask, Anne spoke up. "I'd like a Perfect Manhattan." Turning to Patterson, she said apologetically, "I know it's only noon, but I find I need some kind of lift earlier and earlier these days."

"I've got to return to the office later, but I can't let you drink alone." He ordered the house chardonnay.

She arranged herself in her seat and allowed her jacket to slip from her shoulders, exposing the low-cut white blouse beneath. "Rob, as good as it is to see you after so long, let's dispense with the niceties. Catching up is not why I called to meet."

"I didn't think so, Anne. Does Lance know you're here?"

He noticed her hesitation. "No, and I hope we can keep it that way. Please?"

"Of course. If that's your wish. But understand, due to ethical restraints, I'm limited as to what we can talk about. Hopefully, you'll appreciate that the case is off limits."

"You forget that I'm a lawyer's wife. I know all about such things. But I do want to speak with you about, well, the case—or just one aspect of it."

"Anne, I'm the chief prosecutor. I will be the one calling the shots going forward. So, I can't really share any information, or answer any questions you might have."

"How about we start with 'I'll talk, and you listen.' Sound acceptable?"

"I'm not convinced, but go ahead and we'll see."

"First of all, can we agree that this is all off the record? Okay? I was never here, and we never had this conversation. Agreed?"

"Like I said, we'll see. It depends. I can't make any promises." He paused as the waiter delivered their drinks.

Anne looked around at some other patrons being seated across the room. "So be it." Taking a sip of her Manhattan, she said, "We both know that my husband can be a, well, I'll just say he can be difficult."

Patterson almost spat out the sip of wine he had just taken and lifted his napkin to his chin. "But I know," Anne continued, "and I think you must know too, that he's no murderer. He would never subject me and the children to the consequences, no matter what."

"Look Anne, it's not my job to find him guilty or inno-cent. If we uncover evidence that suggests a person com-mitted a crime, we charge them. It's that simple."

"It's not that simple! Lance didn't do it. I know him better than anyone alive, and such an act just isn't in him. He may be morally ambivalent about a lot of things," she admitted, then paused, taking another sip. "But where the law is concerned, he's as ethical as any of the rest. That includes you, Rob."

"What about ending a relationship that could substan-tially harm his business, or the campaign, or even more importantly you and your children? Might he be morally ambivalent about such a threat? I think virtually anyone would be, especially if it meant protecting everything in life that's important to them."

Anne frowned and leaned in closer, whispering, "You're doing this because of me, aren't you?"

"That's not true!" He looked around at the sound of his own raised voice, then whispered back, "I admit I was once in love with you. But that was a long time ago. We were young and…inexperienced."

"Inexperienced? For sure! As I recall, I was a virgin when we were together, Rob."

"Yes. And as I recall, we planned to change that before your mom came home early that summer afternoon." He chuckled. "I barely got my pants on and hightailed it out your bedroom window, running like hell back to my car down the street."

She giggled, downed the last swallow of her drink, and looked for the waiter. "I wonder if it would all be different…now. I mean if things had worked out as we'd planned."

"But they didn't. And we can't go back. I admit, I was furious when Lance barged onto the scene, and jealous. But like I said, that was a long time ago. I'm married now. I, *we*, have two wonderful kids. I'm happy."

"And I'm happy for you. But what if we could go back? Would you be willing?"

Patterson squirmed uneasily. "What are you saying, Anne?"

"I'm just asking. I'd like to know."

His eyes narrowed. "Did Lance put you up to this?"

"Certainly not. If Lance knew I was coming to meet you, he would do everything he could to stop me."

"I would hope that's the case."

"This is on me, Rob. I came here on my own. I'm prepared to do anything to get you to let this go—anything."

"Anne, stop this. Even if I wanted to, I couldn't. Not now. It's too late."

"It's never too late. You remember my daddy, the senator? He liked you." She moved her hand onto his on the tabletop.

"Yes. Your father and I got along very well, and I still respect him."

"Well, he taught me that lesson, which he learned from a lifetime in politics. No matter how strongly entrenched his opponents were against him, he found a way to change their minds. He always said, 'everything is negotiable.'"

"I'm sorry, Anne. It's not just my mind you have to change. Lance has been charged with murder, following an investigation that lasted for months. We can't just simply drop the case and pretend like nothing happened. What in the world could I say to explain such a thing?"

"You could say that you're convinced he's innocent, or that there's insufficient evidence to take it to trial. You could think of something."

"We didn't charge him on a whim. Frankly, and I'm sure you don't want to hear this, but the evidence is pretty compelling; and there's more to come."

"What do you mean, more? What else?"

"I can't say. I've probably let this go too far already. There's just nothing I can do at this point."

"I wonder. You say 'nothing,' but is that really true? What if … what if Lance decided not to run?"

Patterson squinted quizzically. "Not run? You mean, not accept the Democratic nomination?"

"The caucus is way off. There's a lot of time between now and then. As I said, minds can be changed. This entire ordeal is enough to deter anyone from further exposure. He could decide that he just does not want to subject himself, his family, to this kind of public scrutiny. That would clear the way for your election."

"Bribery of a public official is a crime, Anne. I'll assume you weren't offering that and give you a pass."

She squeezed his hand. "I'm begging you, Rob. If not for me, then do it for the sake of my children. What if it was your family, your kids? If you still care for me at all... if you ever did, please. This is destroying us."

"Try to understand. This has nothing to do with you, Anne. It's simply not my decision. Unless Lance wants to consider a plea deal, I would be shirking my responsibility as the attorney general if I backed out now, not to mention it would be political suicide."

She yanked her hand away. "A plea? To admit to a murder? What kind of deal would that be for us?"

Patterson looked down at the table, twisting the stem of his wineglass with his fingers.

"So, that's what it's really about, isn't it? If you can win the case, you'll also have a clear path to the governor's mansion." She pushed her chair back from the table with both hands. "Now you've finally got your chance to get him back and guarantee your political future at the same time."

"That's just not true. I let all of that go long ago. Now I'm just doing my job!"

"I don't believe you. I should never have come here expecting anything from you." Anne abruptly stood up, threw her jacket over her shoulder, and stormed out.

Patterson took out his cell phone and called Cynthia Worthey. When she answered, Patterson said, "Cynthia, release the press announcement that we'll be taking over the case. Let Bartlett know. It's full steam ahead."

CHAPTER 36

Same day. Near Lakeview.

"Hello, Chief. It's Willy. I found it. It's just like he said." Willy was standing in the forest northeast of the Atwood property, talking on his cell with Mitch Quinn. They had driven to the area after receiving an anonymous phone call at the station that morning. The caller had described a shocking discovery while out for a morning walk in the woods. Noticing some clothing under a rotten tree trunk, he investigated further and found what appeared to be human bones and a woman's purse. The caller provided a general description of the spot where he had seen the bones. On the way to the scene, Mitch dropped Willy at one end of the heavily wooded tract, then drove to the other end so they could work toward the middle.

"Okay Willy. I'm on my way." Mitch ran back to the patrol car. Within minutes he had driven the mile or so down the road, gotten out and carefully begun working his way through the forest to find Willy.

"Hey Chief, I'm over here!" Willy waved his arms as he saw Quinn come into view, winding through the trees and brush. "Take a look."

The chief stopped at the top of a shallow gully, looking down at the large, felled tree lying on the bottom. Willy held up a surfboard-shaped section of thick tree bark leaning against the trunk's rotted end, revealing a depression hidden partway under the tree.

"Don't worry, Chief. I only lifted the bark, didn't touch anything else. It was covering most of the stuff lying in here."

Mitch angled down the gully's steep slope, coming to stand beside Willy, and looked over the organic material spread on the ground, interspersed with an ample amount of pea gravel. "Well, you don't have to be a wizard to figure out those are bones, and what looks like what's left of a body, or at least part of one. The only question is, whose is it?" He walked to the other side of the trunk for a different perspective. "For my money, I bet you we've found what's left of Prudence Wheatley."

"Maybe so, Chief, but what's with all this gravel?"

Mitch shrugged his shoulders and pulled his cell phone from his jacket pocket. "I don't know, Willy, but this time I'm going to call for somebody who knows bones."

As he waited for the connection, Mitch pondered the prospects. If it turned out these were in fact Prudence Wheatley's remains, he knew it could be critical evidence in getting a conviction. This location was not that far from Atwood's beach home. The bits of body had been broken up somehow, but it did not look like they'd been burned. There were still some larger pieces, from which he hoped they would be able to extract usable DNA.

CHAPTER 37

Late afternoon. East Grand Rapids.

"I couldn't get him to budge. He wouldn't even consider dropping the charges. We've got to find another way." Anne Atwood paced back and forth before her husband in the living room of their home, describing the details of her meeting with Rob Patterson. Atwood leaned forward on the edge of a sofa with his hands folded and his elbows on his knees, looking up at her.

Over the years, Anne Atwood had willingly acquiesced to her husband's chronic infidelities. Satisfying his seemingly insatiable appetites elsewhere relieved her of the burden. Provided that he supplied their family with the appropriate level of financial security and kept his trysts unpublicized, she was content with their marital arrangement. But this inability to eliminate the threat of his indictment was testing her resolve. Typically unflappable, for the first time in her memory, she felt seriously concerned about her future well-being.

"Don't worry, Anne. We will. I've got Harley working

on it. He'll get the press narrative going on Rob's conflict, and the fact this is a vendetta prosecution—a move to promote his campaign. Jules Goldman is a master criminal lawyer. With their help, we can turn all of this to our advantage by election time."

The couple sat on matching love seats in their four-season sunroom. Having planned for the overture to Patterson, they thought they would first test him to see if his past affection for her might move him to drop the charges. Dangling the idea of Lance quitting the race was Plan B— never intended as a genuine offer. They knew Patterson could never admit to such a deal should the charges be dropped.

"The public, and our party, will forgive powerful men their occasional dalliances, but we can't have any further distractions like this while the trial is pending. I don't want to hear of anything," she stared at him indignantly, "especially something like that teacher you were screwing for so long."

Anne got up, walked over to the slider in the glass wall, and gazed at the lake below. "My God, Lance, you actually represented her. What in the world were you thinking? That alone could have gotten you disbarred. Now, this trial may be the end of everything we've worked for. We've either got to get the damned case dropped, or—God forbid it goes to trial—you simply have to win. Exoneration would do wonders for your ratings in the election."

Lance viewed his wife as a partner as much as he viewed her as a spouse, although at moments like these his lust was amplified. On those rare occasions when she would submit, her passion was almost insatiable. He hoped this would be one of those moments.

"The fact that I did nothing to Prudence Wheatley will carry the day, Anne. As long as Rob, or whoever it is who tries the case, can't convince the jury to convict me for infidelity, I can't lose. Jules will find a way to counter whatever Patterson comes up with."

Anne sat. "We can't let this stop us from getting to the governor's office. Once you're elected, the sky's the limit. One or two good terms and you will be on to Washington. Harley and my father will help us take care of that."

Lance sat beside her. Placing an arm on the back of the couch, he put his other hand on her leg. "We both really want the same things, Anne. I have not been working my ass off, pumping thousands of dollars into the party coffers for years, for nothing. I've been buying a whole lot of influence, and it's going to pay off, for both of us."

He drew close, whispering into her ear. "Most important Anne, I want you, and I think that you still want me."

Anne turned her head, inched her hips closer toward him, and put her hand on his chest. "If I let you, will you promise not to play around anymore while this case drags out? We can't afford any more bad publicity."

Lance reached around her back and began to unzip her dress. "Alright, I promise you. No more." He leaned in and kissed her passionately as she slipped the dress off her shoulders and unfastened her bra. "I want only you. I need you, now." Biting her ear gently, he ran his lips down her neck and then to her breast as she pulled her bra straps down along her arms.

"Then we have a deal." She stood up, allowed her dress and bra to fall to the floor, slipped her panties down her legs, kicked them off, and stood spread-legged in her high heels.

Lance fell to his knees on the floor in front of her, wrapping his arms around her waist. He kissed her belly and looked up into her face.

Anne peered down at him. "I'll give you what you want... for now. But just remember, we have a long while before the trial, and you had better win. And I mean win it all."

CHAPTER 38

Later in the day Mitch and Willy were joined by Dr. Walter Kilroy, the coroner from adjacent Cairn County. Mitch had summarized the case on a call to his sometimes-colleague, who dropped what he was doing and enthusiastically agreed to assist.

An orthopedic surgeon by education, Kilroy's self-described morbid passion to find whodunit drew him to his chosen specialty. With an ample stomach extending over long, spindly legs, his military-erect profile reminded Mitch of the letter P. Mitch watched from the gully's ridge as Kilroy labored alongside CSI agents the rest of the afternoon, methodically examining, collecting, and photographing the evidence. Finally, Kilroy stood up, snapped off his latex gloves, and trudged up the side of the ravine toward Quinn.

"A real mess. Those are definitely human bones down there. I can identify parts of leg and arm bones, a clavicle, and some teeth for sure. It's not a complete body though.

Much of it is missing. My initial conjecture is they're all from one female. It sounds crazy, but it almost looks like something exploded under that tree trunk."

"Exploded?" Quinn perked up. "You're not the first person I've heard that from, Walt. Dr. Jacoby told us it appeared the pieces of bone we found in the firepit looked like they'd been blown up too."

"Well, it's as if the body was placed inside the trunk, covered with that heavy bark, and then blown up."

"Willy found it just like you saw it when you got here, Walt. Pretty much everything is right where it was initially."

"This is all very odd, Mitch—especially all the gravel mixed in with the remains. I don't see it anywhere else around here. It had to be brought in here and dumped."

"You think this gravel had anything to do with the explosion?"

"Could very well have. If the body was exploded using that gravel, it would explain the mass destruction."

"As I told you on the phone, we grabbed a lot of material out of the suspect's firepit. Dr. Jacoby told us that due to the extent of the burning it may not be possible to get a DNA profile. Is there any other way to tell if these remains match what we found in that pit?"

"That's a tall order. We can do whatever chemical analyses may be possible, of course, but it will be extremely difficult. Unless some of the pieces from the firepit can be mated to others found here, I just don't know. I do think we'll likely be able to identify the deceased from these teeth alone."

"Damn! I was hoping we'd be able to get a match."

"Well, let's think a minute." Kilroy turned around to

look back at the scene below. "If whatever is under that tree trunk was in fact exploded, there had to be some kind of fuel used to cause the ignition. Consequently, there may be a detectable chemical residue. If whatever was in the pit came from this site, that same chemical residue may be detectable."

Quinn grabbed his colleague by the shoulder. "Walt, you're a genius!"

"Don't get too excited just yet. I said *may be detectable*. The fire in the pit could have burnt the residue so intensely that we won't be able to detect any chemicals. We'll need to test the material from both sites, the bark, some gravel, and portions of the tree trunk, and then we'll see what we've got."

"At least there's a chance. Right now, that's pretty damned encouraging."

"If your CSI folks can help me collect samples and the remains, I'll start the ball moving on DNA testing."

Mitch looked over the scene. "And now we wait."

CHAPTER 39

Monday, June 22.

M itch quickly stepped inside the station out of the pouring rain, the shower having started just as he left the diner across the street. Standing in the waiting area just inside the door, he shook the water from his Stetson. Unusual for this early in summer, the Lakeview area had suffered a couple weeks of hot, drought-like weather, accompanied by spates of badly needed rain—though Mitch hated having to wear a raincoat. The only one he owned was a long khaki poncho, which made him sweat even more when he put it on.

"Damn. It could have waited five minutes," he grumbled to no one as he glanced blankly at a person seated in one of the few visitor chairs against the wall. It struck him that the man's western garb and boots were unusual for summer in a beach resort. The brim of a straw cowboy hat hid the visitor's face as Mitch passed and pushed through the gate in the dividing railing.

Stopping by the desk clerk, Mitch raised an eyebrow and nodded his head in the direction of the visitor.

She whispered, "Waiting outside when I opened up at seven. Seemed really anxious to see you."

The chief turned and walked back toward the visitor. "Good morning. You wanted to see me?"

The stranger looked up at him, rose from the chair, and stuck out a hand. Mitch took a short step backward—the cowboy he had expected to see was, instead, a cowgirl. He wasn't sure of her age, but then he was bad at guessing ages, particularly of women. Her hair was pulled back in a ponytail, mostly hidden under the straw hat. It shone somewhere between blonde and orange, reminding him of a summer sunset.

She looked straight up into his eyes, unwavering. "You're the chief of police?" Her voice was as firm as her grip.

Mitch shuffled from one foot to the other, confused over the sudden sensation he felt as the stunning pair of eyes bored back into his. He tried to place the color. Jade came to mind.

"Uh, yes, miss, I am. Mitch Quinn," he said, snapping back into focus.

"I'm Danielle Sparro, Chief Quinn."

"So, what can I do for you, Miss Sparro?"

"I would like to talk with you about the man you arrested a while back. The one you charged for the murder of that missing court reporter."

"You mean Lawrence Atwood?" She nodded. "What about him?"

"You've got the wrong man, Chief Quinn."

"I'm sorry?" He wasn't sure whether to laugh or curse.

"You've charged the wrong man for the crime."

"What in the world makes you say that?"

"Simple. I know who did it, and it wasn't Lawrence Atwood."

He waited, open-mouthed. "It's a long story, Chief Quinn." She looked around. "Is there someplace we can talk, privately?"

"Is this some kind of prank?"

"I can assure you that this is no joke, Chief Quinn. If you'll give me the courtesy of a few minutes, I'll explain."

Mitch squinted as he pinched his nose between his thumb and forefinger. "Okay. Alright. I guess we can use my office. But this had better be good. Follow me, please."

She went to grab her file, Mitch leading the way to his office in the rear of the station room. As he passed Willy's desk, he tapped him on the shoulder, leaned down, and whispered, "If this meeting isn't over in fifteen minutes, come knock on my door and say you need me right away."

Willy looked up to see the woman following behind him and nodded. "Okay Chief."

Closing the door behind them, Mitch removed his coat, hung it on a coat pole in the corner, and motioned Dani to one of two mismatched side chairs.

Dani looked around the room, her gaze resting briefly on the trophy shelves in the corner. Then she laid the file on top of his desk and sat.

"So, who do you claim is the real killer, Ms. Sparro?"

"He's a serial killer who's murdered dozens of people around the country over the past almost-forty years. It's all in there," she said, tapping on the file.

"Whoa! Hold on just a sec there." Mitch grinned.

"Why, that's almost one murder a year, if you allow time off for vacations and holidays." She frowned defiantly.

"I'm sorry to be facetious, Miss Sparro, but you've got to admit it's a pretty incredible accusation you're making. Dozens of killings, plus Prudence Wheatley?"

"I agree, but it's true. You'll see if you…"

"Regardless, just what makes you think this serial killer is my serial killer?"

"The reasons are all in that folder. But more importantly because I saw him on television here."

"You saw this serial killer on TV, here? In Lakeview?"

She nodded. "Yes. During the coverage of Lawrence Atwood's arraignment. I saw it in Colorado. He was standing off to the side among the crowd on the courthouse steps while Atwood and his lawyer were interviewed."

"And just how do you know it was him? Have you met this prolific mass murderer?"

"Well, no. I haven't, but it had to be him. I was able to compare his image to TV footage my dad had in his file. He was caught on camera at an earlier trial of one of his marks, in Wisconsin. They looked almost exactly alike."

"Almost exactly? That's why it had to be him? And why would someone appear out in public like that after he's killed someone? Sounds like a pretty crazy thing to do."

"Because he does that. He shows up at events connected with his marks, like trials, funerals, and arraignments. And, yes, he is insane. Assuming a psychopath is insane."

Mitch leaned back in his chair and put his feet up on his desk, wondering if his staff had put her up to this. He decided to play along.

"Why don't you remind me of the difference between a sociopath and a psychopath? It's been a while."

Dani sighed a *tsk*. "Alright. I guess you could say that a psychopath is a sociopath on steroids. Both lack empathy, and each can be manipulative, but sociopaths typically have a conscience. Psychopaths don't. They're remorseless and consequently much more dangerous. They won't flinch at torture, or even murder, to get what they want."

"That's pretty good, Miss Sparro, but I'll have you know I've investigated this case thoroughly and concluded, along with a very experienced county prosecutor—and the state attorney general, no less—that the evidence supports Mr. Atwood's guilt. Your coming in here out of the blue from, where was it, Colorado, and claiming that some alleged serial killer from God-knows-where has somehow fooled us all is, well, it's pretty galling."

"Chief Quinn, I'm not suggesting…"

"What you're suggesting is that we didn't do our job, that we screwed it up. You know, we're not just a bunch of country bumpkins here in Lakeview."

Dani blushed. "I'm sorry. I didn't mean to criticize you. But my dad studied this man for years. He's fooled more than a few police investigators around the country."

Mitch dropped his feet to the floor, sat up, and leaned his elbows on the desk. "I'm going to give you the benefit of the doubt, Ms. Sparro, and about five more minutes to finish your story. Then I have to get back to work."

"Okay. Fair enough. I'll summarize as best I can. This man has an established pattern of selecting marks…"

"There's that word again. Just what do you mean by marks?"

"I'm sorry—it's like targets. He sets them up by

planting evidence, ingeniously staging the murders so everything seems to point in one direction, toward the mark. A second victim, you could say."

Dani paused, waiting for a reaction. Mitch's eyebrows raised. "The crimes are often horrific," she continued. "The public gets frightened, and the authorities get anxious to charge someone. He relies on that."

"Sounds like this guy is some kind of mastermind."

"Consider this, Chief Quinn. One of the earliest crimes he committed was the double murder of a couple of innocent teenagers. It happened in southern Illinois, in 1977, near Cairo. His mark was a priest who had abused him while he was in an orphanage as a kid. The priest was charged, convicted, and the killer later showed up at his sentencing."

"So how do you know he did it if the priest was convicted? Or are you suggesting some other police officers screwed up that one, too?"

"Yes, as a matter of fact they did. For sure the police rushed the investigation, and he got away with it."

"Maybe he just showed up to get closure?"

"He'd been living in Montana. Why would he travel hundreds of miles just for closure?"

"Victims of childhood abuse might go a lot further than that. Look, Ms. Sparro, I'm sure whatever's in your folder makes for fascinating reading, but I don't have time to bone up on an alleged psycho killer who, as far as I know, has never committed a crime in my jurisdiction."

Just then a knock sounded. The door opened slightly, and Willy peeked in. "We need you out here, Chief. You know, that matter we talked about earlier?"

"Thanks, Willy. We're just finishing."

Dani pushed herself up and placed a finger on the file. "Tell you what, Chief—I'll even pay you to read this file. If you do, I'll treat you to dinner, on me. You can pick the place. All you've got to lose is a little time, and just maybe then you'll go after the real killer."

"I'll think about that, Miss Sparro. In the meantime, I'd also like to talk to your father."

"You can't."

"Why not?"

Dani walked to the door and turned. "He's dead. The man you'll read about in that file killed him."

"What?"

"My cell number is on the file cover." She smiled as she opened the door. "By the way Chief, I like your boots."

Mitch looked down at his feet, then gaped after her as she closed the door.

CHAPTER 40

Sunday.

Settled back in the overstuffed chair in the corner of his small living room, Mitch propped his bare feet upon a tattered ottoman.

Curiosity got the better of him after he had ended his Saturday morning shift, and he started reading right after lunch. Continuing through dinner and late into the night, he had fallen asleep in his chair, only to begin again as soon as he awoke with the dawn. He only stopped to make coffee, and now it was early Sunday afternoon. The files disclosed many suspicious connections between the suspect, and a number of highly publicized murders, but the evidence was all circumstantial. Drawing any conclusions required considerable speculation, but the early history of the alleged serial killer (as retold by a nun traced by Dani's father) he found fascinating.

Sister Mary Elise was assigned to the Catholic orphan-age, where a young man named Gordon Gruca had been placed at age twelve. According to the records,

Gordon's father, George, was an army veteran and an abusive alcoholic, who had separated from his mother a few years earlier. As an army brat, Gordon moved from one base to another following his father's repeated episodes of insubordination and drunkenness. Since George Gruca was a decorated war vet with severe PTSD, his superiors arranged periodic reassignments when it became necessary, as opposed to more stringent penalties.

Ultimately, George was dishonorably discharged after a violent attack on his wife and a soldier with whom she had been involved. Both were hospitalized, and the soldier was put on inactive duty for months to recuperate. Afterward, Gruca's mother stayed in the Columbus, Ohio, area near the Fort Hayes base where George had been stationed. She eventually lost custody of her son after a string of arrests for drug possession and solicitation.

Gordon had previously been enrolled in a local Catholic grade school, and early on began exhibiting problematic behavior, including truancy and fighting with other students. His scraps became increasingly vicious, and he seemed to spend almost as much time in the principal's office as he did in the classroom. He was finally expelled when he was caught by a janitor, having tied up and beaten a fellow student in the school boiler room.

His father had disappeared, so the forfeiture of his mother's parental rights resulted in his being ordered to the St. Francis Orphanage for Children. There he became the charge of Father Peter Quattrocci, who was the chief administrator and self-appointed task-master. Sister Mary Elise described the priest as a particularly severe disciplinarian. He professed that order was maintained through fear, and fear was instilled by the infliction of harsh corporal punishment for infractions of the rules, which Quattrocci himself dictated and supervised.

The nun recalled that the priest took a particular interest in Gordon immediately upon his arrival. Over the next three years, Quattrocci treated him much like a household pet, alternating reward and punishment. Although the sister stopped short of alleging abuse, she observed generally that Gordon's temperament became increasingly sullen and belligerent. She recounted one specific series of events which had profound repercussions.

An assortment of animals had been kept in a barn on the rural property. As a reward, the priest allowed Gordon to help with daily maintenance, thus providing some respite from the priest's pernicious influence. According to the nun, Gordon spent extended periods in the barn and seemed especially fond of the variety of rabbits they kept. She often saw him in their pen, holding and talking to them just as owners often talk to their dogs and cats.

One afternoon, four plow horses reserved for trail rides escaped, and their stall gates were found unlatched. Local volunteer firemen assisted in rounding them up, which took the better part of a day. An older boy accused Gordon, but Sister Mary Elise suspected the older boy himself had released them out of jealousy. Not long afterward, the rabbits suddenly disappeared. She was convinced that Quattrocci had one of the employees kill them, or perhaps he did so himself. Weeks after the incident the other boy disappeared without a trace. It was presumed he had run away.

In the meantime, Gordon was inconsolable, and the priest's treatment of him became even more severe. Relief of sorts eventually came by way of Gordon's absentee father, who showed up one morning on the orphanage doorstep. The meeting with the priest was described as loud and angry. Although the details were unclear, afterward George Gruca left the orphanage with Gordon in tow. The records showed only that custody was given to his father. Shortly after, the priest was transferred to a small parish in Southern Illinois. It turned out his sins had been long known to the diocese but suppressed due to fear of public exposure.

Five years after his transfer, Quattrocci was charged with the brutal murders of two his high school students, whose bodies were found in an abandoned rail shack. John Sparro traveled to the Illinois State Attorney's office, where he was allowed to look at the trial transcripts. A particularly important piece of evidence introduced at the trial was a small-caliber pistol recovered in the nearby marsh. Ballistics testing proved the gun was the weapon used to murder one of the teens. Investigators traced the gun to a former employee at St. Francis, who confirmed it had been his, but that it had disappeared about the time the priest had left the orphanage.

When Quattrocci appeared in court for his sentencing, he had to be restrained, loudly proclaiming his innocence. He insisted to the judge that he had seen a former ward of the orphanage in the hall outside the courtroom that morning, and that he was the one who had killed the two teens. A police search of the building yielded no trace of anyone fitting the description, and the priest was given a life sentence and remitted to the state prison. Six months later, he was incinerated when a package received from an unidentified sender exploded into flames in his cell. It had been examined by the prison guards beforehand, but they'd found only what appeared to be a portable radio and cassette which an accompanying note said was a gift from a sympathetic parishioner. The investigation afterward determined the package had been a sophisticated booby trap of a type often utilized by Army rangers and terrorists. The parishioner turned out to be fictitious.

That was all the nun had to share, except for a postcard she had received in the mail shortly after Quattrocci died. It was addressed to her and postmarked from Fort Bragg, North Carolina. The cryptic message said only, "Dear Sister Mary Elise, I hope you are well. I am fine, but there is much to do." It was signed "G.G." She told John Sparro she had no idea what it meant.

Mitch leaned down, pushed the papers into the folder on the floor, got up, and walked out through the kitchen to the backyard of his house. He stretched and plopped into one of three green plastic Adirondack chairs scattered about the small brick patio. Staring at the sliver of lake he could barely see between two houses across the backyard, he tried to make sense of what he had just read. All the evidence until now had pointed to Atwood's guilt. The tales of large white rabbits had seemed preposterous, but now he pondered whether it all could conceivably be part of some sinister scheme concocted by a psychopath.

He sat for a long while, mulling over the facts contained in the file documents, arguing with himself whether someone besides Atwood could possibly be the killer. But he kept coming back to the same question: Why would some stranger out of nowhere come all the way to Michigan to frame Lawrence Atwood for the murder of a person he had no way of knowing? There was nothing in what he had read to suggest that this Gordon Gruca had any connection to Atwood, let alone Prudence Wheatley. After another hour of contemplation, he had come full circle, resolving that Atwood was guilty and Dani Sparro was just chasing after an explanation for her father's suicide. So...why couldn't he get those rabbits out of his mind?

CHAPTER 41

Tuesday.

"Is this seat taken?" Dani Sparro looked at the uniformed deputy sitting one stool over at the counter of the Satellite Diner. She had waited impatiently in her room again that morning, hoping for contact from Chief Quinn. After days without a call, she decided to confront him again and drove across the river to the west side of Lakeview Village. As she parked her car, she spotted the deputy she had seen at the police station going into a restaurant down the street. She quickly detoured to the diner, hoping she might have a chance to extract some helpful information.

Willy looked around at the empty seats in both directions and shook his head. "Uh-uh," he grunted through a mouthful of coffee.

As she slid onto the stool, Dani grabbed a menu from the fixture on the back edge of the countertop. The waitress came to set a plate in front of Willy, then looked at Dani, eyebrows raised in question.

"Just coffee, please."

She watched as Willy pushed scrambled eggs onto his fork with a piece of toast. "Didn't I see you at the police station last week, when I met with Chief Quinn?"

"Uh, yeah. I guess so."

Dani stuck out her hand. "I'm Danielle Sparro."

Willy wiped his hands on his napkin and accepted. "I'm Martin Willoughby, but most folks just call me Willy."

"Pleased to meet you, Willy. You can call me Dani."

"Me too, Miss, uh, Dani." He chuckled. "You sure don't look like any Danny I know."

"Well, thank you, Willy. I'll take that as a compliment." The waitress returned with a cup and poured.

"So, how long have you worked with Chief Quinn?"

"Just about as long as he's been back, I guess."

"Back? From where?"

"He was in the military police. He went all over the world with them."

"That sounds like quite an interesting job. Why did he come back?"

"I'm not really sure. It wasn't long before his dad died; I guess it was to help out. His mom was having a hard time of it after Iron Mike got the cancer."

"Iron Mike?"

"That's what folks called his dad. He was the first Chief Quinn."

"Chief Quinn's father was also the chief of police here in Lakeview Village?"

"Yep. That's back when I was a kid. He was a pretty tough guy. That's why they called him that. He was chief for a long time."

"So, why didn't Chief Quinn leave after his dad died?"

"When he came back, he became Iron Mike's deputy. That was before me. Then he met Lisa."

"Lisa?"

"Yeah. His wife. Actually...he already knew her. They'd dated a while in high school, but they broke up when he enlisted. When he got back, they started up right where they left off, getting married a year or so later."

"Hum. I didn't realize that the chief was married," Dani said, surprised by her sudden tinge of disappointment.

"Oh, he's not. Not anymore. She died, along with their son. He was three at the time. It was a car accident. Well, I guess you wouldn't say accident. A drunk driver killed them."

"That's terrible. How sad."

"Sure was. Damned near the whole town came out for the funerals. It just about put the chief down. He began dr...um..." Willy hesitated. "He was real torn up over it. Took a year or so away from work."

"But he came back, again?"

"Yep. His friend Mr. Bartlett helped him—he's the county prosecutor. He got him into reh—um, got him back on track. I'm sure glad he did. Folks around here really respect Chief Quinn. I mean, did you see all those trophies in his office?"

"Yes, I did."

"Well, they're really sumthin', but I don't think Chief Quinn likes them there. His dad saved all those awards, putting them up when it was his office. The chief keeps saying he's gonna take 'em down, but he never does. I think that's okay though." Willy took another mouthful of eggs.

"I get the impression you like the chief a lot, Willy. Am I right?"

"Mm, hmm. Yes ma'am," he said, chewing. "I surely do. When I got out of high school, I was goin' in the wrong direction. My parents broke up, and my mom drank a lot. There were some pretty bad guys I was running with. I'd probably be in jail today, or worse, if it hadn't been for the chief."

"What do you mean?"

"He really straightened me out. Took me under his wing, got me into community college, then into law enforcement. And after a while … after his family, well, he made me a deputy. I pretty much owe him everything, I guess."

"Everything? That's a lot, Willy."

"Yeah." Willy glanced at his watch, then got up after taking a quick sip of coffee. "Ah, shoot." He wiped a few spilled drops from his shirt front. "I've gotta get back at it, Miss, uh, Dani. Nice talkin' to ya." He snatched his bill and headed to the end of the counter to pay.

As Dani raised her cup, she spied a man staring at her from a booth across the room. He quickly lowered his eyes. She squinted at him, but the waitress appeared in front of her, blocking her view. "Care for anything else?"

"No thank you." The waitress laid the bill on the counter. When she moved away, the man was gone. Dani swiveled around to see his back passing out the door behind her.

Quickly scurrying to the register, she paid, rushed outside, and scanned up and down the street. The man had disappeared. As she hurried toward the police station, he poked his head out of a storefront doorway down the block. Once he saw her enter the station, he started walking in the opposite direction.

CHAPTER 42

"**M**r. Bartlett, I have the attorney general's office on the phone, line two." Bartlett had asked his secretary to contact Rob Patterson so he could deliver the news he had just received. He grabbed his desk phone and was told by the operator to hold. A moment later, Patterson greeted him.

After the pleasantries, Bartlett got to the point. "It's a good news, bad news thing, so to speak."

"Okay. Let's have it." Patterson had his desk phone on speaker and looked curiously at Cynthia Worthey and their paralegal Virginia "Ginny" Drummond, both of whom were seated across from him.

"I had a call from Dr. Jacoby this morning. You know, Wilhelm Jacoby? He's the pathologist helping with the DNA testing of the remains from Atwood's firepit."

Patterson's eyes widened. "Oh, yeah. He's the one who thinks Atwood blew up the body, right?"

"Well, he thinks someone blew it up, anyway. The most important thing he told me was that the DNA from the tissue in the bones found in the woods are a match for Prudence Wheatley."

"Alright!" Worthey clapped her hands loudly.

"They also identified residue of ammonium nitrate and a Coleman-type fuel at the scene. Most likely it was used to ignite the explosion. The gravel they found would have helped to, uh, break things up."

"Jackpot, Dave! Your hard work is paying off, and much appreciated," Patterson exclaimed.

"Most of the hard work has been Mitch Quinn's. But I'm uneasy about this case."

"What is there to be uneasy about? Atwood is cooked," Worthey chimed in.

Patterson raised his palm. "You said there's good and bad news, Dave. What's the rest?"

"Jacoby has been trying to piece together fragments from both sites, but it's not going well for a DNA match. They're having a hard time with the material from the fire-pit. He's not confident they'll be able to connect the two by the time of trial, if ever, and without that we're all just speculating."

"Speculating? Are you kidding?" Worthey stood up, bending down to the phone. "We've got all we need, even without what was found in the pit!"

"You'll never get that admitted at trial—unless Jacoby or some other expert can testify that the material from the pit is connected with what we found in the woods."

Worthey threw her head back. "Come on, Bartlett. You said Dr. Jacoby believes it was human bones in the pit. Are you saying a judge isn't going to let him testify to that? Even if he won't, don't forget the DNA matches from the bedroom, and the muddy shoes found in Atwood's garage. Those were his shoes!"

"So what? Atwood can explain those away in a heartbeat. He could say he wore them for a walk in the park on a rainy day. There's no one to refute that."

"At least you've got the victim's body now, or part of it, right?" The two lawyers turned to Virginia Drummond's voice. "That's a lot more than you had when he was arraigned, isn't it?"

"That's my paralegal, Virginia Drummond, Dave. She's absolutely right." Drummond beamed. "And Cynthia makes a good point. I think we've got a damn good case— one we can win."

"And if we get the stuff from the pit in at trial, bingo! It's game over." Cynthia wind-milled a fake dunk.

Bartlett sat quietly. "Maybe. But tell me this—why would Atwood blow up the body? And why in the hell would he put the remains in his own backyard? A jury will ask that for sure, and we'll have to come up with an answer."

"We've got time to think of that. Right now, why he did what he did doesn't matter. I'm convinced he's our man. If you're not, Dave, then maybe you need to rethink assisting at trial."

"When it comes down to it, I'll do my job."

"Good. I'm counting on it."

Bartlett hung up. Patterson leaned back and tented his fingers, staring at his two assistants. "Cynthia, it'll be your job to keep a close eye on him. Ginny, give Cynthia all the support she needs in preparing this case for trial. She'll need it. There's nothing worse than a trial lawyer who doesn't believe in his case, and right now Bartlett's not fully on board."

"You got it, boss."

CHAPTER 43

Later that morning.

The muffled lyrics of *Nessun Dorma* resonated from behind the closed door to Dave Bartlett's office as Mitch entered the outer reception area. He frequently joked to his friend that the décor reminded him of early Ikea renaissance. Bartlett's longtime legal secretary and girl Friday, Irene Campbell, sat behind the single rectangular desk adjacent to a black vinyl Luca sofa, flanked by two faded plaid fabric armchairs.

"Sounds like he's on a roll."

She smiled a mouthful of denture-perfect teeth, bobbing her salon-coiffed, almost-red pageboy. "Yes. He is certainly feeling it this morning, Mitch. Go right in. It'll be a relief."

The a cappella amplified as Mitch opened the door to see Bartlett, arms outstretched, serenading an imaginary audience. As he took a breath, he opened his eyes and stopped abruptly at the sight of Mitch's wide-eyed smile.

"Just tuning the old pipes, officer. Gotta keep 'em in working order."

"Sounds like they're plenty well-oiled, Dave. I could hear you down the hall when I hit the second floor."

Bartlett smiled contentedly. "Then I've achieved my purpose. Now, what pressing bit of police business brings you here this fine morning? You said when you called that you wanted to talk to me about something important. What's up?"

"I'm in need of your prosecutorial experience, counselor." Mitch laid the Sparro file on Bartlett's desk and dropped into a side chair.

"A new case? Is that what's in there?"

"You could say that. This file contains a history of various crimes from around the country. Crimes which may or may not have something to do with our present case. A young woman presented it to me just last week."

"We don't handle crimes around the country, Mitch, just those committed in our little county." Bartlett settled back in his chair with a smirk. "Is she suggesting that Lawrence Atwood committed a crime somewhere else that we don't know about, or is she saying that we've got the wrong man?"

"Bingo! Right again. I knew I came to the right place."

Bartlett raised back up with his elbows planted on top of the desk, his palms spread out. "Okay. Stop with the games. What's this all about?"

"I'm not kidding, and she surely isn't. The young woman who gave me this file is the daughter of a former FBI agent. Her name is Danielle Sparro."

"What, like the Johnny Depp character in those Disney pirate movies?"

"I've never seen one of those."

"Go on."

"She said she had proof that Lawrence Atwood didn't kill Prudence Wheatley. She told me the evidence was in this file, and that she'd seen the real killer here in Lakewood."

"She saw who? If she said she saw Atwood in Lakeview, which he was, and claimed that he's the real killer, which he is, I'd agree with her. But who does she think it is?"

"His name is Gordon Gruca, but I'll get to that. I read the material in here over the weekend. There's some pretty compelling information inside."

"Compelling is one thing. Proof is something else entirely. What kind of proof does she have that we could present to a court?"

"Hear me out, Dave. There's a lot to take in. Just bear with me. I'll talk, you listen." Bartlett eased back as Mitch pulled some records from the file and began relating what he had read over the weekend. When he finished almost half an hour later, Bartlett rested his forehead on his hands, rubbing at his temples with his thumbs.

"Mitch, less than an hour ago I called the AG's office to tell them Jacoby matched DNA from the remains at the explosion site to Prudence Wheatley. They're ready to go full-bore on Atwood with all the evidence we have now, and things are looking good for a win. So, what, you're suggesting we try to get the charges against Atwood dropped?"

"I'm not saying you have to drop the case against Atwood. I'm not sure exactly what I'm saying, except that there's enough in that file to raise some doubt. One minute

I'm thinking it's crazy, the next minute I'm, well...the bottom line is what I read is nagging me. Maybe we should open a separate investigation."

"On what grounds? Based on what's in that file? And even if we could, which we can't, what then? We go after some guy who's not even on a radar screen in our state, let alone in Lakeview. For what? Those other murders? Christ's sake, he's apparently not on any radar screen anywhere, because they didn't have any evidence, and neither do we."

"If her father was right on even one or two of those cases, Gruca is a murderer, and we do go after murderers, don't we?"

"But, unless you forgot what you learned about the scope of our authority, Mr. Chief of Police, we don't go after them unless they're in our jurisdiction, and that's typically after they commit a crime *here*."

"But if we found a murderer in our jurisdiction, we sure wouldn't just let him roam around. We'd arrest the son of a gun."

"Remind me—how did this Sparro woman happen to place her supposed mass murderer here in the first place?"

"Simple. She saw him on the television news broadcast from the courthouse right after the Atwood sentencing."

"For crying out loud, man. Has she ever seen the guy? I mean in the flesh."

"Not that I know of."

"Did her father?

"I'm not sure, I...I don't think so," Mitch said sheepishly.

"Then how would they know what he looks like?"

"Dani compared another TV film of him taken at a trial in Wisconsin not that long ago, and there's a photo in the file from when he was in the Army."

"When was that? Twenty or thirty years ago? More? That's it?"

"There's a lot more than just that."

"Like what? Does she have any fingerprints, DNA, witnesses, any hard evidence at all to connect this guy to any of these crimes?"

"In at least two cases, he was a Person of Interest and was actually interviewed. In one of those he was almost indicted when the mark was arrested; that arrest was based upon information that Gruca himself gave the police," said Mitch.

Bartlett barked. "Being a POI doesn't make you guilty. You know that. We don't have a thing connecting him with the Wheatley murder, but we sure have a lot connecting Atwood."

"All I'm asking is that you don't react just on what I've told you but read the actual documents John Sparro put together. He connected Gruca to at least two cases in which the victims' bodies were blown up, and more than one where they were also burned. That's more than just coincidence."

"John Sparro sounds like a retiree who had a vivid imagination and too much time on his hands."

"You should read up on him while you're at it. The guy was one hell of a detective. The fact that he died under some pretty questionable circumstances while tracking Gruca just adds more questions to the mix."

"Maybe so, but they're not ours to answer. How did he die?"

"The investigation concluded it was suicide, but ..."

"Geez, man. He killed himself, and you want me to take this seriously? Now I'm thinking he was just a *depressed* retiree with too much time on his hands."

"Dani, uh, Miss Sparro, is convinced that Gruca killed her father and made it look like suicide."

"Another one of this psycho's schemes, is that it?"

"Maybe he found out that Sparro was after him and decided to stop him. Look, I know it sounds like a stretch, but before we let this go just give it your careful consideration, please. I trust your instincts. If you read the whole file and then tell me I'm out to lunch, I'll call it quits." Mitch laid a finger on the folder, tapping it decisively.

Bartlett swiveled his chair to look out the window, rotating back after a long pause. "Alright. But just because you're the chief of police, and only because of that, not because you're my friend. I'll look at the damn file. But don't think I'm going to have some kind of epiphany." He scooped up the folder and rose. "Now, I'm getting out of here ... before you talk me into some other ridiculous goose chase."

"Thanks, Dave. Maybe you're right. But I'd like to hear what you think after you read what I read."

"My money says he was never in Lakeview, but if he was, there's no reason for him to stick around. And just out of curiosity, what's this Dani Sparro look like?"

"Well, she's sort of... I guess she's..." Mitch looked like a kid caught chewing the cookie he had just pulled from the jar.

"Tell me it's not true!" Bartlett shook his head. "I should have known. She's attractive, and you got hit by the thunderbolt."

"Thunderbolt?"

"Never mind. That's another movie you probably haven't seen."

CHAPTER 44

Mitch dropped his feet from his desk and grabbed the phone when the receptionist told him Danielle Sparro was calling. He had been thinking about her a lot since they met, figuring it was just odd curiosity sparked by the Gruca file.

"Good afternoon, Miss…uh, Dani. I'm glad you called." He glanced absentmindedly at his boots.

"I saw him."

"Saw who?"

"Gruca. I saw him again. He's still right here in Lakeview."

"Again?" Mitch frowned incredulously.

"I'm almost positive; it had to be him."

"You're *almost* positive it was him?"

"Well, for sure he's changed. He doesn't look much like the pictures I have, but that would be expected after so many years."

"Look, Dani, I did read your file over the weekend,

and I'll admit there's a lot of provocative information in there. I even gave it to our prosecutor, and he said he'd look it over. But there's still nothing in there that connects Gruca with the murder of Prudence Wheatley."

"What are you not getting, chief? Didn't you see all the similarities? He's here, and you have to do something." Dani paced about her room, her arm waving erratically as she spoke.

"You're not even positive it was him! You could be mistaken, and what am I supposed to do? We already have a suspect charged and heading to trial. How would I convince the judge to issue another warrant? Just say, Ms. Sparro here is almost positive she saw a man here in Lakeview who she believes killed Prudence Wheatley? Oh, and by the way, she also believes he's a serial killer who killed her father?"

"What about the court reporter's body, chief? The papers suggested that some suspicious material was found in a firepit at Atwood's place. Was it by any chance human remains?"

Mitch winced. "We have no evidence that anything found on Atwood's property is human remains."

"When you do, I'll bet you'll find traces of ammonium nitrate and some kind of fuel at the scene, if you haven't already. You saw in the file those cases where he'd burned bodies before? For sure in both Wisconsin and Missouri. That's the exact same MO. A moron could connect the dots."

"I'll assume you weren't referring to me."

"No, I only..." Her cheeks flushed.

"Look. I said I gave your file to the prosecutor. If he decides there's sufficient evidence to start another investigation, I'll go along. That's the best I can do for now." Mitch heard her sigh, then nothing but a long pause.

"Okay Chief. I can live with that, for now. And since you read the file, I owe you a dinner. Where and when?"

He paused. "Well…alright. How about tomorrow night? Where are you staying?"

"The Shoreline Inn."

"I'll pick you up at the front desk at 7:30."

No sooner had he hung up than Mitch wondered what he might be getting himself into. His law enforcement instinct told him he should do something about Gordon Gruca, but what? Unless Dave Bartlett got on board, which he thought unlikely, there was really nothing he could do but keep an eye out. If Gruca did turn up, he could at least bring him in for questioning. In the meantime, he would just sit tight and await Dave's assessment.

He began to have second thoughts about accepting her invitation. After leaving Bartlett's office, he had googled "hit by the thunderbolt," and learned it came from *The Godfather* movie, describing love at first sight. Surely that hadn't happened to him—but what was he feeling for Dani? Then he envisioned Lisa, asking himself, "Should I be having these kinds of feelings again?" After a few minutes of futility, he snapped out of contemplation, concluding he wasn't going to let his angst ruin a free meal.

CHAPTER 45

As promised, Mitch presented himself in the lobby of her hotel at precisely 7:30 p.m. Wednesday evening. After pacing for almost fifteen minutes, he was about to call her room when the elevator door opened and disgorged four guests. He tried not to stare at the attractive young woman among them, felt dumbfounded when she walked right up to him and said, "So, Chief Quinn, how are you planning to spend my money tonight?"

He hadn't even recognized her and stood saucer-eyed at the striking transformation. The ponytail previously tucked under her straw hat now fell in a profusion of center-parted hair, reaching to her shoulders. The well-worn jeans and vest had been traded for a bright-colored cocktail dress, cut just low enough to tease the imagination. Her eyes sparkled as she smiled at his gawk, continuing, "Are we still going to dinner, Chief, or just hanging around here?"

His lips moved without a sound. Dani shrugged,

walking quickly past him toward the door. As Mitch twisted slowly around, following her with his eyes, he was unable not to notice her shapely legs moving beneath the almost knee-length skirt that swayed with each step. He shook his head, hustled after her and opened the door to the white Ford F-150 pickup parked in the front turnaround. Dani stopped to gaze.

"No police vehicle tonight, eh Chief Quinn?"

"I'm off duty, Ms. Sparro. This one's all mine."

"Quite a rig. What year is it?"

"It's a 2002 Harley-Davidson edition. I got it at auction last year."

"It goes well with those boots of yours." She smiled approvingly.

Once underway, their conversation during the short drive proved light, Mitch pointing out the few local landmarks. The spot he had selected for dinner was a casual waterside restaurant packed virtually every evening from spring through summer, tonight being no exception. After they parked, he led her by the hand through the crowd of drop-in patrons, marching up to a check-in stand by an arbor-framed entranceway.

"Quinn. Reservation for two, at 7:45. We're a couple minutes late."

The young maître d' looked at her list, motioned to a waitress, and passed her the menus. "Table twenty-two." Turning back to Mitch, she flashed a smile. "Enjoy your dinners."

As they walked out onto the upper deck, Mitch slowed his stride, hit with a surge of nostalgia. The evening sun shone through a string of clouds, hanging low on the horizon; suddenly he worried that he had made the wrong choice.

Dani halted tableside. "I've got to say, Chief Quinn, if the food here is half as good as the view, I'll get my money's worth."

"Mission accomplished then. Actually, the food is pretty good." Mitch congratulated himself as he pulled out a chair for her.

The waiter appeared, and Dani ordered the house chardonnay. Mitch declined.

"You're going to make me drink alone, Chief?"

"I'm driving." His dismissive smile suggested an end to the subject.

She shrugged and raised her water glass. "To each his own. Had I known, I wouldn't have ordered anything."

"I'm glad you did. This experience should be enjoyed."

The waiter returned quickly, serving Dani, and they both sat gazing at the brilliant sunset. Mitch eventually broke the silence, saying, "I like to call it God's canvas." Dani's eyes narrowed, and he waved his arm across the horizon. "I mean, the sky over the lake at sunset. Each evening it's like He paints a different picture. Clouds like this always make it more interesting."

"My, my, Chief Quinn, you're full of surprises. Can it be that you're a romantic, or are you just religious?"

"I thought we were on a first-name basis now?"

"Okay, Mitch."

"A bit of both, I guess you could say. My mom was very religious. She was Catholic. My dad was, well, I suppose he was agnostic. Although nearer the end I think he found religion or some form of it."

"If I raised a sore subject, I ..."

"Thanks, but no worries. They had good lives. Not as long as some, but together to the end. They loved one another very much." She gazed back at the lake.

"And how about your folks, Ms., uh, Dani? I know you said your father had passed. What about your mom?"

Dani paused for a sip of wine. Taking a deep breath, she answered, "My mom left us when I was thirteen. She never really wanted a family—or at least, that's what Dad told me. I came to believe she just found someone else, someone she wanted more than him. But no matter. My dad raised me, and we were very close when I was young, at least until college. Then, well, things got complicated."

Mitch sensed he should change the subject. "Where did you grow up?"

"Mostly in Colorado. My dad stayed there a while after he graduated college at CSU. When my mom left, he wanted to get a fresh start, so we moved to Southern California. He'd always intended to join the FBI, but he didn't get accepted right away, so he applied for a position in the LAPD. He spent two years there, then reapplied to the FBI, and it was off to Quantico for training. That's in Virginia."

Mitch grinned. "I know."

"Dad was passionate about becoming a crime investigator. It was that passion that eventually got him onto the trail of Gordon Gruca. Which brings me back to ..."

Just then the waiter appeared to take their orders, Mitch sighing in relief at the interruption. He asked for a few more minutes, suddenly spotting Alan Redmond heading in their direction as he spoke. Alan stopped at their table, and they exchanged hellos.

"I'm here for our homeowners' association board meeting." Redmond's eyes darted back and forth between Mitch and Dani. "So, what's the occasion, chief? It's been a long time since I've seen you out. Especially here. Wasn't this once a haunt for you and..."

Mitch cut him off. "Alan, meet Ms. Danielle Sparro. She's visiting... from Colorado."

Redmond's eyes widened as he focused on Dani. "Well, my heart be still. It is a genuine pleasure to meet you, Ms. Sparro. I'm Alan Redmond. Please call me Alan. It's seldom we see our number one policeman out enjoying himself and particularly in such lovely company, if I may say so. What brings you to our little community?"

"Thank you, Alan. Compliments are always welcome. As a matter of fact, I'm here to..."

Mitch interrupted again. "Ms. Sparro takes exception to our having charged Lawrence Atwood with the murder of Prudence Wheatley. She thinks the real killer is still on the loose. As a matter of fact, she says he's right here in the village."

"Is that right?" Redmond's smile disappeared. "Well, that's... very... interesting, Ms. Sparro. Pru Wheatley was a very good friend of mine. Just who is it you think killed her, then?"

Mitch couldn't help himself. "Ms. Sparro's father was an FBI agent specializing in serial killers. He did a lot of research on a man named Gordon Gruca, becoming convinced he was responsible for numerous murders across the country. Ms. Sparro believes she saw Gruca in the village just yesterday."

"I know that I saw him. And he is here. At least he was last week," Dani insisted.

"That's quite some theory, Ms. Sparro. With all due respect, some good folks around here have concluded otherwise, not the least of whom is sitting right across from you. The evidence they have seems persuasive. How is it you're so sure it's not Atwood?"

Before Dani could answer, Redmond looked up at the sound of his name being called. They all turned to see three men waving at them from a table at the far end of the deck. "Looks like your group is beckoning, Alan. Maybe we could discuss this another time?" said Mitch.

Redmond waved back. "Oh. Well, sure. I would very much enjoy speaking with *you* further about this, Ms. Sparro."

"Any time, Alan. I'm staying at the Shoreline Inn. And please, you can call me Dani."

"Then I'll call on you tomorrow, if that's okay... Dani? If it's okay with the chief, of course."

Mitch raised his hands in mock surrender as Dani replied, "Any time after nine a.m."

"Tomorrow it is then, Dani." Redmond shook her hand and walked away.

"Sorry if I got you into something there. Alan is an attorney from Grand Rapids. He apparently worked a lot with Prudence Wheatley. I think it may have been something more than merely professional, at least for him. Her death hit him hard."

Dani ran a finger around the edge of her wineglass. "According to Alan, it sounds like you used to come here often?"

Mitch shifted awkwardly. "This is a popular place. It has the best lake view dining in the area."

"So, am I out of line in asking who else he was referring to when he said this was a haunt of yours?"

"I'm sure he was talking about my wife, Lisa. We came here pretty frequently."

"You're married? I didn't see a ring." Dani feigned ignorance, not wanting to betray Willy's disclosures.

"I was married."

"Divorced then?"

"She died."

Dani sat back. "I'm sorry. I didn't mean to ..."

"No worries. It happened a few years ago. Car accident. Just bad karma, I guess." Quinn was staring intently into the water glass in front of him. "I wasn't there."

Dani reached across the table and placed her hand on his. "I didn't mean to pry."

Her touch sparked the same vexing sensation he had felt earlier, but Lisa's face kept popping into his mind. Neither spoke for a long moment.

Mitch waved at the waiter. "Maybe we should order."

Dani forced a smile, withdrawing her hand. "Good idea."

CHAPTER 46

The man sat fixed at the end of the bar as he swallowed a shot of Jack Daniel's. Placing the empty glass next to the IPA draft in front of him, he peered curiously through a large window behind the bar overlooking the dining deck outside. Earlier he had been strolling the boardwalk along the channel when he happened upon this restaurant. The crowd waiting outside was a deterrent, until he saw the police chief pass by leading an attractive woman by the hand. He then pulled his hat lower, looking for another entrance.

Entering through a separate side door, he hustled a vacated stool with a view of the deck. He observed with interest the exchange between the chief, his female companion, and a man who interrupted their conversation, who he recalled seeing during his watch at the prosecutor's office. Something about the woman was familiar, and he concentrated on her after the other man left.

Half an hour later he flinched at a tap on his arm. "Are

you saving this seat?" He looked up to see Alan Redmond's face staring down at him.

"No. All yours."

The man took a sip of his beer, then addressed Redmond as he plopped on the stool. "Quite a crowd tonight."

"It's always like this in the summer," Redmond answered over his shoulder as he waved at the bartender.

"I've never been in this place before." He noticed the bartender nod back at Redmond and begin mixing a drink. "You must come here often."

"Why do you say that?"

Nodding at the server, the man said. "He seems to know you."

"I guess you could say that I'm a regular. I drop in here whenever I can get out to the lake." Redmond extended his hand. "I'm Alan Redmond. Do you live around here?"

As they shook, the man said, "No. I'm just here on business. I have a couple of customers here in Lakeview."

Redmond took a big swallow of the martini the bartender set in front of him. "Is that so? A great time for it, Mr., uh?"

The man hesitated for a long moment. "Um … James. Stewart James. So, you live here then?"

"Oh, no. I actually live back in Grand Rapids. My law office is there. I own a cottage nearby."

"That's a coincidence. I've been reading about someone else in your profession."

"Oh? Who's that?" Redmond gulped the rest of his drink and signaled for another.

"A guy named, uh, give me a minute … it will come to me." He tapped the bar and looked skyward. "Atwood!

That's it. His last name is Atwood. His first name was…
uh…"

Redmond answered for him. "It's Lawrence. You've
been reading about him and the Pru Wheatley murder,
then? I thought coverage had died down."

"The article I saw said his trial will be in the fall. Do
you know him?"

"Yep—both of them. Ms. Wheatley was a close
friend. And I've had a few cases with Atwood. He's a hell
of a lawyer."

"The article I read makes it sound like they were
lovers. They said they found her remains in his firepit."

Alan looked confused. "I don't remember that being
reported."

"I read it just recently."

"Can't imagine I missed it, but I've been busy this
summer. I need to catch up. It's true that, if he did it,
there's a strong case for some kind of psychosis for sure.
But that's a big if." Alan took a gulp of the fresh cocktail
placed in front of him.

"Why is that?"

Redmond turned on his stool to face him. "As I said,
I've had cases with Atwood. He's a pragmatic strategist—a
very cool customer under pressure. I've never seen him
flinch, even in the tightest of situations. So, I just can't see
the crime-of-passion claim the prosecutor is pushing."

The man leaned closer. "Well, the papers said that
he's quite a womanizer. I read he's married, with kids.
Maybe this woman caused problems for him? That might
be a reason to lose your cool. It happens, right?"

"Oh, he's known as a player for sure. There are too

many rumors for it not to be true. But I just don't think it's in him to kill someone, especially like that. Makes little sense—and in my profession, most things ultimately do." Redmond downed his drink.

"You sound awfully convincing, Alan. Maybe you should represent him?"

"Ha! Even if he wanted me, no can do. I'm not a criminal lawyer. I only handle civil cases. The state attorney general will be the lead counsel at the trial." Redmond twisted around and raised the empty glass, pointing it toward the server.

The fourth martini was an invitation. The man ordered another beer. "Isn't that unusual? I mean, the attorney general getting involved?"

Redmond turned as he grabbed the refilled glass, not noticing that he spilled a few drops on the man's pant leg. The man brushed them away without looking. "Rarely. He has the authority to take it over, and it's not all that unusual when the case has a high profile. Especially if winning it can bring the comprehensive press coverage so many prosecutors long for. And this case has an extra special appeal."

"Oh? What's that?"

"Robert Patterson, he's the attorney general, will be the Republican candidate for governor. So winning this case not only nails one of the most renowned lawyers in the state, if not the country, it puts his main competitor behind bars. Quite an accomplishment, wouldn't you say?" He hesitated. "But it's no slam dunk."

"Sounded in the papers like they've got a lot of evidence against him. But I'd sure like to hear what you think would make it a slam dunk."

Alan made a signing motion toward the server, pointing to himself and the man. The server acknowledged he would be paying for both.

"I've talked with Dave Bartlett, the county prosecutor. He's co-counsel on the case. Most of what they have is circumstantial." He slurred slightly as he talked. "See, they can't prove the remains in the firepit are Pru Wheatley's. No DNA connection. Without that there's only speculation, which is exactly what the judge will instruct the jury not to do."

"Don't juries do that all the time?"

"Of course. But that's where a good trial lawyer makes the difference. He doesn't let them go too far afield." Redmond stood up as the waiter handed him the tab. He then looked curiously at his companion. "You seem to know an awful lot about, well, a lot, Stewart." He looked at the bill and pulled out his wallet. "Gotta go. This should cover both of us. I need to get to the cottage in one piece. I met someone tonight who may shed a whole new light on all of this."

The man jumped up, grabbing Redmond's hand. "I can't let you do that. I'll get this."

"Well, thank you Stewart. I'll never argue."

"But now you've got me even more interested. Who'd you meet?"

"A charming young woman who believes that Atwood didn't do it. She seems quite sure of herself." He placed his hand on the bar in a steadying motion, shoving the wallet back in his pocket. "Matter of fact, she claims the real killer is right here in Lakeview Village. Said she saw him the other day."

The man stiffened. "Did she identify the person she thinks did it?"

"I think she said his name is, uh, Gorka? Or Greco? No. That's not it. Something like that though. I'll find out tomorrow when I meet with her." Redmond swiveled to leave, then turned back and held out a business card.

"You said earlier that you have customers in the area?" The man nodded. "So, give me a call the next time you get back here. We can meet at my cottage. The view is great, and the bar is well-stocked. I'll buy *you* a drink then, or maybe two."

Watching the lawyer wobble out the door, the man looked down at the card and said to himself, "Can't wait." He tucked the card in his wallet, paid and left, thinking on his way what a truly fortuitous evening it had been.

CHAPTER 47

Thursday. Early morning.

Mitch rolled awake and stared through his bedroom window at the emerging dawn. Confusion pestered him as his mind wandered to the night before.

They had outlasted most of the crowd, then moved to a vacant table nearer the edge of the deck. She ordered another glass of wine. He struggled to keep the conversation away from the Gruca file, which inevitably led to Dani's probing of his background.

"So, Mitch, tell me why a man like you would stay in a town like Lakeview Village?"

"What's wrong with Lakeview Village?"

"Nothing. You just seem to be the type who'd venture out ... look for something more, I guess."

"I did. I was gone for quite a while."

"Where to?"

"First to the Army and Fort Leonard Wood for basics. After that, a couple years' active duty on U.S. bases. Then I applied for the military police and returned to Leonard

Wood, completed the program, and went on active duty stateside. Ultimately, I became a CID special agent."

"What's CID?"

"That's short for Army Criminal Investigation Command. Don't ask me why it's not CIC. No idea."

"But a military policeman? What made you want to be that?"

"I suppose it was my dad. He was chief of police here, you know."

"Uh, no. Really?" Dani feigned ignorance again.

"Maybe I was trying to make up for ... well, maybe it just runs in the family. Who knows?"

"What was that like? I mean, how is it different from what you do now? Besides being military, that is." Dani leaned in closer.

"It was nothing like what I do now," Mitch said. "Not even close."

"You sound like you resent that."

Mitch took a sip of water. Setting the glass down, he said, "I suppose that I did, at least for a long time I did. This Wheatley case woke me up. It's kind of a double-edged sword. On the one hand, it's motivated me in a way I haven't felt for a long time. Otherwise, it opened a Pandora's box of old wounds."

"Old wounds?"

"Things that happened when I was in CID."

"Like what? When we first met you intimated that you had some experience with psychopaths."

"Once or twice. One was in the States, before they transferred me to Europe. Another serial killer. He was military, and he murdered quite a few before we caught up with him."

"But you got him? That's a good thing, isn't it?"

"I guess you could say that." Mitch recalled his two murdered team members and the weeks he spent recuperating after catching the monster they'd chased for over a year. Absentmindedly he rubbed at the old scar on his side. *"We got him, but it wasn't a positive experience."*

"But can't you use that experience to get Gordon Gruca?"

He wouldn't take the bait. *"Enough about me. Tell me more about Dani Sparro."*

Dani paused, disappointed, but took a breath and started up where she had left off almost two hours earlier. She confessed not knowing what she wanted to do after graduating from USC. Following a year of dating, she married an engineering student she had met at a sorority mixer, but they divorced after eighteen months. They were hopelessly "in like," she said, but not mature enough to maintain a long-term relationship. After school she remained in California, migrating south to Newport Beach, where she found work as a gofer in a small law firm. She took a number of prelaw courses at a local community college but never got motivated enough to apply to law school. Two more years of the beach life convinced her to return to Colorado. Once settled, she and her father began a slow dance of reconciliation, while she acted as his part-time secretary, research assistant, and student sleuth.

As she continued, Mitch found it more and more difficult to listen, unable to focus on anything besides her every move—her habit of constantly pulling back her hair from her face with both hands, the tic of raising her left eyebrow when making a point, and she always smiled with her eyes. He wondered what it would taste like if he kissed her. The *increasing knot in his chest overcame his earlier guilt over betraying Lisa's memory.*

"My father and I had grown apart for a variety of reasons; I was a lot more liberal than him, for one. He was a man of strong convictions, but I hadn't yet developed that level of commitment. Regardless, he didn't deserve to be murdered, especially not by a serial killer he was trying to bring to justice. That's why I want you to do something, Mitch."

Mitch sighed and snapped back to attention. "Look, Dani, I've told you I can't do anything without the prosecutor's go-ahead. Atwood's trial is coming up soon, and I doubt the prosecutor will support my allocating resources to chase after Gruca. But I'll let you know if he changes direction. So, for now, can we please just drop it?"

As he watched for Dani's reaction, the words "if looks could kill" came to mind. "Maybe we should go," he suggested.

She replied curtly, "Can you get the waiter? I want to make sure I pay my debt."

After she settled the bill, they drove to the hotel in silence. Mitch paid little attention to the road. His mind wandered, thinking of how to mend the fence he may have just broken and what more he could do to make Dani appreciate his dilemma.

Then, just as Mitch pulled in, Dani asked offhandedly, "By the way, you haven't seen any white rabbits around here lately, have you Chief Quinn?"

Mitch stepped hard on the brakes, bringing the truck to a jerking halt in front of the entrance. Turning to her, he asked, "What the heck do white rabbits have to do with any of this?"

Dani could see her comment had struck a chord. "Wait a minute! You know something, don't you?"

"Never mind what I know or don't know. What's this about rabbits?"

"Well, in a number of the more recent cases you'll find in the file, witnesses claimed to see a white rabbit at the murder scene, or close by. Those crimes all took place in different cities or states, so investigators had no way of coordinating the information. They just didn't know. In each case they concluded the stories were either wild imaginations, pranks, or the witness was in shock. But the material in my dad's file shows there are just too many incidents to ignore as unrelated. He was the only one who put them all together."

"I saw nothing at all about white rabbits in the file," Mitch said as he exited the truck. He recalled the claims of both Willy and Atwood.

Dani didn't wait for him to open the door, stepping out as he started to walk around. "I didn't give you the whole file, Mitch... just enough to understand why my dad was right. There were no references to rabbits in any of the earlier cases. But given the repeated stories, my dad thought they may have become a fixation, or possibly he uses them as some sort of... well, a sign of some kind."

"A sign? Of what?"

"I'm not sure. Maybe a signature. Something to show..." Dani's words trailed off as she saw the look on Quinn's face as he drew closer.

"Okay, so who saw the white rabbits, Mitch? Was it you?"

"No. I saw no rabbits."

"Who then? Someone did, didn't they? Tell me."

"Look Dani, let's talk about it later."

"When?"

He walked her into the foyer, said good night, and turned to leave, saying, "Soon."

"Tomorrow?" Dani called after him.

Mitch pivoted and beelined back to her, reaching his arm around her waist. Dani leaned back, but he drew her closer, kissing her. It wasn't a long goodbye kiss, but long enough to make an impression. He released her, saying, "As soon as I can." His heart pounding, he strutted away sporting a self-satisfied grin, but determined not to look back. She stood wide-eyed, staring after him.

Now he sat on his bed with his head in his hands, trying to decide what to do next. He felt exuberant but still conflicted and hating it. Before she mentioned rabbits, he had been thinking about Dani in a way that had nothing to do with murder or criminals. Afterward, the gnawing suspicions about Gruca re-emerged. He needed to talk to Willy, then to Dave Bartlett again. He had unfinished business with Dani, too—much more than just what to do about Gordon Gruca.

CHAPTER 48

Shoreline Inn. 9:30 a.m.

Dani sat across from Alan Redmond, trying not to show her impatience. He had phoned her at exactly 9 a.m., asking to meet; having made the offer, she felt obliged to agree but regretted her invitation almost immediately after he called. For a change, her first thoughts that morning were far from Gordon Gruca. Instead, she just couldn't put Mitch's kiss out of her mind. When she reached over to take his hand the night before, the touch had been almost electric—she felt mad at herself for bringing up the case again. At this moment, she wanted to be anyplace else but talking with Alan Redmond.

They had convened in the hotel restaurant at ten. Most of the guests had departed earlier for the beach, and they now sat alone in the small dining room. As soon as they ordered, Redmond began asking her about Gruca. Listening to Dani recite his long history of mayhem, Alan perked up when she began to describe the rape and murder of a young woman in Wisconsin several years before. He vaguely remembered the case, but it was the details of the crime which most interested him.

"You say he somehow cut her up and then burned the remains?"

"Not just 'cut her up,' Alan. That would have left much larger bone fragments. Her body was violently blown apart, leaving only smaller pieces. Easier to burn—and harder to identify. But otherwise, pretty much the same. He even used the same ingredients." She immediately regretted her comment when she saw the lawyer wince. "I'm sorry, Alan, but understand Atwood didn't do it. Gruca did."

Redmond shook his head in disbelief. "But how could that be? I mean, you said the trial in the Wisconsin case happened in early 2007, and that your father saw him there, right?" She nodded her head. "How could he have had the time and brainpower to plan all that's happened here, let alone pull off Pru's murder?"

"The trial ended in March 2007. That's when my dad saw Gruca in the courthouse. He was standing in the background during a hallway interview filmed by a local TV station. Dad didn't realize it until he saw the spot air later that night; the killer had been only a few feet behind him! Anyway, once they convicted the mark and Gruca had made his appearance, it was over for him. That's what he wanted. Nothing more. Then, he had over a year-and-a-half to get here and put things together. For all we know he was planning the murders at the same time."

Redmond sat in contemplation, struggling to process what he had just heard. "And you said last night you've seen him here, recently?"

"Just the other day. In a diner on Main Street. At least I'm pretty sure it was Gruca. It just had to be him. He'd been watching me while he ate breakfast at that diner down from the police station. When I noticed him watching me, he left in a hurry. I followed him out, but he'd disappeared by the time I got outside."

Redmond thought he saw her shiver. "Any idea where he is now?"

"No idea. I haven't seen him since."

"And Mitch doesn't buy your theory?"

"He said he gave my file to prosecutor Bartlett, and that he'll go along with whatever he decides, but I don't think he's on board."

"Mitch is a darned good cop, and he's probably right. But, right or wrong, if you could convince Dave Bartlett, he's all you need to get a warrant. He's the prosecutor, not Mitch."

Dani realized that Redmond was right. She felt like an idiot. Why hadn't she approached Bartlett from the beginning? She knew why, but she did not want to admit to herself that it was Mitch. She became infatuated when they first met, letting her emotions get control. But now she needed to concentrate on the objective—to get Gruca and avenge her father.

"Gruca could leave at any minute, Alan. If he does, he'll probably come back, but he might not, and I won't take the chance."

"So, what are you going to do now?"

"I've got to find him. I'll try to convince Bartlett to go after him, even if Mitch won't."

Redmond mulled over the possibilities. "Can I help you? I would really like to. I know the area and most of the key business owners in Lakeview. I can ask around. Have you got a picture of Gruca, so I could recognize him if I saw him?"

Dani reached for the satchel on the chair next to her. "I kept some things, and only gave Mitch part of the records I brought. And what I do have isn't very good. It's old. I also have a still from the TV program I told you about, but he's somewhat in the shadows."

She pulled out two pictures and placed them on the table between them, pointing to a small, black-and-white photograph of a young man in a military uniform. "That's his Army ID photo. He was only about twenty at the time they took it." She pushed a larger photo closer to him. "That's the scene in the Wisconsin courthouse, which dad pulled off the video. It's grainy, but at least it gives you an idea of his body type. And then there's this." She pulled a large print from the bag.

Alan picked it up and examined it closely. "Is this him now?"

"Maybe. Understandably, the man I saw in the diner was a lot older and heavier, and he was wearing a hat and had on glasses. I didn't get a really close look at him. He put his hand up to his face, like he was trying to hide it. That's why I'm just sure it had to be him. Why would anyone else in Lakeview spy on me like that and then try to hide himself? I don't know anyone here but you and Mitch."

"Frankly, I can think of reasons why a man would stare at you Dani, but that's beside the point. Where did you get this?" Alan said as he pointed to the print.

"After my dad retired, he still had friends in the agency. That's a computer facsimile they made for my dad using Gruca's ID and a program the FBI has which creates an age progression of what someone might look like when they get older. But keep in mind, this shows him with a receding hairline, which might be natural for a person his age now. Today, he could have a full head of hair or no hair. I couldn't tell the other day because of the hat he was wearing."

Redmond examined the images. "There's something about this guy that seems familiar, but I don't recognize him. Must be my imagination—or maybe just wishful thinking?"

"Well, what I saw of the man was not particularly distinctive. He was just ... the only word that comes to mind is ordinary."

"Sort of an everyman?"

"Just don't let appearances fool you. He's a methodical, cold-blooded killer and ruthless."

Alan shrugged. "Then I guess I can't rely on this much to identify him now, can I?"

"Probably not, I'm afraid."

"What else can you tell me?

"After his parents broke up, a court placed Gruca in an orphanage. Later his estranged father showed up and took him away. My dad tracked them to Fort Bragg, in North Carolina. Gruca's father was a vet, and I guess he must have had some connections there. Anyway, dad learned that Gruca eventually enlisted and trained for the Rangers. For some reason he was discharged; dad couldn't find out why. His records were sealed."

"It must have been something pretty bad."

"Whatever it was, understand, he's a psychopath."

"That doesn't scare me, Dani. Besides, it sounds like

he only kills with a specific purpose in mind. I'm not a good enough, uh, what did you call it…a mark? I just wouldn't qualify."

"Well, we don't know what he'll do if he gets cornered. If you really want to get involved in this, Alan, you've got to appreciate what you're getting into."

"If it could help catch Pru's killer, I'm willing to take the risk. Let's get this guy." Redmond removed a notebook from his suit pocket and began writing furiously.

"Are you going to take notes?"

He grinned. "I always do these days. I don't want to let any senior moments interfere with my objectives."

"Okay, then I've got some ideas. You say you know the local merchants? I'll get some photo prints made, and you can start asking around. You must describe Gruca as best you can. He's about six feet tall. I'd say he's got a stocky build—athletic, like a boxer or a football player. He has … uh, *had* … brownish-colored hair, and of course he was wearing glasses and a hat when I saw him."

"Any scars or birthmarks of any kind?"

"Nothing like that, but he does have a tattoo. I'm not sure what it is, but it covers most of his lower right forearm. You can see it in a quick clip of the TV footage of him leaving the courthouse. It just wasn't clear enough to identify exactly what it is."

"Well, that's something people will probably remember." Redmond stood up. "Let's get at it, Dani."

CHAPTER 49

When Mitch got to the station, he met with Willy and had him repeat what he could recall of seeing the white rabbits the previous October. He then called Dave Bartlett to see if he had read the Gruca file, get his take-away, and vet him on what to do next. Bartlett's secretary had just answered when Mitch saw Dani come in the front door, stopping at the reception desk. He watched as she handed over a large envelope, looked at him and waved, then walked toward the door. He told Irene he would have to call back, hung up, and quickly ran out to catch Dani, bursting onto the sidewalk just in time to see her car driving away. When he returned inside, the reception officer handed him the folder.

"Ms. Sparro said to make sure you got this, Chief."

"Did she say what it is?"

"Nope. No idea."

Mitch opened the envelope as he returned to his office. Pulling out the contents, he found what appeared to be transcripts of the statements Dani had referred to. For the next hour he pored through the records, and in fact they confirmed what she had said. There were four cases around the greater Midwest in the past twelve years, including the most recent case in Wisconsin, in which witnesses testified to seeing white rabbits at the murder scenes. Two cases concluded in convictions after trial, one ended in a hung jury, and the last was unsolved.

When he finished, he called back to Bartlett's office. Irene answered again. "Irene, Mitch Quinn. Sorry I had to break off earlier. Is Dave available?"

Waiting as she put him on hold, he decided not to mention the rabbits right away. After a short pause Bartlett answered, and Mitch asked if he had read the file.

"I'm working on it."

"Well, how long before you can finish it? I need to talk to you about this whole thing and to show you more records Dani Sparro left for me this morning."

"I had hoped you'd forget this fairy tale."

"Uh, well, no, not exactly. There's way too much to ignore."

"Look Mitch, I'm busy as hell. I've got another trial starting Wednesday, and I just don't have time for this. I'll finish it when I can. Remember, the Atwood trial is not that far off, and the AG is loaded for bear. There's plenty for us lawyers to do getting ready without chasing after some phantom serial killer."

"But Dave, if you'll just…"

"There are no buts about this, Mitch. It would take a miracle to generate an investigation based upon what you've told me is in that file, and I'm out of miracles today. I'm sorry, but this discussion is over and done."

After they disconnected, Mitch began sorting through the materials again. He tried to convince himself that Bartlett was probably right—but that was only one horn of his dilemma. How could he possibly reconcile all of this with Dani? He didn't even know how she felt about his kissing her, what exactly it was he was feeling for her, or whether she felt anything in return. The question he asked himself was: "What next?"

CHAPTER 50

One week later.

Alan Redmond had not returned to his law office since his meeting with Dani the week before. He stayed at his cottage, spending each day canvassing every retailer, restaurant, bar, gas station, and hotel he could cover south of Lakeview near his cottage. So far, no one recalled a person matching the computer simulation, nor had any of them seen a man with a forearm tattoo. Today he was focusing on a handful of cheaper motels north of the village, always the last considered by vacationers who were late to make summer reservations.

The Beltline Motel was a one-story remnant of the fifties, badly in need of paint and fronted by a gravel lot a hundred yards off the state highway. Although two miles outside the village limits, it was still close enough to merit a look from frugal travelers. Having just finished another disappointing interview with the Randy Quaid look-alike desk clerk, Alan almost ran right into a man carrying a packing box who was not looking where he was going.

The man's expression quickly changed from surprise to concern when he looked up to see Redmond.

"Alan Redmond, right? What are you doing here?"

It took a few moments for Alan to recognize him as the man he had met over a week ago at the lakeside restaurant bar. He seemed to look different for some reason. "Uh, yes. Stewart, isn't it? I was about to ask you the same thing."

"I'm back to see one of my customers. I missed him the last trip." He shrugged toward the motel disapprovingly. "That's why I'm staying here. My expense account is running low."

Alan scanned the front of the motel. "To be honest, it wouldn't be my first choice."

"So, why are you poking around this dump, then?"

Alan glanced over his shoulder, then looked back at the man, lowering his voice. "You remember our discussion last week, about the Lawrence Atwood case? I mentioned I was meeting with a woman the next morning."

The man nodded. "Um-hmm."

"Well, we met and talked, and she knows who the real killer is."

"The real killer?"

"Yes. His name is Gordon Gruca. It looks like he killed Prudence Wheatley—and many others, as a matter of fact."

"A matter of fact? You sound like you're sure of that."

"As I told you before, I never really thought it was Atwood. Well, maybe I did at first, but after thinking it through it just made no sense. Dani Sparro convinced me."

The man's eyes narrowed slightly. "Oh?"

"She showed me all kinds of police files, statements—a

bunch of stuff that shows the man's a serial killer. He even murdered a young woman in Wisconsin the year before Pru. He blew up her body in the same way as…" Alan looked away and didn't finish.

The man interrupted. "Sparro? That's her name then? She seems to know a lot about this Gruca person."

"Yeah. Her father was an FBI agent. He tracked the guy for quite a while. I think I told you she thought she saw this Gruca guy here in Lakeview Village, right? Well, she saw him again, just in the past two weeks. I've been helping her search for him since. She had a computer-generated likeness made of what he could look like today. I'm showing it around to see if it can shake someone's memory."

"Does that really work? I mean, how could that work?"

"Apparently you scan in a photo of a person when they were younger and the computer program, well, it just ages them. So, you can project how the person might look at any age—say, fifty or sixty, whatever."

"Can I see it?" The man put his box down on a bench next to the door. "Could be I've seen him around on one of my visits."

"Sure." Anxious for any help he could get after days of plodding from one stop to another, Alan pulled a paper out of the manila file he was holding and handed it over.

The man exhaled as he realized the image bore little resemblance to his present appearance. The Universe, once again, aligned in his favor. "Hard to tell. Not really a photograph, is it?"

"No, not really. But it's the best thing I've got."

"Looks like no one I've seen around. Do you have an actual picture of the guy? Seems like that would be more useful, even if he is younger in it."

"Dani has an old service photo, and a short TV clip of him in a courthouse in Wisconsin—where he killed that girl. But get this. That clip, or a part of it, showed he has a large tattoo on his right forearm. You couldn't miss it. So, be on the lookout."

The man glanced covertly at his right arm. Relieved to see his jacket sleeve pulled down, he bent and picked up his box. "I have to go … be late to meet that client. But I'll for sure watch out for the guy."

"No problem. I've got a bunch of spots left to check on this side of the village, but I should finish those by tomorrow." He turned to leave, then looked back. "Say Stewart, are you going to be around tomorrow night? If so, why don't you come over to my cottage for that drink I promised?"

The man slowly cocked a smile. "I just might take you up on that. Come to think of it, I might even have some legal work for you."

"Oh yeah? So much the better." Alan gave him directions. "Shall we say 6:30 then?"

"See you then."

Alan opened the door for him as he carried the box into the hotel. Walking to his car, he pondered what the new business might be.

CHAPTER 51

"Well, Mitch, you got it! The big FM." Bartlett had just hung up with Dr. Jacoby, who called to report more DNA results. The doctor wanted Mitch to be the first to hear, but he was out on patrol, so Bartlett tracked him down on his cell.

"Got what? What's an FM?"

"FM. Fuckin' miracle. You got what you wanted... at least a shot."

"What are you talking about?"

"I just heard from Dr. Jacoby. You remember that tie we took from Atwood's bedpost?"

"Yeah. What about it?"

"They recovered DNA from the tie, and it didn't belong to Mrs. Atwood."

Mitch bolted up in the seat of his cruiser. "So, who the hell did it belong to?"

"Some of the DNA was Prudence Wheatley's."

"I'll be ... So, he did tie her to the bed."

"Lawrence Atwood didn't tie Wheatley to the bed. The other DNA wasn't his."

"What? So whose was it?"

"No idea, but they know for sure it's DNA from a male."

"Holy shit!"

"Why did it take so long to get these results back, anyways?"

"Simple bureaucratic blunder. Jacoby and his team were so focused on the bones from the pit, one of his techs forgot the tie. They sent the bone fragments and hair out A-S-A-P for testing, while the tie sat back in the lab. Jacoby apologized profusely."

"No matter. The important thing is we now know somebody other than Atwood tied Prudence Wheatley to that bedpost. But where does that leave us?"

Pausing, Bartlett replied, "Well, there's no question this complicates things for the trial. When Atwood's lawyer finds out he'll have a field day. This is a huge advantage in creating reasonable doubt. I have to call the attorney general and let him know. A major question will be, if not Atwood, then who?"

"You can't deny that Gruca just moved to the top of your list."

"Sorry, my friend, I can't go there. At least not yet. But now I just might read that file you gave me."

"Damn it, we've got to do something. If Atwood didn't kill Prudence Wheatley, whoever did is still out there."

"Mitch, there's nothing to prove that Atwood didn't hire someone to kill her, or even help them do it. That's a lot more believable than this Gruca person coming out of nowhere to kill a person at random—in Lakeview, of all places. Now, I've got to go call Patterson."

"Wait. Before you go, tell me one thing. If it was Atwood's tie, and he wore it, wouldn't his DNA have been on it?"

"Sure. If he wore it. But it was at his beach house, not his home. How many times do you think he got dressed up and wore a tie when he was at that beach house? Probably had it just in case and never wore it. Now, goodbye, my friend."

CHAPTER 52

Early evening. East Grand Rapids.

"This could be a huge break in the case, Lance." Jules Goldman sat in a classic, upholstered library chair in the cavernous living room of Atwood's suburban home. Harlan Milbank filled an identical chair across from him, set at the end of one of two opposing twelve-foot red leather sofas. A massive fireplace dominated the end of the room. Lawrence and Anne Atwood each sat on one sofa; it was 6:30 in the evening, and Jules had called the meeting to share some important news.

Atwood sat up. "What kind of break are we talking about, Jules? It's about time for some good news!"

"It is. I called Rob Patterson this afternoon to talk about the upcoming trial, trying to see if we could agree on some evidentiary issues. He seemed awfully edgy. I eventually pressed him, and he reluctantly, and I mean very reluctantly, told me that he would move for an adjournment. He asked me if I would stipulate to an order."

Anne Atwood interrupted. "Why is that good news, Jules?"

"Yeah, Jules. Isn't the idea to fast-track this case?" Lance asked, echoing her concern. "How is an adjournment good for me?" He glanced at Anne. "For us?"

"I told him I would have to talk to you. And you're right—our strategy has been to get this case to trial as fast as we can. But it's not merely the fact that our AG may want an adjournment. It's why that has me thinking."

"A delay only helps him, right? Why should we help him to convict me of a crime I didn't commit?"

"He wouldn't tell me exactly what he has going on, but we know he's been awaiting DNA results. He tried to persuade me that those results could help the defense."

"How?" asked Anne.

"He argued that finding the DNA of anyone or anything besides Pru Wheatley could clear you."

"Could? Shouldn't that be an emphatic would?"

"Not necessarily, Lance. What if the results come out inconclusive? Or, even if they are the remains of an animal, as you suggested, what then? That just means it's not Ms. Wheatley's remains in your firepit. It's not conclusive that you didn't kill her. They've still got the other evidence, and we don't know what they may have taken from your bedroom. You told me Quinn and the CSI were in there a long time and that they left with some evidence bags."

"Whatever it was, it sure as hell wasn't from Pru Wheatley. She was never in that bedroom."

"She certainly better not have been," snapped Anne.

"She wasn't, damn it."

Goldman raised his palm. "Understand, if we don't

stipulate and Patterson argues to the court that he needs more time to get the DNA results, he'll get it. But my experience tells me it has to be something more than that and awfully important. Something in his demeanor… it's much bigger than merely a strategic delay to buy time. I'm thinking the DNA test results came back and there's a problem, or they have a new suspect."

The significance of such a prospect didn't escape Lance Atwood. He knew that, without DNA, Patterson had a difficult evidentiary case. Identifying a viable alternative perpetrator would make it more difficult to get a conviction. If Jules's instincts were right, this was a breakthrough.

"Well, that does sound like good news." Anne stood up and headed toward the staircase in the adjacent foyer. "This is cause for celebration. How about dinner here? Jules, Harley, won't you join us?" She turned back at the arched doorway. "I'm going upstairs to change." They watched as she left the room.

"Let's not to be premature, Lance. I could be wrong. It may be something else entirely," Jules cautioned.

"Why don't we let her have this, Jules? This has been stressful as hell on both of us, but especially Anne. Most of her friends have stopped calling. Invitations have dried up. She feels like an outcast. Even the prospect of a positive turn will lift her spirits. Join us for dinner. Harley, you're coming too."

Just as Harley smiled in assent and Goldman opened his mouth to answer, the doorbell rang.

"Who the hell can that be?" said Lance as he got up to answer the door. He pointed across the room. "Why don't you two help yourselves to drinks while I answer that?"

The two men rose and ambled over to the large

built-in bar. Goldman climbed onto one of eight elevated director chairs bordering the semi-circular granite counter as Harley moved behind the bar. The ceiling-high glass shelves on the mirrored wall behind held dozens of bottles containing every conceivable alcoholic concoction. Harley grabbed a rare single malt. "Scotch, Jules?"

"Don't mind if I do."

Gripping the Glenmorangie, Harley reached for glasses beneath the bar. He heard Lance open the front door, then shout loudly, "What the hell are you doing here? I told you never…" The door slammed shut, and the hallway filled with the muffled sounds of two persons arguing. Their words were incomprehensible, but his voice was angry, hers sounding desperate. Then there was a loud blast, followed quickly by two more. The bottle dropped from Harley's hand, shattering as it hit the bar.

CHAPTER 53

Lake Michigan shore.

As the man pulled his SUV into a dirt parking area on the side of the road, he realized it was above Redmond's cottage. Treetops blocked a clear view ahead, but he could make out a roof through the wooden rails of a section of fence edging the drop-off on the other side. He spent a few moments mulling over the legal matter he had concocted as a ploy to switch Alan's focus, thinking a lawyer would surely look forward to a new case. Then he left the truck and followed a trail of stone steps leading down a slope toward the sound of breaking waves. Suddenly, motion floodlights exploded the dwindling twilight, brightly illuminating the grounds.

As he looked for the entrance, Alan's head popped through an open doorway inside the screened porch forming the end of the main cottage.

"Welcome, Stewart. Come right on in."

"Hi, Alan. Sorry I'm late." He opened the screen

door and stepped across to the doorway where Alan had appeared. The lights outside shut off, returning the outside surroundings to dusk.

"Not a problem, my friend. Although I'm a couple cocktails ahead of you."

Alan was standing beside a Formica counter displaying an assortment of liquors.

"Help yourself, Stewart. If you don't see what you like there, I've probably got it around here somewhere."

"How about just a beer?"

"Oh yeah. You're a brew man, aren't cha?" Alan opened the door to the refrigerator and leaned down. "I think I might have one or two. I'm not much of a beer drinker." He reached in toward the back of a shelf and turned around holding a Heineken. "Your lucky night." Alan opened the bottle and handed it to the man, then refilled his tumbler with Grey Goose vodka. He adjourned to the porch, and the man followed. "It's been unusually warm lately. I thought we could sit out here, and I can have a cigar." He reached for a humidor sitting on a brick mantle over a fireplace grill in the porch wall. "Care for one?"

"I don't smoke," the man said, shaking his head.

Alan picked out an Ashton and grabbed a cutter. "Cigars aren't really smoking, you know. Not unless you inhale. I don't."

The two sat silently as Alan cut and lit his cigar. He noticed the man looking around, examining his property.

"It may not look like much now, but when I'm through, it'll be a gem. I got it for a song almost two years ago, part of an estate one of my partners was handling. Never got on the market. They had just added the bunkhouse there." The man turned to look over his shoulder where Alan pointed.

As he exhaled a cloud of smoke, Alan asked, "You said yesterday you may have a legal question for me?"

Gruca smiled to himself, quickly changing the subject. "Is that an observation deck you're building out there?"

Alan raised up to see where he was looking. "Yes, it is. It should provide a great view stretching out over the dune. You can't really see very well from here…not in this light."

The man turned back to him. "How high up are you?"

"Forty-nine steps. You can't leave anything up here when you go down to the beach because you only want to come back up once." Alan chuckled to himself.

"Could I see your deck?"

"Sure." Redmond held up his empty glass as he rose unsteadily. "Just let me top off my cocktail, and we'll go over. You need something? I might have another beer in the fridge."

"Uh, uh. Thanks." The man rose, set his empty bottle on the mantle above the grill and moved to the side of the porch looking out toward the lake. "Have you learned anything more about that Gordon Gruca?"

Alan set his cigar in an ashtray by his chair and walked back into the kitchen. "Not a thing. But we'll keep after him. If he's here, something will turn up."

"So, do you expect to keep working with that Sparro woman in trying to locate him?"

"Oh yeah. Dani's not going anyplace."

"She sounds committed."

"I think she might be a bit obsessed. I figure she'll never stop until she gets him. We just can't believe someone hasn't seen that tattoo of his."

"Do you know what it's a tattoo of?"

"Nope. Just that it supposedly covers most of his right forearm." Redmond took a sip of his drink and smirked. "You don't have a tattoo on yours, do you Stewart?"

"Heh!" He grinned back at Redmond. "Wouldn't that be a joke?"

"That'd be a real cruel joke on me—if it were true. Even real life isn't that cruel."

After a pause, the man pushed open the screen door, walked out, and said, "What about that deck?"

"Sure. Let's go." Alan moved to the door.

As the man proceeded away from the house, the yard erupted in brightness.

He called back to Alan, "Can you turn out those lights? I would really like a glimpse of the water." He heard the flip of the switch, and the yard returned to darkness. "Much better."

They walked out to the deck and stepped up onto the wooden platform, which rose about a foot off the ground, extending a few feet over the edge of the drop-off. Stacks of rails, pieces of deck planks, and spare two-by-fours were piled on one corner of the deck. The man stepped to the edge, leaning against a partially completed railing abutting the deck's far side.

"Oh well. Can't see the water. It's too dark. You say its fifty feet down to the beach?"

"At least. Maybe even a few more."

Alan took a long swig of vodka. The man picked up a stray length of two-by-four.

"You know how you said real life isn't that cruel?"

He lowered his glass and turned around. "What about it?"

"It's not true."

The man raised the board like a bat, swinging with as much force as he could at Alan's face. The blow caught Alan square in the nose, breaking it immediately. He fell to one knee. Bone protruded just below his eyes, blood pouring from the open wound; he screamed and held his hand against his face. "Fuck, Stewart! What the hell... you broke my..."

The man swung again, this time hitting the side of Redmond's head and driving him to the ground.

Alan lay with his head hanging partially over the side of the deck. The blood was running into his eyes, and he tried to speak. "W... why?"

The man pushed up his sleeve to expose the blue-black figure extending from just above his wrist to the crook of his arm. Bending down closer to Redmond, he grabbed his hair and pulled his head up, jabbing his forearm in front of his face. "You see Alan, life really is that cruel. The joke is on you."

Alan squinted through his semi-consciousness, trying to bring the markings into focus. He fought to recall their first meeting, struggling to remember what the man had looked like and what had changed since he next saw him at the motel. Then it came to him. "You shaved your beard," he murmured. "And your hair was... more..." His head dropped.

The man grinned. "Appearances can be easily altered, Alan." Then, he dragged the lawyer across the deck toward the stairs.

CHAPTER 54

Rob Patterson had just dialed home to tell his wife he would again be late getting home. With the Atwood trial only a few weeks away, he and his staff had not had a full night's sleep in a long while, but now he was staying over for a different reason. They had to decide what to do about the latest information from Dave Bartlett. The unidentified male DNA found on the tie was potentially devastating to their case; Rob hoped Goldman would agree to the adjournment he had requested, so he wouldn't have to disclose the problem to the court in a motion.

As Patterson listened to his home phone ringing, he heard the chatter of high-heeled footsteps echoing loudly in the hallway outside his office. Cynthia Worthey burst through the open door just as the recording on his home phone replied, "Sorry, we can't come to the phone right now." She breathlessly mimicked that he should hang up. No sooner had Patterson put the phone down than Cynthia blurted out, "He's dead."

Patterson gazed back at her, shaking his head with one palm held up. "Who's dead?"

"Lance Atwood!" she exclaimed.

He jerked up in his chair, mouth gaping open and eyes wide. After a long pause, he swallowed and asked, "You're sure?" Cynthia nodded. "I can't believe it. When? What the hell happened?"

"He was shot earlier this evening, at his home, just answering the door. They pronounced him dead on the way to the hospital."

"Jesus. Who shot him?"

"It was that teacher; you know, the one he got reinstated? The one he got the big jury award for last year." Seeing her boss's blank stare, Cynthia added emphatically, "The one he had the affair with; her name was Helena Mercer."

"Holy…" He placed his fingers on his temples.

Cynthia recounted the officer she talked to had told her the woman was sitting on her knees in the yard when they arrived. She surrendered peacefully. Atwood's lawyer already had taken the gun from her without a fuss. During the ride to the station, Ms. Mercer said they had started an affair during Atwood's representation of her in that wrongful discharge case, and they continued for quite a while afterward. Then he suddenly broke it off—probably about the time he decided to run for governor. Although she tried to reconnect with him, he snubbed her. Her husband filed for divorce and took the kids. Perhaps the last straw was the fact that she also lost her job again.

"A woman scorned I suppose?"

The issue of an adjournment was now irrelevant, but his mind raced about the ramifications. If not handled carefully and sympathy turned for Atwood, the whole thing could become a public image debacle for the AG's office, not to mention the fallout for his campaign.

Worthey plopped into a side chair, lamenting, "No more super trial now…just when things were really looking up. Too bad Mr. Atwood ruined it by getting himself killed."

Patterson grimaced. "That is cold, Cynthia. Even for you. And what if Atwood was innocent?"

"Well, even if he didn't kill Prudence Wheatley, he sure as hell wasn't innocent." Dropping her chin onto her chest, she lowered her voice. "But I still think he did it."

Patterson leaned back, reposing into quiet contemplation. The Atwood trial would have been a once-in-a-lifetime opportunity. Now what, he thought. After a few moments, he stood back up and turned to the window, gazing out with arms crossed.

Worthey knew better than to disturb him, but her impatience got the better of her. "So, what next, Rob?" He ignored her, and she waited obediently.

Turning, Patterson said, "I need to get back to Bartlett. I think I have a way to right this ship. If it works, we can still come out looking good."

Worthey leaned in. "Never a doubt. What's the plan?"

"Listen closely and I'll explain."

CHAPTER 55

If it had not been for the neighbors' inquisitive golden retriever puppy anxious for a morning walk, Alan Redmond's body might have gone undiscovered indefinitely. The dog sniffed out the body, sprawled in a clump of dune grass, and the owners immediately called the police. Mitch was in his office when the call came in. Although the address didn't initially ring a bell, the caller said it was at a Mister Redmond's cottage. Upon hearing that, Mitch was eager to find out just who it was at the bottom of those stairs. As he hurried out, he ordered the dispatch officer to contact Willy and tell him to meet him at the location.

When he arrived, he found Willy already standing beside his cruiser in the parking area above Redmond's cottage. The two of them rushed down the path to the house, racing across Redmond's yard toward the deck. Mitch noticed the top of the stair rail grip hanging by a nail and immediately suspected a fall. As he peered over the bluff at the EMTs working down below, he felt confident his hunch was correct.

Willy had started down the stairs to the beach, but he stopped and bent over, reaching into the dune grass about ten steps from the top. "Got something, Chief." He held up a clear plastic tumbler on the end of his pen.

"Bag it, Willy. Then search the rest of the stairs. See if you can find anything else. I'm going down to see who they've got down there."

Mitch proceeded down the stairs to the beach. At the bottom, he found three EMS techs and a small group of onlookers. They had just turned over the body to load it on the gurney. Despite the dried blood and serious swelling and bruising around the head and face, he recognized it was Alan Redmond.

The lead technician examined the body sufficiently to confirm the injuries were consistent with a fall down the steps. The advanced stage of rigor mortis suggested that death was at least thirty six hours earlier.

"Looks like there are even some splinters in his face, Chief Quinn. His neck is broken, which could have happened in the fall. That's gotta be forty or fifty feet to the top."

Mitch questioned the dog owners and the other gawkers. None had anything of importance to add. He and Willy then checked the interior of the cottage but found nothing notable.

"Well Willy, from the looks of it, Alan had a snoot full, ambled outside to his new deck, and either tripped or lost his balance, falling down those steps." They agreed there was nothing left to do, and Willy went back to the station, leaving Mitch standing alone in the kitchen. His gut told him that something was wrong, but he just couldn't think of what it was. There was no evidence of foul play, and Alan was a notorious drinker. On a dark night, that deck was an accident waiting to happen.

He leaned back against the counter, staring across the room at the row of assorted liquor bottles. He considered whether Alan may have entertained someone. After a long while, he reached over, opened the refrigerator door, and stooped to look inside. Raising back up, he closed the door and walked back out to the enclosed porch. As he scanned the room, he spied the single, almost unsmoked cigar and eventually focused on the empty beer bottle over the grill. He mumbled to himself, "I thought you were a vodka man, Alan."

Within minutes he had found a large plastic bag and a wooden ladle in the kitchen drawers; he bagged the bottle using the ladle handle. As he sealed the bag, he wondered whether he was being overly skeptical. After all, Alan was well known and gregarious, and it had been a pleasant evening. A neighbor, or even a client, may have just dropped by for a visit. Nonetheless, he made up his mind to do some follow-up, just in case there might be a witness who had not come forward.

CHAPTER 56

Lakeview.

Reports of Lawrence Atwood's death made front-page headlines, becoming prime-time news on radio and television stations around the country. The salacious details of his demise, his courtroom successes, and unattained political aspirations even rated a feature article in the *New York Times* Sunday edition. But what had been a surging interest in his impending murder trial quickly dissipated. Public sentiment seemed to be that the guilty party already got the justice he deserved.

Still worried about the way he had left things hanging after their dinner, Mitch was pleasantly surprised when Dani called. She was anxious to learn more about Alan's death, which she had heard about on the local news stations. Mitch didn't care what the reason was; he would accept any excuse to see her again. When he arrived at her hotel, he rushed into the lobby, only to slow to a stroll when the desk clerk jerked to attention, eyeing him curiously.

"I'm just here to meet someone," he said as he strode on to the restaurant.

Dani sat sipping coffee at a corner table as he entered the room. Spotting him, she rose abruptly, clanking her cup onto the saucer. The sight of her delighted him, but he wasn't sure exactly what to do or say, so he just gave a quick, "Hi," pulled out a chair, and sat. Dani spoke first.

"I just can't believe it, Mitch. I met Alan right here in this same room, just after I dropped off those files at your office. He wanted to help me find Gruca and even volunteered to canvass some area motels and businesses. We planned to meet back here tomorrow."

"Alan was helping you look for Gruca?" Mitch's investigator's antennae rose.

"Yes. He was going to scout different hotels and restaurants—any places he could think of where Gruca might go. But what happened?"

"Apparently, he'd had a lot to drink. Looks like a railing broke on a deck he was building, and he fell. Some neighbors walking their dog found him at the bottom of the stairs leading down to the beach. The autopsy will confirm just how much he had in him, but even if he hadn't been drinking, a fall like that could've killed just about anyone."

"But don't you think it's suspicious that Alan no sooner started working to track down Gruca than he's killed in a freak accident?"

"All indications are that Alan's death was an accident. I don't want to jump to a conclusion, but I wish I'd known about this when we were out there after they found him." Mitch decided not to mention the bottle, which he had sent to Jacoby for testing. If it yielded some helpful prints, or matched the DNA on the necktie, he could then let her know. The news that Alan may have been tracking Gruca around Lakeview shed a different light on his death. He was now wondering whether he may have missed something at Alan's cottage.

Dani could see he was lost in thought. "Mitch, what are you thinking?"

"I'm thinking this certainly raises a lot of questions. I do have some positive news, though. It looks like the attorney general's office may consider going after Gruca. Patterson asked Dave to arrange for a meeting, and he wants you to be there."

"Why me? And why now?"

Mitch explained that Robert Patterson called Bartlett the morning after Atwood was killed, inquiring about other possible suspects. He told her about the DNA evidence found in the bedroom at Atwood's beach house, which suggested that another person may have been there before Pru Wheatley disappeared. Patterson had been particularly interested in Bartlett's thoughts about the possibility of a new suspect.

"What a tragic coincidence," Dani lamented.

"Coincidence?"

"All of this occurring so close to Alan's death is a coincidence—and tragic because Atwood didn't murder Prudence Wheatley, but it took his being killed to get someone to go after the real murderer."

"I don't know if the AG is convinced that Atwood didn't kill her or if Gruca did. But at least you've got the right people talking. Dave mentioned you and your theory when Patterson asked about any further suspects and I guess it must have piqued his interest."

"It's more than just a theory, Mitch."

He shrugged. "Anyway, he wants to meet with you, hear what you have to say, and I'm sure he'll want to look at all of your files. Dave offered to help you prepare. He said you may only get this one chance to persuade Patterson, so you'd better be convincing."

Dani looked at him in a mix of joy and disbelief. He thought he saw her eyes well up. "Thank you, Mitch. That is very good news." She scooted her chair closer and put her arms around his neck. "And I'll eventually convince you, believe me."

"Well, I..." Mitch twisted awkwardly as Dani leaned in and kissed him. Content that it wasn't a mere thank you kiss, he slipped his arms around her waist and kissed her back.

CHAPTER 57

Late August.

G ordon Gruca sat on the dune's edge, staring at the reflection of the full moon glistening over the lake below. The boom and crackle of fireworks from the Coast Guard festival had thinned to silence over the past hour. He had regained entry to the Atwood beach house via the unlocked window on the second floor, surprised that no one had found it. The yellow tape was long gone—the prospect of visitors to the former crime scene now unlikely. He had read a news article saying that Anne Atwood had left the state for her parents' home in Florida. This would serve as a safe harbor for the time being.

News of Atwood's killing had turned his mounting anticipation to frustration. Compared to what he had envisioned, the ending was anticlimactic. Ultimately, he had resigned himself to the outcome. With nothing of his original plan left to accomplish, his focus turned to getting away, but without anyone following. After his chance meeting with Redmond at the motel, killing him became necessary. Now, he was already yearning to get on with his next project—investigating the corrupt American Rabbit Breeders Association judge—but just leaving the area for good was not an option. Like her father, Dani Sparro evidently wouldn't give up, so he would also have to deal with her.

He gazed over at his two companions sitting contentedly a few feet away. Their fur reflected a bluish luminescence in the moonlight. He had them tethered to a single stake in the sand, feasting on the lettuce and carrots he had set out. Reaching to pet them, he murmured, "Patience. We will leave soon. In the meantime, we still have some work to do before we make the next show. It's in Ionia." He unfastened the tether, picked them up, and headed across the patio toward the garage.

After placing the rabbits in a makeshift pen on the garage floor, he walked into the hall toward the kitchen. Suddenly, he caught a flash of light in the corner of his eye. Staring through the darkness into the living room, he froze when he saw the silhouette of a man peering back at him from the patio outside. Gruca stood motionless as the reflection of the flashlight beam slowly crossed the room on the other side of the wall. Then the room went dark, and Gruca jumped across the open doorway between living room and foyer.

Pulling a pistol from the holster on his belt, Gruca peeked around the corner. The man outside had his hands cupped on the sides of his face, which he pushed against the window. Gruca's body eased as the man casually walked on to the far side of the house, and he hurried over to the glass pane next to the front door. The man came into view and crossed the lawn, stopping in the drive to look back at the house. He then got into an SUV, backed out, and drove slowly away. Gruca could barely make out the logo of a security company on the passenger's door.

Exhaling, he returned to the kitchen, settled on a stool at the center island, and laid his pistol on the countertop. The visit by the security guard was worrisome. He had hoped to stay here longer, but he would now have to move, if just for a while. It was inconvenient moving around with his two pets, but they were much less trouble to care for than other animals, such as dogs. When necessary, his truck was adequately equipped to accommodate them, at least for short periods, but it was no answer for him. After a few more minutes of contemplation, he nodded to himself and made his way upstairs to pack.

CHAPTER 58

"Yes, that's right. I said rabbits—white rabbits." Dani Sparro was responding to questions from Robert Patterson, who looked up from the summary report she had given him when they convened in his office in the capitol building. During their drive over, Bartlett told her that Patterson had jumped on the idea of other possible suspects, insisting upon meeting with her as soon as possible. She and Dave had hurriedly put together a summary to expedite Patterson's review of the evidence pointing to Gruca. She now looked apprehensively at the incredulous expression on Patterson's face.

"Ms. Worthey shared with me that ridiculous story Lance Atwood concocted for his pre-arraignment interview. About the only believable part of what he confessed was his adulterous affair with Prudence Wheatley. I had to agree with Chief Quinn's assessment that this white rabbit sighting was nothing more than Atwood posturing for an insanity defense. With all due respect Ms. Sparro, surely you don't expect anyone to believe this is anything more than an eleventh-hour strategic ploy, do you?

Dani was seated at the opposite end of the large oval conference table in the middle of the room. She straightened, folding her hands prayer-like, fingertips to her lips. "Mr. Patterson, I'd ask you to withhold judgment until you've read the witness statements from all the cases we followed up on. I know it sounds crazy as we're sitting here, but this is actual testimony from real people describing what they saw."

Patterson looked over at Bartlett. "Dave, I want you to know that I was optimistic after we talked. Now, after hearing this, I'm having second thoughts. From what I've gathered so far, you have no evidence showing that this Gordon Gruca had anything to do with Prudence Wheatley's murder. It's all either pure conjecture, or…"

Patterson turned to Dani. "Or perhaps just the rants of a terrified witness to a murder?" She opened her mouth to speak, but Patterson raised a finger. "If this went public, and we didn't have a suspect in custody or at least some hard evidence like an eyewitness, we'd be a laughingstock."

Dani quickly shot back, "It's not just *a* witness, Mr. Patterson. If you will please just try to be objective, you'll see that I'm not imagining these connections. We are talking about crimes spanning years and occurring in different states. This is not a case of overexcited witnesses."

Patterson winced and turned back to Bartlett. "Okay. I'll humor you. Tell me about these rabbits, and what the hell they have to do with the Wheatley killing, or any others. I'll listen, but don't tell me this is some Jefferson Airplane fixation, or you can walk right out of here and take these records with you."

Dani's head bent pleadingly toward Bartlett, and he winked. His experience told him that Patterson was just being skeptically pragmatic, looking for more solid reassurance before gearing up his office for an investigation based almost entirely on suspicion. His instincts said that the AG would likely go after Gruca, and he was just looking for cover. A brutal serial killer suspect was just what an ambitious prosecutor might look for in the anticlimax of the Atwood case.

"Rob, we both know that a lot of crime solving starts with a gut feeling about what happened, and who did it. Often, we don't have much more than that. Here, we have a whole history of bad acts and an MO which fits the murder to a *T*, not to mention…"

Patterson interrupted. "But that is exactly my point, Dave. There are a whole bunch of killings recorded in that file of Miss Sparro's, most of which were solved, and this Gruca was not linked to any of them. All that ties him in is speculation from a dead FBI agent and his…" He turned to Dani. "Sorry, Ms. Sparro. No disrespect intended. His devoted daughter. And now you tell me your best evidence is a bunch of white rabbits?"

"As I was about to say," Bartlett cleared his throat. "We have much more than mere speculation and white rabbits. You know that virtually all serial killers share several common background experiences. I'll call them their motivators. They typically manifest these during their adolescence. Take Jeffrey Dahmer, for instance—The Milwaukee Cannibal. He had an early fascination with animals, especially dead ones. He started out dissecting animal cadavers."

"You're saying Gruca is another Jeffrey Dahmer?" Patterson said, grimacing.

"Well, yes and no. He's not a cannibal and, as far as we know, he doesn't keep body parts in his refrigerator. However, they do have some similar experiences and characteristics in common. For example ..."

"So, how do you explain the rabbits?"

"I'm getting to that. Work through this with me, will you ... please?"

Dani twisted loudly in her chair, getting Bartlett's attention. "Uh, with us?"

Leaning forward on his elbows, Bartlett nodded. "We're thinking the rabbits are just a part of what's developed as his MO. The files Dani gave you show that he apparently had a negative experience involving rabbits when he was in the orphanage. If we're right, it must have affected him somehow, developing into a sort of ... fixation. Moving forward, we have two witnesses who saw white rabbits on the same day Prudence Wheatley disappeared: Lakeview Deputy Willoughby and Atwood himself. Neither of them had any connection with one another before that, nor did either have a history of, uh, well, of making things up."

"That's interesting, but it proves nothing."

"Agreed. But that's not all. There is a lot more to his patterns. For example, he also gives tips to law enforcement if they're going off track. Mitch Quinn will tell you Gruca likely did exactly that in this case."

"Likely is not fact." Patterson shrugged.

"It's a reasonable inference from fact. They were hitting a wall and suddenly, out of nowhere, an unidentified caller directs them straight to the spot where they found the rest of Prudence Wheatley's remains."

"So? Some local was out walking in the woods, stumbled upon a gruesome scene, and called it in. Things like that happen."

"Maybe. But don't forget the fact that Dani saw him in Lakeview, twice."

"From everything I read in your summary, there is no way to identify the person she saw as Gordon Gruca. The pictures you have are either old or vague, and she had never met the man before or even seen him in person. I'd have to say her so-called sighting was, at best…," glancing at Dani, he continued, "inconclusive. Or at worst, wishful thinking."

"Even if it wasn't Gruca, the fact is in that file you'll see there were cases of bodies being burned, just like this one. In two of those there were markings on the bones suggesting they were sawed or cut somehow, one possibly even blown up, just like this one. And, all the crimes occurred on holidays, just like this one. And …"

Patterson raised his hands in mock surrender. "Alright, alright. You've convinced me there's something worth looking into, at least for now. But here's the deal, Dave. If I let you go on with this, nothing, I mean absolutely nothing, can get out to the press about it, at least not until we have something concrete. And then it's my call on when and to whom—mine alone. If word gets out, my office will deny everything. If nothing pans out, then no harm, no foul. If it does, we'll be back in business. Understood?"

"You've got our word on that, Rob." Bartlett motioned at Dani.

She nodded. "Yes. Mine too. Publicity isn't the objective—we just want to get Gruca."

"And you especially do not, under any circumstances, breathe a word about these rabbits, or I'll deny I knew anything about that and close the entire operation, pronto. Am I clear on that?"

"Crystal clear."

Patterson looked at Dani, who nodded vigorously. "All right then. You've got your authority. Now go find Gruca, and bring him in."

Dani anxiously jumped up. "One more thing, Mr. Patterson. Can Chief Quinn join the investigation?"

Patterson hesitated. "I guess that's all right, but I'd rather someone with more experience be in charge."

"Rob, remember what I told you about Mitch Quinn. You will find no one better. Plus, Mitch is way ahead on this. He should be the one to lead it," said Bartlett as he rose.

"Okay. Have it your way. I'll trust your judgment, but if he doesn't get results quickly, I'll find someone who can. In the meantime, he'll have the full support of the state police and all the assets of my office. By the way … what makes you think Gruca would even stick around here? There'll be no trial, and Atwood has already been cremated."

"We're playing a hunch. There's good evidence that he's showed up to watch things unfold in several past cases."

"Why the hell would he take that chance?" Patterson said, incredulous. "Or is he one of those guys who just wants to get caught?"

Dani spoke up. "It's like a challenge—like he's outwitting law enforcement and flaunting it. If he follows form, we're thinking he'll show up again."

"When and where might that be?"

"The next opportunity would likely be Atwood's memorial service. Mrs. Atwood was so emotionally upset, they delayed it. It's scheduled for next month. If Gruca shows up there, we'll be waiting," said Bartlett.

CHAPTER 59

Later that day.

"Welcome back, Mitch." Bartlett grabbed Mitch's shoulder as he slid his leg over the bar stool next to him. Mitch jerked up with a puzzled expression.

"We tried to call you on our way back, but you weren't at the station. No one there could reach you, and you didn't answer on your cell. After I dropped Dani off at her hotel it occurred to me that I might find you here."

Following the deaths of his wife and child, Mitch dealt with his depression as so many in like circumstances. His watering hole of choice became the Cryin' Shame Pub, a rundown eyesore sufficiently far enough out from Lakeview to assure anonymity. The cruel irony of the name lured him in one night when the grief became intolerable. More than a year of blacked-out nights, while former colleagues looked the other way, put him on the edge of self-destruction. After Mitch was placed on paid leave from the police force, Dave Bartlett intervened and shamed him into choosing between ruin and redemption, and so his rehabilitation began. Once renewed, Mitch began making a weekly stop at his old hangout as a personal challenge.

Bartlett waved at the bartender, pointed at the bottle on the bar top and said, "I see you're indulging yourself with your drink of choice."

Mitch stared down at the bottle of O'Doul's sitting in front of him. "Yeah, I'm really pounding 'em down. What's up?"

"Patterson gave us the go-ahead. We're in business, and you're on the team. Actually, you're the leader of the team."

Quinn sat up, beaming. "How'd you pull that off?"

"I think we have to credit Dani Sparro. She's the one who stayed the course and turned the spotlight on Gordon Gruca."

"Yeah. She's something alright."

"That she is, and I'm sensing she's something more with you, my friend."

Mitch twisted on his bar stool. "What makes you say that?"

"Let's put it down to my keen sense of observation. For example, I note your reversal on the subject of Gruca. Not to mention that look you get when she's around."

"The material in those files of hers is persuasive. That's what sold me. Not her good looks."

"Maybe. But I haven't seen you react to a woman like that since, well, you know."

Mitch stared at the mirror behind the bar. He knew Bartlett was right. There was no question he had strong feelings for Dani. He just wasn't sure what he would do about it.

"Earth to Chief Quinn." Bartlett snapped his fingers, and Mitch broke from his thoughts.

"So, what now, fearless leader?"

"We have to resume looking for Gruca. Only this time with more searchers. I'll use a bunch of the Lakeview force and put word out in the surrounding counties. Alan was only one man. There's no way he could cover this entire area in the time he was out looking, even if Dani was working with him."

"The attorney general will send in the state police to assist if you want. But understand my friend, this is on the down low. You have to alert your people that it's all strictly QT. Any word gets out to the press, and Patterson will shut us down."

Mitch shrugged. "Not a problem. We can trust my people."

"You'd better be right."

"The only focus will be on tracking down Gordon Gruca. Now I need to talk to Dani, find out where Alan went, and what he might have found out."

They left the bar, Mitch driving straight to Dani's hotel, calling her on the way. He felt a rush when she answered. "Dani, it's Mitch. I heard about the attorney general giving the go-ahead on the investigation. I need to talk to you about…"

Dani interrupted, saying, "Yes, we need to talk. How about right now? I'm in my hotel room."

"I'm on my way." She gave him the room number, saying she would wait for him there.

It was almost dark as he screeched to a halt in the hotel lot. He rushed from his car through the lobby, bypassed the elevator, and bounded up the stairs. As he hurried down the hall, looking from side to side at the number on each room, a door opened at the foyer's far end. Dani's head poked out as she waved at him. "Mitch, down here!"

Halting at her doorway to catch his breath, he said, "Dani, I've got to thank you for..." He couldn't finish, as she threw her arms around his neck and eagerly kissed him. Lifting her up, her feet dangling in the air, he carried her back into the room, kicked the door shut with his heel, and pitched his hat onto the bed behind her.

When the long kiss ended, Mitch lowered her to the floor and said, "Dani, I need, uh, I want, to talk to you about ..."

She moved forward, placing a finger to his lips. "Don't talk. Not now. Later." Then she started undoing his shirt buttons. He hadn't noticed until then that the only light came from the slightly parted bathroom doorway.

They undressed in silence, then stood apart as the dim half-light bathed their bodies in a chalky, violet hue. He picked her up, and they kissed again, falling onto the bed in a naked embrace. Time evaporated as they explored one another without restraint—hungrily—yet taking time to assure one another's satisfaction. Neither spoke a word, communicating only by the ebb and flow of passion and tenderness. Exhaustion finally led to sleep.

Mitch's right eye opened to a ray of light shining through the slightly parted drapes. Dani sat cross-legged on the side chair, staring down at him. They both smiled tentatively.

"I want you to know, Chief Quinn, as far as last night goes, I'm not in the habit of such, er, behavior."

Mitch rolled over onto his back, arms behind his head. "Well, that's too bad. I thought your behavior was delightful. I was hoping it could become a habit."

She giggled and jumped onto the bed next to him, sitting on her knees. "Perhaps with just the right motivation, I could be convinced."

"As I recall, there wasn't much talking going on last night."

Leaning down closer, she put her hands on his face. "Maybe that's a better way to develop a habit?" She kissed him tenderly. Suddenly he broke away.

"What time is it?"

"I don't know. What does it matter?"

Mitch sat up and spied the alarm clock on the bed stand. "Almost 7:30. Got to get moving; if we're gonna catch Gruca, I've got a lot of work to do."

Dani grabbed his arm. "Say, mister. Shouldn't we at least talk a bit about what happened last night? I mean, I'm not into the wham-bam-thank-you-ma'am thing."

"Well, sure. We should, but I..."

She laughed loudly as he twisted out from the covers. "From the look of things, I'd say you're ready to pick up where we left off."

Mitch blushed, embarrassed by the fact that he was naked and had an erection. He put his hands over his crotch, retrieved his boxers from the floor, hustled into the bathroom, and closed the door. Dani heard his muffled reply. "For sure we need to talk about, uh, things, and I want to, very much. But you're the one who started all of this about Gruca. I would think you'd be eager for me to get the search going."

"You mean *us*."

The water running in the sink stopped, and the bathroom door jerked open. "What do you mean *us*?"

"You meant to say I'm anxious for *us* to get the search going."

"No way. You're not getting back into this."

"I sure as hell am. You're absolutely right that I'm the one who started this, and I will see it through to the end. I won't just sit on the sidelines while you and whoever else track down Gruca."

"Dani, we'll be hard-pressed to get him with trained professionals doing the job as it is. No way can I have you along for this."

She jumped up defiantly, fists raised. "I was chasing Gruca long before you even knew he existed. And don't forget, you thought Atwood killed Prudence Wheatley."

"Look, I just don't want you to get hurt. I…"

"I've already been hurt, damn it! That monster killed my father. He'll pay, even if I have to chase him into hell all by myself." She leaned into him.

Mitch held her, realizing he would give in, but trying to think of a way to compromise. "Okay, okay. I will try to find some way. You're in."

She pulled back from his chest to look up at him, sniffled, and said, "You mean it? I'm serious, Mitch. I need to be a part of this."

"I said okay. Now, sit down for a second. I need to ask you something."

"What?"

"When you met with him, did Alan give you any notes or records of who he'd talked to?"

"No. He hadn't even started yet. We planned to meet again after a few days, but he… we couldn't."

"It's important that we find any record he might have made. We searched his cottage after they found him, turning up nothing helpful. But then, I didn't know what he'd been doing." Dani frowned at his look of disapproval. "I need to make another sweep through there, just to see if we missed anything."

Dani grabbed his wrist. "I'd like to go with you. I remember now … during that first meeting with Alan, he took notes. He had a small, black leather notebook, one of those about the size of an envelope. If we could find that it might tell us who Alan talked to and where he went."

Mitch hit his palm on the desk. "That could be big."

"Do you think anyone has been over there to clean out his belongings?"

"I sure hope not. But if someone has, we'll just have to track them down." Mitch knew that Redmond got divorced a few years before, and had no children, but he had no idea about other relatives.

"I'll get dressed and go to the station, get things organized. You take your time. Then I'll come back and pick you up. Okay?"

Dani opened her robe widely, saying with a smile, "All right, Chief Quinn. I think we've just had our first spat. I forgive you. Should we take a few minutes to make up?"

Mitch began anxiously pulling off the shirt he had just put on. "You are a persuasive woman, Ms. Sparro. You should have gotten that law degree."

CHAPTER 60

Late morning.

When they arrived at Alan Redmond's cottage, they found a car parked in the gravel lot by the road. Mitch noticed that it had Illinois license plates and called the station to run a check of ownership. They started walking down the path toward the building, Mitch's cell ringing as they approached the back porch door. He recognized the voice on the line as the Lakeview dispatch officer.

"Chief? It's Penny. Those plates are registered to a Mrs. Lois Conway of Evanston, Illinois. The Chicago suburb. You need the address?"

"No Penny, but hold onto it just in case." Quinn shut his flip phone and knocked on the door.

A muffled female voice answered from within. "Who is it?"

"We're from the Lakeview police. Can we come in?" He spoke loudly so the person inside could hear.

He and Dani looked at one another as they heard hurried footsteps getting closer. A slender, middle-aged

258

woman in light-colored blue jeans and a black cowl-neck sweater entered the porch. Her almost-black hair was streaked with gray, pulled back into a tight bun, and she wore an expression of both suspicion and concern.

"Is something wrong?"

Quinn replied in a reassuring tone, "No, ma'am. I'm Lakeview Police Chief Mitchell Quinn. This is, uh, my assistant, Ms. Sparro." Dani looked at him quizzically. "We were both acquaintances of the owner, Alan Redmond. As you probably know, he passed away recently. May I ask who you are?"

"Not until you show me some identification."

As Mitch opened his jacket to show his badge, he pulled out his wallet, saying, "Certainly. Sorry. Here's my ID."

The woman opened the screen door wide enough to grab his wallet and inspect the ID, comparing Mitch's face to the photo. "I'm sorry too, Chief Quinn. But you can't be too careful these days. I'm Alan's sister, Lois Conway—Lois Redmond Conway. I'm here collecting Alan's things." She handed his wallet back through the partially opened door. "I live in Illinois. Evanston, Illinois."

"Yes, I know," Mitch said, surprising the woman.

"Oh. You do?"

"I called in your plate number when we drove up. You can't be too careful these days, you know."

The woman relaxed, smiling. "Point taken, Chief Quinn. Please come in." She pushed the door open and extended her hand. "I didn't mean to be rude. Welcome. And you likewise… Ms. Sparro, is it?"

Dani nodded and shook her hand warmly. "Yes. Thank you, Mrs. Conway."

"So, what can I do for you?"

Mitch thought momentarily, deciding it was best to be direct and brief. "We're investigating a missing person case, and we're looking for a notebook Alan kept which may contain relevant information."

Her eyes widened. "But how was Alan involved?"

"Not to worry. It just so happened Alan knew the victim. She was a court reporter he worked with. We're just checking any possible leads. I happened to remember Alan kept a notebook and thought it might possibly contain relevant information." Unsure just how much Alan's sister knew about Prudence Wheatley, Mitch decided not to say anything more about their relationship or Alan's involvement in the investigation.

"Could that have had anything to do with Alan's death?"

"By all appearances, Mrs. Conway, Alan's death was an unfortunate accident." Dani looked up at Mitch, who ignored her. After a pause, he said, "I wonder if we could look for that notebook?"

"Of course. You can help yourselves. In fact, I think I remember packing a notebook like that. It would be in one of the boxes in the living room."

They followed her into the adjacent living room, and she pointed toward a couch covered with cardboard moving boxes. "Try the one on the left. I'm thinking I may have put it in there."

They both rushed to the couch, Mitch prying open the box to find the notebook lying right on top of various papers and folders. "That's it." Dani grabbed the notebook. "This is the one he was using when I last…" She turned to Lois Conway. "I'm sorry. I didn't mean to…"

"That's all right, dear. Truth be known, Alan and I were not especially close. Our relationship was defined by Christmas and birthday cards, with an infrequent phone call."

Mitch interjected. "We'd like to take this with us, Mrs. Conway. Also, I'd like to take another look around outside—if you don't mind?"

"Not at all. Look around all you want. Anyway, I'm sure Alan wouldn't mind."

Mitch left Dani with Mrs. Conway, crossed through the screened porch, and walked out to the stairway where Alan fell. Everything appeared exactly as it would have if Alan had just been working on his deck. He stood for a few minutes surveying the scene, staring intently down the precipitous stairs to the beach. When they initially found him, Alan's wounds, the broken stair railing, and the recovered glass were all consistent with a drunken trip and fall to the bottom. Later confirmation of his blood alcohol level supported that conclusion. There had been no reason to suspect foul play. However, the single beer bottle he found nagged at him. Now he pondered whether Gruca may in fact have killed Alan, and if so, how. He decided to take another look at the beach.

Once he reached the bottom, he paced gradually along the beach to the south. Not sure what he was looking for, he thought he would scout the perimeter of Alan's lot and walked to what appeared to be the border. A cutback formed a divide between Alan's lot and the next. It was filled with cut brush, heavy weeds, and some littered trash tossed away by beachcombers. As he made his way back into the gully, something caught his eye. Wading over to get a closer look, he discovered a single deck board almost hidden by the dense undergrowth. He grabbed it and gazed back up to look at the deck, but the walls of the ravine blocked the view. As he started walking back to the stairs, he turned the board over in his hands, noticing a reddish-brown stain on one end. Looking closer, he saw what appeared at first to be fibers stuck in the raw end of the board. Then he realized they were hairs.

CHAPTER 61

Same day.

"Well, hello Roy!" Gruca looked up to see the woman he had left sleeping at the hotel weeks before. He was sitting alone at a four-top table in an almost-empty roadside restaurant east of Lakeview Village. "Remember me?"

Gruca didn't speak but forced a welcoming expression.

"Surely you didn't forget me already?"

He pressed his lips into a smile. "No. Just surprised."

She grinned back contentedly. "Mind if I join you?"

"Hmm." He nodded to the chair across from him.

Instead, she hooked the strap of her purse around the chair's back and sat down next to him. He scooted his chair closer to the wall.

"I was wondering if I might ever see you again. That was quite a night we had—but then you just up and left. Not even a goodbye. Makes a girl wonder."

He considered what excuse she might accept. "You were sleeping. I decided not to wake you."

Grabbing the waiter's sleeve as he passed, she ordered a Bloody Mary and asked, "You want anything, Roy? It's five o'clock somewhere, right?"

"Nah. I'm good." She nodded to the waiter as Gruca pushed his plate aside.

"One of my customers wanted to talk about expanding her business, so we met this morning. I thought I'd stop for a bite on the way back. This little spot just called out to me. Must be fate, eh, Roy?"

"It's too bad you're headed out of town."

"Well, if you're nice to me, I might stick around. Remember? I make my own schedule, so all I have to do is book a room."

His eyes widened. "No need. I already have one. I planned to check in after lunch."

"That sounds like one of those offers I can't refuse." Just then the waiter returned with her drink.

"Then let's get out of here," said Gruca.

"Well, you are an eager boy." She gulped her drink as he motioned to the waiter for the bill.

CHAPTER 62

Convinced that the blood and hair on the board he found were likely Alan Redmond's, Mitch wanted to get it to a lab for testing as quickly as possible, worried it had been exposed to the elements for too long. Returning to the cottage, he found Dani and Mrs. Conway in the kitchen talking. As he stood in the kitchen doorway, each of the women stared at the board he held. He shifted squeamishly, looking at Alan's sister.

"I thought I'd take this back to the office for closer examination. It's, uh, apparently one of the boards that broke when Alan fell. Maybe there's a defect or something." He could tell Mrs. Conway was skeptical, not to mention Dani, so he quickly extended his hand. "Thanks so much for your help, Mrs. Conway. We really appreciate it." He glanced appealingly at Dani, and she took the cue.

"Yes. It was a pleasure, Mrs. Conway. Our sincerest condolences for your loss. Alan was a good man."

Once they got back to the car, Mitch opened the trunk

and pulled out a sheet of plastic. Dani came to stand beside him, asking, "So, what's with the two-by-four?"

Mitch tied the plastic around the end of the board. "I found this stuck out in the dune grass. Since all the initial evidence clearly pointed to a drunken fall, we didn't search much beyond Alan's cottage and the stairs to the beach. I'm thinking that maybe Alan didn't fall after all; possibly he was hit by this board, then thrown down the stairs to make it look like a fall. If so, he was likely dead, or close to it when he went down. And if that's the case, then our friend Gruca's the one who did it." He shut the trunk and they got in the car, heading back to Lakeview.

"So, now you actually believe that Gruca killed Alan?" Mitch nodded.

Dani swore. "Then Alan must have identified him. Or he was pretty close to it."

"Yep. And, we have to assume that Gruca's got it in mind to do the same to you."

"Me? How do you figure that?"

"Think about it. Why would Gruca kill Alan? Atwood was his, uh, what did you call him ... his mark? So Gruca must have somehow found out Alan was tracking him. I don't know how or where they met, but obviously Gruca made his way here. Anyone who knew Alan realized he was a talker. Chances are he spilled your story to Gruca somewhere along the line. My guess is he got Alan talking, and now he knows who you are and what you're up to. If my hunch is right, he'll try to get you out of the way. Then, as far as he knows, no one's after him."

Dani slowly shook her head. "If he's still here, I think he'll keep to his script. He'll show up just to give us the finger, whether at the Atwood service or someplace else.

After that, he'll want to be on his way like always. That is, if we don't get to him first."

Suddenly Mitch swerved over to the side of the road, parking on the shoulder. He stared straight ahead, gripping the steering wheel tightly, and took a deep breath. "I can understand why Gruca would want to come to Atwood's trial, but this is just a memorial service. There is no reason for him to expect us to be there, so who'd he be gloating at? Nope. I just don't buy that."

Dani started to speak, but Mitch talked over her. "You said 'we.' You're talking about the team hunting Gruca. But it's time to put a stop to that 'we.'"

Dani turned in her seat to face him. "What do you mean, put a stop?"

"I mean this whole thing has become deadly serious. Alan Redmond was probably murdered by the maniac you have been trying to catch. It doesn't take a genius to figure out you'll be in his crosshairs soon enough."

"We've already had this discussion, and it's not your call. I'm not under your command, and I can do what I want."

"You're wrong about that. This is now a formal police investigation, and I'm in charge. You're a civilian, with no authority whatsoever, and we're pursuing a dangerous murder suspect. If I decide you're an obstacle to the success of the mission, I can order you to stand down."

"You wouldn't dare do that... would you?"

Mitch put his hand on her shoulder. "Only if I have to. But not for the reason you might think." He hesitated as he saw her confused expression. "Look, I've got a job to do, and I've got to keep a clear head. I can't have any distractions."

Dani's eyes widened. "You don't have to worry about me. I'll be just fine. I'm not afraid of Gruca, and I'm well aware of what he's capable of. I can help—and I'll be careful."

"I'm not being clear about, well, what I mean. I am trying to say that I, I don't want anything to happen to you. It's you I'm concerned about. I don't know where we're going, Dani. I mean us. Last night was great, but I would like to think it was more than just that … the beginning of something between us. And I want to make sure nothing interferes with it. Especially not Gordon Gruca."

She stared into his eyes blankly, expressionless for what seemed an interminable period. He finally pleaded, "Well, say something, will you? Please?"

Slowly Dani smiled, her face brightening. "I'm thinking. I need to process what you said, or at least what I think you said. If I'm right, I like it. I like it a lot. If not, then I'll feel like a fool 'cause I've felt the same way about you for a while."

Mitch felt a rush. He had let go of the guilt he had felt at first, when he had thought about his wife and child. Pushing all of that out of his mind, he was now only concerned about what Gruca might do next.

"Then you can understand why I'm worried and want you out of Gruca's reach?"

"The only thing I understand right now is that you'd better kiss me, or I'll go crazy."

Mitch stretched over the car's armrest, encircling her in his arms. "One thing I'm good at is following orders. The rest, we'll talk about later."

CHAPTER 63

Days later.

Rafferty's Saloon was always empty in the mid-after-noon. Bobby Litwin stood behind the bar, cleaning and stacking glasses to prepare for the expected Thursday night crowd. Looking through the large front window, he saw a police cruiser pull up in the parking lot. He watched as the police chief got out of the car, put on his Stetson, and walked to the door.

Mitch had reached a compromise with Dani. He agreed that she could help in the search, but only during daylight hours in the more populated areas in and around Lakeview. Still, he worried her zeal for capturing Gruca might push her to do something rash and quietly directed the rest of the force to keep a lookout for her.

As Mitch entered and adjusted his eyes to the dim bar-room, Bobby waved a hello. "Hey, chief. What's up?"

"Hi Bobby. I need to ask your uncle a few questions. Is he here?"

"Yeah. He's in back. I'll go get him. You want anything?"

Mitch shook his head. "Nah. I'm good."

Bobby disappeared through the swinging door leading to the kitchen. Charlie Rafferty emerged moments later, wearing a combined expression of curiosity and concern. It wasn't common for the chief of police to pay a visit—not unless there was trouble. "What can I do for you, Chief?"

Mitch laid two pictures on the bar. "Can you look at these and tell me if you've seen this guy before?"

Rafferty picked them up and held the two pictures side by side, studying them carefully. "Can't say that I have, Chief, although something about him looks familiar. What's he done?"

"We think he killed a woman here in Lakeview and possibly a man. He may still be around here, and we're trying to track him down." Mitch looked past Rafferty to see Bobby coming back through the swinging door behind him.

"How about you, Bobby? Have you seen this guy?" His uncle handed him the photos.

Bobby held the pictures at arm's length, squinting. "This bigger one looks kinda weird."

"It's a computer simulation. It uses a program designed to age a person. They take a picture of them when they're young, like that one in your right hand, and the program shows what they might look like when they're older."

"Boy, I dunno. Sorta looks like that guy who took out those bikers a while back, don't it?" He held the image out to Rafferty. "You remember that guy, Uncle Charlie? He got in a throwdown with those bikers, and I told 'em to take it outside. When we went outside to check, the two bikers were on the ground, but the other guy was already gone."

Rafferty nodded in recognition. "Oh yeah. Both those guys were laid out. When they got up, they said not to call the police, and then they skedaddled. But I dunno. This don't look much like that guy to me. I recall him as older. And didn't he have a beard, Bobby?"

"Maybe." Bobby turned to Mitch. "But if that is the guy, Chief, he sure must be able to handle himself."

Mitch's eyes narrowed. "Meaning?"

Bobby shrugged. "You know … like a boxer, or maybe even a karate guy. From the looks of 'em, those two guys were no pushovers, man. But he dropped 'em both in no time."

This revelation worried Mitch. A serial killer with that kind of lethal skill was especially dangerous.

"Did he ever come back here?"

"Can't say I've seen him," Rafferty said.

Mitch turned to Bobby, who shook his head. "Me neither, Chief," Bobby added. "I can ask the staff, but I think they woulda mentioned it. We talked about it a lot after."

"I'd appreciate it if you would … and soon. Let me know right away if anyone tells you they've seen him again. Or if you see him again. Okay?"

Both men agreed, and Mitch turned to leave. "Thanks, fellas. We need to get this guy. He's a bad one."

As soon as he got back in his car, Mitch began wondering how Dani was doing with her search. He recalled her claim, that she knew what Gruca was capable of, and wondered exactly how much she knew, or didn't. He regretted that he had let her talk him into involving her, worrying that she might be in even more danger than he imagined.

CHAPTER 64

Dani pulled into the gravel parking lot of the Woods Motel on the south end of Lakeview Village. Redmond's notebook contained a list of all the various businesses he had checked out by date, and she was working her way further north from his last stop. She felt relieved that Mitch had relented, agreeing to let her assist in the search. It was late afternoon, and this was her last stop for the day.

Secluded in a thick stand of pines and barely visible from the state road fifty yards away, the log-style building lived up to its name. Dani entered the reception area through a squeaky glass-and-metal storm door, approaching the front desk. Seeing no one, she tapped the service bell on the counter. She heard rustling through a doorway that opened on what appeared to be an adjacent office. A tall, slender man, wearing a faded madras shirt hanging out over stained chino jeans, slowly shuffled into the small lobby.

"Yes ma'am? Want a room?"

Dani shook her head. "No, thank you. I'm working with the Lakeview police department. We're looking for someone. I'm hoping that you may have seen him recently. I'd appreciate it if you could look at some pictures for me, Mr., uh?"

"Prestwick. Randy Prestwick." Dani removed the military photo and computer replica of Gruca from her coat pocket. Placing them on the counter, she asked, "Have you seen this man before?"

Prestwick leaned over, peering down at the pictures through the thick lenses of his horn-rimmed glasses. As he did, a greasy comma of hair fell from his comb over across the side of his face. "Uh, uh. He doesn't look familiar to me."

Frustrated after a day's worth of getting the same answer at each stop, she pressed him. "The one on the left is old. He was much younger. The other larger one is a facsimile of what he might look like today. He may have gained weight, or he could have some facial hair, or even be balding. Please look again."

He looked down again and began to shake his head negatively. "I just don't think I …"

Dani cut in. "And we know he has a large tattoo on his right forearm. We don't know what it's a tattoo of, but …"

The man looked up at her abruptly. "Tattoo, huh? Why didn't you say so in the first place? Yeah, there was a guy like that a few days ago. I remember he paid cash in advance. Stayed two nights and left early in the morning. Must have been in a hurry. Is he in trouble?"

Dani ignored the question. "Is there anything more

you can tell me about him? Did he say what he was doing here or where he was going?" Prestwick shook his head in denial. "Well, did he give you a name?"

"He didn't talk much about anything. But he had to give me a name. He checked in."

"Can I see those records?"

The clerk reached under the counter, pulled out a folder containing the check-in forms, and slowly flipped through the sheets. Handing her the relevant form, he said, "Yeah. Here it is. Williams. Roy Williams was his name. At least that's what he put on the check-in sheet. See?"

She grabbed the sheet, saw the address given was in Minneapolis, and knew it had to be false. The space for the description of the guest's car and for a license number was blank. "Any reason you didn't have him fill this in?"

He looked down at the sheet to where her finger pointed. "Hm. I guess I didn't notice. Nope. No reason. I just didn't. But he was driving a huge black pickup. It had one of those tops over the back and tinted windows."

"Did you recognize what make it was or see what state the plate was from?

"No. Sorry. Maybe a Chevy, or a Ford? I dunno. I didn't get a look at the plate."

"Anything else you can tell me? Did he have anyone with him?"

"Well, that last night he had a woman in with him. At least, that's what I was told."

"Told by who? Didn't you see her yourself?"

"Nope. That's what Hal told me. Uh, that's Harold. Harold Blandford. He's the night clerk. He told me when I came in to relieve him. He said they were making a lot of noise…if you know what I mean?" He smiled at her leeringly. Dani gave a sternly disapproving stare, and he looked away. "She must have left with him the next morning."

"Did Mr. Blandford tell you anything about the woman? Her description? Or her car?"

"Nope. You'll have to ask Hal. Like I said, I didn't see her."

"Where can I find Mr. Blandford? I'd like to talk with him. Does he live close by?"

"No. He lives down in Platteville. About thirty miles south of here."

"Does he work today?"

"Should be in at six tonight. Like I said, he's the night clerk."

Dani looked at her watch. It would be at least two hours before Blandford arrived, and she didn't want to just sit around waiting. Not with this character. She grabbed a postcard from the small stack on the counter, taking a pen from her purse. "I'm giving you my cell number. Could you please have Mr. Blandford call me when he comes in? Tell him it's very important that I speak with him as soon as possible."

Prestwick stared at her figure as she walked away. "Sure. Okay. But it won't be long before he's here. You're welcome to wait." Dani winced. "Where ya goin'?"

Looking back over her shoulder, she answered, "Somewhere ... else."

CHAPTER 65

Next morning.

Willy climbed back up the steep hillside to the country road where he had left his squad car. He stood, standing where he had first seen tire tracks in the gravel beside the shoulder heading over the edge of a thirty-foot decline to the creek bed below. Returning from serving a witness subpoena, he had seen the tracks and had stopped to investigate. He now rushed to report what he had found.

After sliding into his patrol car, he grabbed the radio handset, pressing the button to connect with the dispatcher at the station. "Penny, come in. It's Willy."

A few moments passed before the dispatcher replied. "Come in, Willy. Dispatch here. It's Penny. Sorry, I was on another call. What's up?"

"I've got a single auto fatality on State Road 27. I'm at that *S* curve near Pierson Creek. Looks like a woman didn't make the curve. She went over just before the bridge. I can't tell how long she's been here. A while from the … looks of it. Anyway, she's dead. I'll need an ambulance out here to recover the body. Can you send 'em out right away?" The dispatcher replied in the affirmative.

Willy replaced the mike, retrieved gloves and a mask from his trunk, and descended back down to the wreck for a closer look. When he got to the bottom of the gully, he stepped carefully around the small SUV, which was lying on its side in the shallow creek bed. Peering over the roof through the open window, he saw that the woman sprawled below him was not wearing a seat belt.

"What's going on down there, Willy?" The deputy turned at the call. It surprised him to see the chief looking down at him from the rim of the embankment.

"Geez, Chief. What are you doin' here?"

"I wasn't far from here following up on the Wheatley investigation. I called in, and they told me you had reported an accident. I wanted to take a look for myself. The description of this car got me thinking." He began making his way down the steep hillside. When he got to the bottom, he moved quickly past his deputy, looking through the open window down into the vehicle.

Pivoting back to Willy, he took him by the shoulder. "Willy, get up and lay on the side of the car. I want you to reach down inside and grab the purse lying at the bottom next to that woman. I'll hold your legs."

A few wiggles after stretching down into the vehicle and Willy grabbed the bag. "Got it, Chief!" he gasped.

Quinn helped him back up, opened the purse, and pulled out the wallet inside. The license read Sheila Patrice Doane. Mitch believed he now knew the name of the woman Dani had learned about during her interview with the motel night clerk. The clerk described a buxom woman with reddish-brown hair; he had seen her enter the hotel room of the guest registered as Roy Williams. He didn't get her name, but said she followed Williams into the lot in a red SUV compact—exactly what was now sitting on its side in the creek.

CHAPTER 66

After dealing with the woman, Gruca sensed that a temporary absence was called for, and he had left the area to attend the rabbit show in Ionia. During the return trip, he heard on the news that Mrs. Atwood was prolonging her Florida hiatus, and that a memorial celebration for Lawrence Atwood would be delayed until October. He then headed to the Atwood beach house. After carefully scouting the neighborhood, he had switched his truck, now out of sight in the garage, with an older car he had stolen in a mall lot near Grand Rapids. Each time he used the vehicle, he traded out one of the many license plates he had collected over the years.

He now sat in the darkness, recalling his fateful tryst with Sheila Doane. She had been suspicious and mentioned his tattoo as they left the restaurant. He decided then that she would have to be silenced. She had seen too much. Killing her was not a problem, but staging her accident required imagination. Fortuitously, after their arduous lovemaking in the room that last night, she said she was heading home early in the morning, and he proposed breakfast together. That presented the perfect ruse.

The chosen location was a sharp S curve he had driven past the previous week. It was isolated enough that early morning traffic would be unlikely. He told her he would lead them to a restaurant further down the highway. After they left the motel, he pulled over just ahead of the curve and lured her out of the car, saying, "Come. You have to see this view."

He led her toward a slight clearing, then quickly spun around, causing her to halt. Just as she jerked back, he pulled a tire iron from beneath his jacket, aiming a blow at the bridge of her nose. Grabbing her as she fell, he snapped her neck, confident the wounds would simulate trauma caused to a beltless driver by her car's thirty-foot drop into the creek below. He reasoned that the umbrella used to jam the accelerator would not be suspicious considering the recent showers, but afterward he had to make sure it hadn't stuck in place. After he placed her in her car and directed it over the edge, he worked his way down the stream bed ahead of the wreckage to minimize any tracks. He was pleased when he saw the brace had dislodged in the crash.

Returning his thoughts to the present, Gruca reached over toward the coffee table, grabbing a copy of the local newspaper he had bought earlier. He paged to the obituary section and focused his small penlight on the announcement of the service for Atwood. After a few moments of contemplation, he walked into the kitchen and grabbed a head of lettuce from the refrigerator. Entering the garage, he tore off the leaves and tossed them on the floor. His pets were barely visible in the dim half-light as they scampered for their meal.

"Eat hearty, my friends. We're going places."

CHAPTER 67

"There was no sign of another vehicle or of alcohol or drug involvement, although it's possible the toxicology report might show something. They found nothing suspicious in the car."

Dave Bartlett looked down at his desktop as he listened, slowly shaking his head, and twirling a pen between his fingers. Mitch was describing the Sheila Doane accident, which he and Willy had investigated the week before. Mitch and Dani had convened in Dave Bartlett's office to go over the results of their search efforts before an impending meeting with the attorney general and a state police representative, preparatory to planning security for the Atwood memorial service. Aside from what Dani learned from the motel clerks and the revelation from Rafferty, no one else had offered any information about Gruca.

"So, what caused her to swerve off the road into a thirty-foot-deep ravine, Mitch?" Bartlett didn't wait for an answer.

"For all we know, it could have been a deer." He glanced briefly at Dani, then back to Mitch as he continued. "You and I know deer collisions are commonplace all across this state. It could have been a heart attack or a stroke. Or she could have reached for something in her purse, her cell phone, or dropped something on the floor. Almost anything could have been the cause." He had hoped to have a lot more to report to Patterson at the meeting.

"But the fact is that she spent the previous night in a hotel with Gordon Gruca, and they left together early the next morning," Dani interjected.

"The fact is," said Bartlett, "that she apparently stayed with a man who checked in as Roy Williams, and no one can say exactly when they left, let alone that they left together."

"Dave, the man had a large tattoo on his arm. Are you saying that's just a coincidence?" said Mitch.

"All I'm saying, my friend, is that there is no solid evidence Gordon Gruca had anything to do with this woman's accident. Saying Gruca was the man she was with just because he had a tattoo is nothing more than conjecture." Bartlett dropped his pen and leaned back. "Regardless, it doesn't matter, because you haven't located this Roy Williams, nor do you have any idea where Gruca is, or even if he's still in Lakeview." Only sheepish looks answered these factual statements.

"The only other new information you've got suggesting Gruca's been in Lakeview are statements by Charlie Rafferty and his nephew that they saw someone in their bar months ago who may fit Gruca's description, and that this person had a fight with two guys in their parking lot."

"And he probably used martial arts," Dani exclaimed.

Mitch looked away disapprovingly, but feared she was right.

"If I had a buck for every bar fight in Lakeview, with or without somebody using martial arts, karate, kung fu, whatever, I could retire early."

Mitch knew that when the AG arrived, he would want to hear they had found Gruca, or at least had sufficient evidence to support a warrant. He appreciated Bartlett playing devil's advocate against their theory that Gruca killed Sheila Doane. Bartlett had supported their pitch to get the AG to authorize the investigation, and Mitch figured he was not about to be made a fool of. He was pressing to get something convincing so Patterson would commit his resources to stake out the Atwood memorial service, in case Gruca did show up.

"Look, guys, we've only got a few minutes before Rob Patterson walks through that door and demands information. If we don't give it to him, he can shut this whole thing down and just let the Atwood tribute go on by itself."

"But we have …" Mitch twisted anxiously in his seat.

Just then the call button on Bartlett's desk phone lit up. He winced, shushing Mitch with an upraised palm. "I told her not to disturb us. Yes, Irene, what is it?"

"That Dr. Jacoby is on the line. He says it's important. I thought you'd want to take it."

"Thanks," said Bartlett, immediately picking up the phone. "Hello, Dr. Jacoby. What can I do for you?"

After Mitch returned from Alan's cottage, he first had CSI dust the bottle and the board for prints, then submitted both for DNA testing. He asked Bartlett to push Dr. Jacoby for help in expediting the process. Since the case was already on the lab's docket, they hoped for a fast turnaround. Mitch then sent CSI to the cottage for possible print retrieval.

After a few uh-huhs and a quick thank you, Bartlett hung up the phone and broke into a satisfied grin. "Man, if that wasn't fortuitous. I had asked the good doctor to call me by this morning, but I frankly thought it was unlikely. He must still be stinging from his office screwing up the tests on that tie." Mitch and Dani both gaped curiously.

"The DNA test on that board you found is in. It's a match for Alan Redmond."

"That's sure better than what CSI came up with. No prints but Alan's and his sister's were found anywhere at the cottage, and none on that bottle."

"What bottle?" Dani asked.

"Oh. Yeah. I took a bottle from the mantle on Alan's porch."

"Why did you do that?"

"Well, when I saw the bottle, it occurred to me that Willy found Alan's glass on the beach steps the day they located his body. And I knew that Alan wasn't a beer drinker. So, I thought someone else might have been there with him before he died. It was a shot in the dark that didn't pan out. No prints."

"That's no surprise. Gruca removed his own prints long ago."

"You never told me that."

Dani looked at her lap. "I guess I … forgot."

Mitch cringed and turned to Bartlett. "But the DNA on that board is proof that Alan didn't fall down those stairs by himself, isn't it? Somebody threw him—or if he did fall, it was after they whacked him with that board."

"It had to be Gruca!" Dani exclaimed.

"Both of you hold on," said Dave. "We're not there yet. I've got to think this through. Jacoby did say they got DNA from the bottle."

"And?" pushed Dani.

"And it was male. Also, it matched the DNA from the tie. But we still have nothing to show it was Gruca's, and nothing to connect him with Alan's death. Or Prudence Wheatley's, for that matter."

"But we're a hell of a lot closer than yesterday," Mitch said. "Alan was all over Lakeview looking for Gruca, and within a week he got killed. I'd say that's more than a coincidence."

"I'm not saying it wasn't Gruca. In fact, I'm not saying he's not our number one suspect. I'm just saying we don't have enough to make a case," said Bartlett.

The call button lit up again, and Irene announced that people from the attorney general's office had arrived. Dave told her to let them in. "At least now we've got something to give Patterson."

When the door opened, Cynthia Worthey and state police Captain William Ryerson, accompanied by two of his lieutenants, entered the room. Worthey announced that the attorney general couldn't join them because of a last-minute conflict. Mitch and Bartlett both knew Ryerson well, having worked with him on several cases over the years, but it surprised them that Patterson was absent. They exchanged disappointed glances at Worthey's reappearance.

Bartlett then explained what Mitch and the police had been doing over the past month in pursuit of Gruca, including his suspected murder of Alan Redmond, the DNA results on the board and bottle from Alan's cottage, and the suspicious death of Sheila Doane. Noting Worthey's attention, he decided to make his pitch.

"Based upon the history provided to your office previously," he gave a nod in her direction, "we believe it's likely that Gordon Gruca will show up at the Atwood memorial service. As you'll recall from Ms. Sparro's file materials, it's exactly the type of event he's attended in the past. If he does, we've got a plan that will ensure his capture."

"Which would go a long way toward soothing the sting of having charged the wrong man in the Prudence Wheatley case," Mitch interjected.

Worthey sat up rigidly. "So far, I haven't heard anything but rank speculation that Gruca might, and I emphasize might, make an appearance at the service, and nothing substantive proving that he had anything to do with any of what you've been talking about. That's what I'll be reporting to the attorney general."

Bartlett took a deep breath. "Whatever. As the representative of the AG's office, are you going to listen to the plan we have for the memorial service, or not?"

"I'm only here to listen and to evaluate what you have to offer. So, get on with it."

Mitch rose from his chair, walked over to an easel in the corner, and flipped up the overlay.

"Although our investigation is far from over," Mitch looked over his shoulder at Worthey, who answered with a smirk, "we've for sure learned a few things that we all need to keep in mind. First, if we're right, he's killed twice since the Wheatley murder. So, we know that he won't hesitate to kill if threatened. Second, we must assume he's armed, and he may be skilled in some form of martial arts, so we'll instruct our personnel that no one should try to take him on single-handed. Finally, although the clerks at the Woods Motel provided us with a description of what he looks like, we should expect that he'll disguise himself in some way. We'll pass out the pictures we have, but they're not current and we can't assume they're an accurate reflection of what he looks like now. He does have that large tattoo on his forearm, but he'll surely try to hide it. The biggest challenge, though, will be the venue."

Mitch pulled a pointer from a tray on the easel and pointed to the displayed chart. "This is the floor plan of St. Matthew's Church, where they'll hold the service. As you can see, there is a large central area with two sections of thirty rows of pews, one on each side of an aisle, starting just in front of the altar and running all the way to the rear of the church. Each pew seats up to fifteen people, which means they can accommodate around nine hundred in just those pews alone."

Everyone shook their heads in concern. Captain Ryerson raised his hand, asking, "What are those lines shown on the sides of the floor plan? Are those more pews?"

"I'm afraid so. There are corridors with more pews along the entire length of the church, each holding up to six people. And that doesn't include this large alcove to the right of the altar. We're talking possibly over fourteen hundred if they fill…"

Worthey cut in. "Rob says the Dems will come out in numbers. Quite a few are scheduled to speak. In addition,

Atwood was a star in the state trial lawyers' association, and his wife's dad is a former senator. So, we've got to plan on a packed house."

"What will make this an even bigger problem is the number of entry points to the church. There are eight doors directly accessing the main level and two more outside stairwells to the lower level. We've got a lot of square footage to cover, and..."

Worthey interrupted again. "If this turns out to be the crowd we expect, Quinn, it will be standing room only."

"That's just the point I was about to make. We must position our people at every entry point, and scatter more throughout the vestibule and the main church itself. There should also be a couple men downstairs, as there are several window wells allowing access below ground."

"I'll pull in all the troopers I can, Chief. I should have at least twenty," said Ryerson.

"Questions?" Mitch asked, trying to avoid eye contact with Dani, who sat stoically with her arms crossed. The others joined Mitch at the easel, and he answered their questions for the next fifteen minutes, periodically glancing at Dani, who hadn't moved. Finally, he dismissed the group, and one by one they headed out of Bartlett's office and into the hallway.

Dani grabbed his arm to stop him as they exited behind the rest, asking sarcastically, "So, what's my assignment going to be?"

Mitch had thought all morning about what he would say to her, but he couldn't come up with anything she might accept. Gently taking hold of her shoulders, he said, "Look, it's best that you sit this one out, Dani. There's no telling what might happen, and I think you should be as far away from Gruca as possible."

"Here we go again with you deciding what's best for me," she blurted loudly, shrugging his hands away. "You know very well I have both reason and right to see Gruca go down. You can't stop me from attending that service."

Seeing the others had all stopped and turned at the sound of her protest, Mitch lowered his voice. "We've been through this, Dani. I told you before that I can do what is necessary to protect the public, and that includes you. You can either do what I say, or I can put you in protective custody."

"Are you kidding me? You wouldn't."

"Yes, I would. But only if I have to."

"You know what getting Gruca means to me, damn it! He killed my father." She pushed him away, stomping toward the exit door at the end of the hall. "You bastard!" she yelled over her shoulder.

Mitch looked at the wide-eyed onlookers, shrugged while giving a weak smile, and chased after her. As the boom of the exit door shutting behind them echoed in the stairwell, he spun her around. "Look Dani, I ..."

"Why don't you understand? I just have to be there!" she pleaded.

Mitch sighed and paused. He hated that he was giving in again. "Okay. I'll make you a deal. When the time comes, I'll get Ryerson to assign a trooper to stick by you until this thing is over. He can accompany you to the event, but you have got to promise me you'll stick with the guy, whoever he is, through the whole shebang, until we either get Gruca or we're sure he doesn't show. Deal?"

"Deal." Dani broke into a smile, placing her hands on his chest. "And I do appreciate your ... concern."

He pulled her to him and kissed her passionately. "I've been wanting to do that all morning."

She looked up at him, eyes glistening. "And I've been wanting you to."

CHAPTER 68

October.

M itch stood in the entranceway between the vestibule and the standing room area at the back of the church, folding chairs lining the rear wall to accommodate the anticipated crowd. He stared at the frescoed ceiling a full three stories above, thinking how much larger it all was than he had imagined. His attention turned to the various state troopers moving through the pews with bomb-sniffing dogs. Just then, Captain Ryerson walked up beside him.

"Big, isn't it?"

"That's an understatement, for sure. You think you've got enough men?"

"I guess we'll know soon enough. There will be twenty-four troopers on site. Including your guys, that's almost thirty. They can cover every square foot of this building, inside and out, including every entrance. A roach couldn't get in without being spotted."

"Maybe so, but we all know what a roach looks like.

I can't say the same for Gruca. Who knows what disguise he'll wear if he comes? And you can bet he won't be showing off that tattoo."

"Well, at least we can eliminate maybe half of the folks coming in here today," Ryerson said through a wry smile. "With his frame, unless he puts on one hell of a costume, he'll never pass for a woman."

"Ha! I suppose that's something. We better get those dogs out of here soon. I expect the crowd will want to get seated, and we locked all the doors for the search. We don't want to alarm anyone before this party even starts."

Ryerson nodded in agreement and walked toward the gathered troopers. Mitch hailed after him, "Bill, have you heard anything from that trooper you assigned to stay with Ms. Sparro?"

"Not yet. When we spoke last night, he said he would book a room at the same hotel she's been staying at in Lakeview. He planned to bring her over here this morning. That's a forty-mile drive. I'm sure they'll be along shortly." Noticing Quinn's expression of concern, Ryerson looked down at his watch. "We've still got twenty minutes before this shindig starts." After a pause, he asked, "She's important to you, I guess?"

"I'll put it this way. If it wasn't for her, none of us would be here."

"As soon as I get these guys out of here and set up at their stations, I'll call him if they're still not here. But I'm sure they will be."

"I hope you're right. More than anyone involved in this case, Dani Sparro has an interest in catching Gruca. A very personal one. I would have expected her to be early."

"Steve Turner, he's the trooper I assigned, is a damned good policeman. He'll take good care of her. You'll see. I'll meet you back here after we get things set up."

Over an hour later, Mitch's cell phone began buzzing in his pocket. He had muted it so it wouldn't disturb the seemingly interminable speaker eulogizing Atwood. The interruption was a relief, and he walked from his position among those standing in the back of the church through the vestibule and out onto the front steps. Seeing the office number on the screen, and assuming it was the dispatcher, he answered, "Quinn here. What is it, Penny?"

"It's Willy, Chief." It surprised Mitch to hear from Willy. When Dani had not shown up after the service started, followed by Ryerson saying he couldn't get in touch with his trooper, he had sent Willy back to Lakeview to check on them. He couldn't have been there for more than a few minutes, so the fact he was calling was reason for worry.

"What's going on, Willy?"

"Well, I haven't checked on Ms. Sparro and that trooper yet because dispatch called me just as I came into town. She didn't want to bother you at the church, but the call she got concerned her, so she contacted me, and I went right over to the office."

"What was this call about, Willy?"

"The manager of the Dunes Motel, you know that newer one out on Old 31?"

"Yes, Willy, I know it. What about the manager?" Mitch was getting impatient.

"Well, he called to report that a guy checked in late

last night, driving a big black pickup with a canopy and tinted windows. He didn't call until this morning 'cause he hadn't gotten the notice we put out. Anyway, I just called him, and he said it's still parked outside of the room the guy checked into. He walked out to look, and he spotted two big white rabbits inside. Just like the one I saw last year in Lakeview."

"Did you go over there?"

"I just got off the phone with him and I'm headed out the door, but I thought you'd want to hear this ASAP."

"All right. You did the right thing. Now get on over there and check things out. But don't go into the room. Just keep your eyes open, and make sure that whoever is in there doesn't leave. Call me when you arrive. Also, send someone over to Dani Sparro's hotel to check on her and that trooper who's with her."

"Okay, but there's one more thing, Chief."

"Yeah? What?"

"Just after the manager got back to his office after scoping the pickup, he heard a loud bang. He thinks it was a gunshot. He said he didn't see anyone leave and that the truck is still there, but he's afraid to go in."

In his mind's eye, Mitch saw Gruca with Dani, wondering if he had somehow gotten to her. He quickly buried the thought.

"Get over there as fast as you can and call me when you get there. Go now!" He yelled the order, quickly closed his phone, and headed back into the church to find Ryerson.

CHAPTER 69

Willy had been sitting for almost forty minutes in his squad car, which he had parked to have a clear view of the door to room number seven—the room rented by a man thought to be Gordon Gruca. When Willy first arrived, he had asked the manager to keep watch inside, quickly evacuating the only other occupied room. He had then returned to his car and set up watch, waiting for Mitch.

After Mitch pulled into the lot, they each got out of their cars and stood together. Mitch could see the black pickup sitting alone about forty yards away. "Is that truck parked directly in front of the door to his room?"

"Yeah, that's what the manager said. Number seven, right next to it."

"Anyone still in there?"

"No activity since I got here, Chief. The manager's in the lobby watching the inside, but he told me he's sure no one's left."

"Okay. Stay here and cover that outside door. I'm going over for a closer look, then I'll get a key. Who did you get to check up on Ms. Sparro?"

"Pete Thompson. But I haven't heard from him. I told him to call as soon as he had something." Willy noted Mitch's look of concern. "Pete's a good man, Chief."

Mitch nodded and walked toward the vehicle, saying over his shoulder, "Second time today I've heard that said. So far, I'm not impressed."

He drew closer and peered into the vehicle, seeing the two white rabbits perched in the passenger seat. Because the drapes were drawn, he couldn't see into the hotel room, so he walked around to the main entrance.

A small, middle-aged man with curly black hair leaned over the counter, staring off to his right. Mitch thought him to be of Italian descent, and in fact he introduced himself as Robert Fricano. Mitch turned to see what the manager had been watching. A vacant corridor stretched all the way to a glass exit at the end of the building. He could see room doors on both sides of the hall. After asking for the key to room seven, he proceeded cautiously down the corridor.

When he reached the door, he drew his gun. Standing off to one side, he knocked loudly and shouted, "This is Lakeview Police Chief Quinn. Open the door!" No sound came from within, so he pounded again, yelling, "Police, open the door!" Again, there was no reply. Quinn then inserted the key and threw the door open, shouting, "I'm coming in! Kneel down and put your hands behind your head."

Edging around the doorjamb, he stopped cold when he saw blackish spatters covering the opposite door and adjacent window drapes. The room was dark, and Mitch could barely make out the feet, legs, and torso of a person across the room. He stepped in with his gun pointed ahead of him, inching around the corner. Seeing the bathroom to his right, he stepped further inside to get a closer look. It was empty, so he walked back to the door, stuck his head into the hallway, and yelled to the manager, "Sir, tell my deputy to come in here."

Moving in closer, he recognized a body propped on a chair leaning against the door. A shotgun lay on the floor beside the chair. The face of the corpse was completely gone, along with much of the top of its skull. Mitch quickly concluded that, whoever was lying there in front of him, he had committed suicide Hemingway style—messy but effective. Just then Willy burst into the room, gun drawn.

"Put it away, Willy. This guy won't do us any harm. Turn on a light, will you?"

Willy obeyed and flipped the switch, light flooding the room. Quinn gingerly tiptoed to the cadaver for a closer examination.

"Looks like it's him, huh Chief?"

"How do you figure that, Willy?"

"See there? Look at that tattoo on the arm."

Mitch stooped down and used his gun barrel to carefully turn over the right forearm, exposing a large tattoo he couldn't quite make out because of blood spatter. Mitch used his pistol to extend the fingers of the right hand. He could see that the tips were abraded, recalling what Dani had said about Gruca removing his own prints.

"It sure looks that way, Willy. Anyway, go call this in and ask for a CSI and coroner. I'll look around."

Mitch holstered his gun and took a quick visual tour around the room as Willy bolted out the door. Spying a sheet of paper lying on the desk, he used his flashlight to illuminate a faint scrawl of handwriting. The message he read gave him a chill, and he plopped onto the desk chair.

CHAPTER 70

While finishing up at the motel, Mitch had called Deputy Peter Thompson, who reported that he had driven to the Shoreline Inn to look for Dani Sparro and trooper Turner. Receiving no response to persistent knocking, he ordered the hotel manager to open both rooms with his master key, finding them empty but with clothing still hung in the closets. Mitch then called Ryerson, asking him to put out an APB for both. The captain advised him he was shutting down the stakeout at the church, the service having ended without disturbance. There had been no sign of Gruca, and they agreed to meet early the next afternoon to determine a course of action.

Mitch had then returned home and sank into despondency, fearing his life was about to come crashing down again. He had not slept at all that night, unsuccessfully trying to come up with any explanation for Dani's disappearance besides Gruca's intervention. Nor could he stop thinking about the suicide note, which summoned nightmarish visions of what Gruca may have done to Dani before killing himself. He knew that she was the one he referred to:

"I'm ending this on my terms, and I've taken the bitch with me."

A knock at the front door startled him. When he answered, Mitch found a smiling Dave Bartlett standing on the doorstep, though his smile immediately wavered.

"You look like crap, buddy."

"You don't look so great yourself, big fella." Mitch turned around and trudged back to the kitchen, leaving the door open with Bartlett standing outside. He followed, stood momentarily staring around the room, walked over to the counter, and helped himself to a cup of coffee from the time-worn coffee maker.

"So, what brings you out here, counselor?" said Mitch.

Dave sat down across from him. "I'm here to snap you out of your funk, my friend. We've got work to do."

"I'm kinda numb at the moment. Hard to turn my mind to that. And I'm supposed to meet Bill Ryerson this afternoon. So, if you don't mind, right now I'd like to be alone."

"The best medicine, my friend, would be to get up and get serious about finding Dani and that trooper. You're not doing anybody any good sitting around feeling sorry for yourself. Which, by the looks of you, is exactly what you're doing."

"You haven't seen the suicide note, have you?" Mitch barked. "If you had, you'd know there's no question Gruca was talking about Dani."

"I wouldn't be too sure about that, buddy. I just might have some positive news for you on that front."

"What the hell are you talking about?"

"Well, once I got word of all of this yesterday, I visited the morgue...after they brought in the body."

"So, you saw what remains of Gordon Gruca. So what?"

"So, I gave it a good once-over and noticed some, well, let's say suspicious things about your allegedly dead Mr. Gruca."

"Allegedly? What the..."

"Didn't you tell me Gruca was in the Army?"

"Yeah. Why?"

"Well, if he was, then why would he have a tattoo of an anchor on his arm? You ever know an Army vet to have a Navy tattoo?" Bartlett let that sink in.

"Navy? I couldn't make out the tattoo. Too much blood."

"And, Mr. Police Chief, didn't Dani tell you Gruca removed his fingerprints years ago?" Mitch nodded. "That's what I thought. But, if I'm not mistaken, someone removed the prints on that corpse quite recently. In fact, I'd say possibly as recently as a week or two."

He could see that Mitch was trying to process this new information. "What I'm saying is, that body down in the morgue is looking a lot less like Gordon Gruca's, and a lot more like some poor slob he used to cover his tracks. Think about it. That shotgun blast blew away the entire face. We don't have any of Gruca's dental records available, not that there's much left to compare, and no fingerprints. So, right now there's no way to identify whoever it is in that morgue drawer."

It was dawning on Mitch what this could mean. "And if that's not Gruca, if he's still alive, then maybe..."

Bartlett stood and put his hands on Mitch's shoulders. "Then Dani may be alive, too. But we've got to get a move on. If Gruca's got her, I don't think he'll wait a long time to…"

His voice trailed off as Mitch pushed past him, shouting, "Ten minutes… no, five, and I'll be ready to go!"

CHAPTER 71

Mitch and Bartlett met Captain Ryerson and one of his troopers in a fifties-style roadside diner halfway between the city and Lakeview. The building resembled a shiny, silver train car, with a long counter and stools running the room's length parallel to a band of glass windows stretching across the front. They convened in a semi-circular booth next to a corner window, which looked out onto the parking lot.

"I guess you could say he was pretty upset." Ryerson was describing with delight Attorney General Patterson's reaction to the news Gruca had apparently killed himself, meaning there would be no public arrest to celebrate. "God only knows how he'll react when he finds out Gruca might still be alive," he added, grinning broadly.

Mitch replied, "Emphasis on the word 'might,' Bill. Nothing's for sure at this point, but we'll proceed as if he is alive—and Dani and trooper Turner, too."

"That brings me to a curious fact. I had twenty-four

troopers assigned to cover the service. We all met at our local headquarters on Friday afternoon, and I passed out walkie-talkies to each one so we could easily communicate on site the next day. After we cleared the church, I asked my sergeant here," he gave a nod to the trooper on his left, "to collect those radios. They returned all twenty-four."

The two men blankly gazed back at him. Eventually Bartlett spoke up. "So, I don't get it. What are you saying?"

"Steve Turner got one of those walkie-talkies. It was before I asked him to shadow Ms. Sparro. He didn't turn his in before he left, but..."

Mitch finished the sentence for him. "But somehow it was turned in afterward?"

"You got it."

"So Gruca was there!" Bartlett exclaimed. "That means he's alive. He took Turner's radio, then turned it in after the Atwood memorial."

"That's what I'm thinking, but let's not get ahead of ourselves. I didn't pick up on it until this morning, when I talked to Sergeant Fuller here and he reported all equipment returned. I put two and two together and asked him to join us today."

"So, you must have seen him then?" Mitch asked.

The sergeant shook his head. "No. I gave the order for the men to return their walkie-talkies, but I called everyone on my radio from the rear of the church, inside. I said my trunk would be open—they could drop them off as they left. I was back and forth over the next half hour, so I didn't stand there and watch them."

"Since this is a weekend, I didn't reconvene the guys after we were through," Ryerson lamented. "Most of them just left directly for home or wherever they had to go, so I won't be able to connect with all of them until tomorrow. I got ahold of a few this morning by phone, but none of them saw an unidentified trooper."

Mitch let out a breath in frustration. "Dang! I was hoping we would at least have some kind of description. I'm betting that somehow he got a uniform, maybe Turner's."

"I'd say that's more than a good guess, Mitch. I've stepped up the APB from a missing person call to a possible abduction-homicide. The new alert says the suspect may be in one of our uniforms, although I expect he ditched it. All officers in the field will be on the lookout. If there's nothing by the next shift tomorrow morning, I'll call in more help."

"Well, I can't just sit back and wait. I've got to do something." Mitch's imagination raced again, sweat forming on his forehead. He was feeling desperate.

"What can we do, Chief? We have no leads and no idea of where he might be. He left that pickup at the motel, so we don't even have a make on whatever car he's driving."

"If he has Turner's uniform, he's likely got his car. But I doubt he'd drive a state patrol car around for long. He'll look to grab another one, and we'll be on the lookout for any stolen vehicle reports."

Mitch motioned for Bartlett to move so he could exit the booth. They both slid out and shook hands with the officers. "If you get anything, and I mean anything, please call me right away, Bill."

"Just don't do anything stupid, Mitch. If you find Gruca, follow your own advice and get backup."

"Nothing stupid. I'm just going to play a hunch. I'll be in touch."

He and Dave left the restaurant and stood outside by Mitch's car in the parking lot. Bartlett stretched his arms into the air to loosen up, saying, "So what next, my friend? Where do we go from here?"

"We're not going anywhere. Like I told Bill, I've got a hunch. It's probably a long shot, but often my gut instincts are pretty good. I'm going to follow them."

"So, what's your gut say, Sherlock?"

"Often a killer, especially a serial killer, will revisit the scene of his crime. I'm thinking Gruca might do something like that...possibly return to one of the last places we'd likely look for him."

"Makes sense. Why don't I go with you, as a second set of eyes?"

"No way. This is not your bailiwick. Police business."

"Maybe I could help?"

"No offense, but it's more likely you'd get in the way. Either that or I would worry about you and then I would end up doing something stupid. I'll call Willy if I need backup."

Bartlett paused, disappointed. "All right, all right. I'll head home. You go get him yourself, tiger, but let me know right away if something breaks."

Mitch patted him on the shoulder, quickly got into his car, and headed back toward the lake.

CHAPTER 72

D ani's eyes slowly opened, then flew wide. She recoiled as she focused on the face of Gordon Gruca rising over her. He flashed a sardonic grin. "I can see you're wondering what's in store for you. All will soon be made clear."

Raising her head, she rolled her eyes around the room. She had no idea where they were, or how long they had been there. Laying face up on a bed, her hands were tied to opposite headposts, crucifix style. Her feet were tied with the same rough twine, stretching to opposite posts at the foot of the bed. She was wearing only a bra, naked from the waist down, her bottom half covered only by a comforter. He had neatly folded her clothes on a side chair across the room.

"First, I have some chores to do." He turned and walked over to a dresser near the bed, recalling to himself the events of Friday evening and early Saturday morning.

Having waited interminably in one of the computer cubicles in the Shoreline Inn lobby, he had almost given up when Dani walked through the entrance around 9:30. He rose, but then sat down abruptly when he saw a uniformed state policeman follow her into the hotel. The two briefly exchanged words he couldn't hear, then she boarded the elevator. As soon as the doors closed, Gruca hurried over to the counter, where the trooper was now speaking with the night clerk. Standing directly behind him, Gruca fiddled with his cell phone, pretending not to listen. The clerk handed Turner his key card, whispering the number, which Gruca was just barely able to hear.

When the trooper turned around, Gruca dropped the car keys he was holding and bent over so the officer couldn't see his face. As Turner walked toward the elevators, Gruca asked loudly, "What's the best restaurant nearby?" Hearing the elevator doors close, Gruca walked out, leaving the clerk's voice trailing off mid-answer.

He waited in his truck in the rear hotel lot until 3:30 a.m., then tripped the lock to the back entrance and made his way up the stairs, where he stood at the trooper's door listening for any sound of activity. Hearing none, he knocked loudly and waited for the cop to answer. When he heard the groggy trooper ask who it was, Gruca slurred in his best drunken ad lib, "Hey, Jim, I'm back. Let me in." He then produced a loud belch, banging even louder.

The voice inside answered, "This isn't Jim's room, mister. Go away!"

"C'mon, Jim. Let me in, man," Gruca slurred.

Turner angrily jerked the door open. "Look buddy, this isn't Jim's ro..." His rebuke was cut short by a powerful ridge chop to his throat, which shattered his hyoid bone. As Turner fell back holding his neck, Gruca punched him forcefully in the solar plexus, sending him to his knees, gasping. He then stepped into the room and looked back into the hall. Seeing no activity, he shut the door, grabbed Turner under the arms and dragged him—groaning and barely conscious—into the adjacent bathroom. There, Gruca quickly applied a headlock and strangled him.

Twenty minutes later he stood in front of the door to Dani's room, this time knocking gently. When no response came, he knocked again with slightly more force. He heard Dani ask, "Trooper Turner, is that you?"

"Yes, it's me." Gruca tried to muffle his voice. "Sorry to disturb you ma'am, but my captain called. I think you'll want to hear this." He lowered his face under his cap as he heard her approach the spy hole, knowing she couldn't see the ill-fitting uniform. Gruca smiled to himself as he heard the chain lock and door latch release.

Dani's smile turned to shock as she opened the door. Gruca swiftly grabbed her wrist and twisted her around with her arm behind her, forcing a gloved hand over her mouth. He lifted her up and shoved the door closed with his foot. Momentum propelled them as he carried her back into the room. He threw her face down onto the bed and jumped on top of her, pinning her arms to her sides with his knees. Dani kicked her legs wildly and opened her mouth to scream, but his weight pushed her breath away. As he pressed her face into the mattress with his forearm, Gruca pulled out a syringe, yanked the cap off with his teeth, and stabbed it into her neck. Then, he waited.

He carried Dani down the back stairs, stowed her in the front seat of the police cruiser, and returned for Turner's body. As he slogged with the deadweight down the same stairwell, he froze as he heard two people talking on the first floor below. Pulling his pistol from his belt, he waited until he heard their room door close, then he continued down the stairs and out to the lot. Once he had dumped Turner's body in the back seat of the car, he checked that Dani was still unconscious and drove off to the one place he felt sure no one would look for him. He had only one stop to make before he got there.

CHAPTER 73

It was difficult to see in the late afternoon twilight as Mitch tramped through the remains of the deserted strip mall. He had been searching the rental spaces one by one, with only two left to go. As he combed through the rubble in each, he prayed that his instincts were wrong and that he wouldn't find Dani's remains. So far, his prayer had been answered. He gritted his teeth as he entered the area where they first found Wheatley's bloodstained Mustang.

Using his flashlight to survey the open room from right to left, Mitch suddenly jerked the beam back to something protruding from under an old service counter. He held the light steady as he walked toward the object. As he drew closer, he realized it was a human foot sticking out from under a large piece of cardboard. Pulling the cardboard aside, he shone his light on the body of a man dressed only in undershorts, a T-shirt, and socks. He noticed bloody residue on the body's chin and mouth and quickly checked for a pulse. Finding none, he called the station to report the body, requesting an ambulance and CSI. Then he called Willy.

"Oh, hey Chief. What's up?" Willy sat slumped in his sweats on a sofa in his apartment's living room, dozing to the sounds of a late afternoon NFL game.

"Willy, I want you to meet me at the Atwood place right away."

"The beach house?" He bolted up. "What're we gonna do there, Chief?"

"I just found a body at the old Four Fronts Mall. I think it's the state trooper who was guarding Ms. Sparro."

"Jeez, a body? At the Four Fronts? That's where I found that lady's car last year."

"Yeah. I know. I'm pretty sure Gordon Gruca killed the trooper and left his body here, probably figuring we'd never guess he'd dump it in this place. I've got a hunch he may have Ms. Sparro at the Atwood place."

Willy hurried to his bedroom and began dressing, cell phone squeezed between his ear and shoulder. "Okay. I'll be on the road in five minutes, Chief."

"Let's meet in the lot of that park at the association's entrance. If you get there first, just wait for me."

"Sure thing, Chief." Willy threw his phone on the bed and grabbed his uniform shirt off a nearby chair.

The ambulance arrived at the scene first, but Mitch waited for the CSIs before leaving to meet Willy. It had begun snowing while he waited, and when he left, it was starting to cover the roads. He found Willy at the lot, sitting in his idling squad car, and parked next to him.

Willy turned off his car, got out, and slid inside

Mitch's vehicle. Closing the door, he huffed a cloud of breath, rubbing his hands together as he asked, "What's the plan, Chief?"

"I don't know if Gruca's even up there, but if he is, we need to be ready. I want you to head up the street with your headlights off. Park in one of the driveways across the road, then make your way up to that bluff next to Atwood's driveway. I will park on the opposite side and go around from behind, on the lake side. Once I get into position, I'll signal for you to come down. Then we'll move in." Mitch handed him a two-way radio.

"You'll have a good view of both front and back from there. If anyone tries to get away before I signal, use this two-way and let me know. Got it?"

"I'm on it, Chief." Willy cracked the door open and turned back to Mitch. "You know, I've never shot at anyone before—never even fired my gun on duty. Only at the range."

Mitch put a hand on Willy's arm, staring intently into his eyes. "We don't even know if anyone's in there, Willy. But if it is Gruca, just be careful. I know you'll do fine." Willy nodded, took a deep breath, and returned to his car. Mitch watched him pull out of the lot, then followed him up the street.

CHAPTER 74

Dani glared up at Gruca, straining to look defiant, intent on not betraying her fear. She concentrated on his facial features, hoping to later have the chance to describe him. His eyes drew her attention. Looking closely, she could see no distinction between iris and pupil, reminding her of pictures she had seen of sharks.

He grinned back at her intense stare. "They're not black." Dani flinched.

"My eyes. They only look black. It's a condition caused by an excess of the pigment melanin. They are actually dark brown, very dark. You can only tell the difference in bright light. I usually wear colored contacts, so as not to draw attention. And of course that helps with confusing descriptions."

She thought to humor him, all the while trying to work free from the ties on her ankles, hoping the comforter would hide her efforts. "You're very, uh, meticulous, Mr. Gruca." He raised an eyebrow. "Though your brilliant strategy for dealing with Lawrence Atwood failed." Dani bit her lip when her voice cracked ever so slightly, quickly continuing, "But of course you couldn't have foreseen what happened to him."

"Strategy? Hmm. Yes, it was brilliant, if I do say so. But then that little tramp schoolteacher had to ruin it. At least I was able to salvage the climax. It's almost comical that they still don't even know."

"Who doesn't know? What climax?"

"Well, I suppose it won't hurt, under the circumstances." He stepped over and sat on the side of the bed next to her, placing his hand on the comforter covering her stomach. She flinched as he looked her over.

"I suppose you could say anticlimax. But first things first. Mr. Atwood was a liar, and a cheat, and worse. He deserved to suffer for his sins, to be vilified and cleansed. I saw to it that he suffered the indignity of being charged for the murder of his whore, who was also deserving of atonement."

"No one deserves what you did to her," Dani said, clenching her teeth.

"It had to be extreme," he said indignantly. "The more brutal, the greater the tension between public outcry and the desperation of law enforcement to solve the crime."

"You burned her in that pit!"

He leaned in so that their faces were almost touching, lowering his voice. "That was the genius of my plan. It was critical to place the focus on Atwood. How better to link him than to place her remains there, at his house? But rest assured, she passed quickly … painlessly really."

Dani turned her face away, wincing in disgust.

"Admittedly, her death didn't go according to plan.

She started regaining consciousness and began to panic. So, I told her I was taking her to meet Atwood. I said that I was a client and needed to settle a debt he owed to me from one of his cases. I told her she was just my insurance policy, but she didn't believe me. She became hysterical, so I had to act. But it turned out to be fortuitous. Those children who found her car couldn't have done better if I'd directed them myself."

She sensed his gratification at someone hearing his story, and turned back to face him, determined to keep him talking. "But you left so much of her in the woods. Why?"

"Pure happenstance. I wasn't able to complete the task as quickly as I'd hoped. A neighbor returned to one of the homes across from Atwood's, and I didn't dare try to go back while they were there. As time passed, with the police making insufficient progress, I felt the need to hurry them along. So, I decided to give directions. It worked."

"And what about the anticlimax you mentioned?"

"That's the best part. I managed to appear for Atwood's grand eulogy service. The big shot attorney general and all the rest of them. They didn't even realize I was right there with them the whole time. I watched all of those sanctimonious politicians and lawyers fawn over Atwood, like he was some kind of hero."

Dani shook her head in disbelief. "But how? How could you manage that?"

Gruca paused. "Of course. You wouldn't know, would you? That was yesterday." Dani frowned in confusion; the last thing she remembered was Gruca charging into her hotel room.

"I simply borrowed that state trooper's uniform. You know, the one who was with you at the hotel? I took his cruiser, drove over to Atwood's memorial, and walked right into the church." Gruca chuckled at his own brazenness. "I've never been sure if I'm just supremely smart or the rest of you are supremely stupid."

Looking around, Dani noticed an alarm clock on the nightstand. The time was 4:45, so she assumed it must be Sunday afternoon. She couldn't believe that she had been unconscious any longer than a day.

"You've been drugging me! Where are we, and why am I here?"

"Almost exactly one year ago, Prudence Wheatley was lying right where you are now."

"This is Atwood's house on the lake?"

"Very good Danielle. Alright. I will indulge you a bit longer. It took a great deal of ingenuity, of course. They now surely think I am dead. I even left a note, and I mentioned you, Danielle."

"Me? Why? What about me?"

"They had to believe, and it occurred to me your Chief Quinn would lose his perspective if he thought you were in danger. So, I decided to orchestrate my own demise." He raised his eyes and hands upward. "I like that word, don't you? Orchestrate."

"But how? They would need a body to believe that."

"Of course. And they have one." He watched as her eyebrows furrowed. "I'll explain. There are any number of overpasses and alleys in the city where homeless men live out their days in anonymity, either drugged, drunk, or just mindless. Many are veterans, and lots of veterans have what I have."

When she looked perplexed, he rolled up his shirt sleeve, extending his arm to display the large tattoo.

Her eyes narrowed as she strained to make out what it was. Her mouth opened. "Is that a…"

He smiled and nodded. "A masterpiece, isn't it?"

"It looks like a monster, a fiendish rabbit monster."

"Not to me!"

She leaned closer. "It's ugly!"

"No matter. To believe, the police would also have to see a tattoo. Alan Redmond didn't know what mine looked like. That told me you didn't either, which meant neither did they. Whatever tattoo the body might have wouldn't matter. At least not for a while."

"How did you manage to…"

"It took a while to find a homeless vet who had one. He passed out after a bottle's worth of cheap vodka, so there was no struggle." He held his palms toward her. "I had to erase his fingerprints, of course. I used sandpaper and pumice stone. Afterward, I kept him in a kind of box I use."

"Box? What, like a freezer?"

"Not exactly. More like a casket. It just stored the body until it was needed. Disappointing that I'll now have to get another. I had to leave it with my pickup, along with two of my pets."

"You're insane."

Gruca's expression went blank, and he slipped one hand under the comforter, squeezing her thigh. She recoiled, but he gripped harder. "Don't get nasty, Danielle. You don't want to anger me."

He let go and rose from the bed. "I knew that Quinn and the others would compare the dead man's face to those pictures you and Alan Redmond showed around, so naturally I had to do something. A 20-gauge shotgun did the trick, and voilà, I was dead."

Dani's face contorted as she lowered her head then jerked it back up. "You said something about a note."

"Yes. Just a simple suicide note."

"Suicide? What does that have to do with me?"

"I said that I was taking you with me."

"But why? Atwood's dead, and you attended his service. You can leave now. That's what you do."

"Not this time, Danielle. Oh, I will go, and soon. But I do not intend to keep looking over my shoulder forever. That note assures Quinn will come after you."

"Why would he if he thinks we're both dead?"

"It will nag him. He'll have hope."

"When he finds you alive, he'll take you down."

He chuckled. "That won't happen."

"Oh? And how can you be so sure?" Dani hoped to keep him occupied, still working at the ties on her ankles.

"Look at what he's managed so far—nothing. I have no reason to suspect he'll improve." Gruca walked over to the dresser, picked up the Browning Buck Mark .22 pistol resting there, and stuck it in his belt. Then he grabbed the syringe and a small vial next to it, returning bedside with a widening grin.

"You had sex with Quinn in your hotel room. And he did not use a prophylactic, did he?" Her expression betrayed her. "I thought not. I did check the room after you left… when the maid went in to clean. I told her I had forgotten my watch. I found nothing."

"He flushed it down the toilet."

"I don't think so. Your rendezvous was not a planned event. And now you've confirmed what I suspected."

"So what?"

"So, a postmortem will disclose that you have Quinn's DNA inside of you. I've read that it can remain up to a few weeks, but certainly many days. I will make sure that your horrific end is linked to Quinn, and they'll have to investigate. That fight you two had outside the prosecutor's office was seen by a number of people."

Dani's face betrayed her shock. "How did you …?"

He laughed contentedly, "I was there. I was watching through the little window in the stairwell door when you ran away from Quinn. I nearly broke my leg jumping down to the next landing so you wouldn't see me. I have been following both of you all along. The back and forth has been a challenge, but I managed. Scanners help tremendously."

He began filling the syringe from the vial. "I have a few more things to do, so I have to sedate you again. Just hold still. It won't hurt."

Seeing the syringe, Dani recoiled, twisting and pleading. "Wait, wait. I need to know. The rabbits."

Gruca paused. "What about them?"

"Why do you…? What do they mean?"

"That's not your concern."

"But if you're going to … I mean, what does it matter if you tell me now?"

He looked away, then back at her. "I raise them. I mean, breed them."

"Then they're what, a hobby?"

"That, and more. They're a … reminder."

"Of what?"

"A man. A priest. He taught me all about cleansing,

that sinners must be cleansed. But he was a sinner himself, of the worst sort."

"He took the rabbits away from you at the orphanage, didn't he? What else did he do to you?"

Gruca stared at her. "That's enough. You're stalling."

"No. I want to know." Dani began trembling, then started to thrash.

"Nothing to be gained by trying to escape, Danielle. This will all be over soon. It will be quick, and I will make sure there is no pain. That's my tribute to your diligence."

Just then, Gruca saw her eyes dart to something behind him.

CHAPTER 75

Mitch parked at the last house on the opposite side of the woods bordering Atwood's property. He jogged around the back, then moved along the ridge above the beach. The increasing snowfall hindered visibility as he worked his way through the trees and brush. When he finally made out the rear of Atwood's house, he saw a slender beam of light cutting across the yard. The rest of the building was dark. Bending low to the ground, he ducked behind the short brick wall circling the patio.

When he reached the midpoint, Mitch peered over the edge. His heart leapt when he saw Dani through the slightly parted drapes of the master bedroom. Crawling closer, he peered in and saw that she was tied to the bedposts. Although he couldn't see the face of the man she was talking to, he knew it had to be Gordon Gruca. Surprisingly, they seemed to be having an almost casual conversation, as if nothing at all were wrong. He continued quickly around toward the entrance to Atwood's office and gripped the doorknob, confirming it was locked.

Mitch tried to focus on what his next move should be, but all that came to mind was the immediacy of Dani's predicament. He now wished that he had followed his own advice and called for backup. Concluding it was too late to expect a prompt response and knowing Dani could be killed at any moment, he rushed over to the side of the garage and called Willy on the two-way.

A muffled voice replied, "Chief? Is that you?"

He answered with his hands around his mouth. "Yes. Come on down here. I'm at the back corner, by the garage."

Willy quickly appeared through the veil of snowflakes. Mitch grabbed his shoulder. "Gruca's inside. He's got Dani tied up in the master bedroom. Remember? That's the room on the other end of the house, in back. I'm going to break in via Atwood's office, then let you in the front door. If anyone comes out before I get there, you stop them. Okay?" Willy nodded, and Mitch pushed him away.

In seconds he was back by the office. As quietly as he could, he used his pistol butt to break one of the small panes next to the doorknob. Reaching inside, he flipped the bolt, pushed the door open, stepped in, and gently pulled it shut. He stopped to listen, and hearing no sound, tiptoed out to the hall, then over to the foyer. Willy was standing outside, and Mitch quietly let him in, pressing a finger to his own lips in a shushing gesture. He motioned for Willy to stay there, whispering, "Don't let anyone get past you," and proceeded down the hall.

Stopping just outside the slightly parted door, he heard Gruca say, "I'll make sure there's no pain..." Mitch gritted his teeth and slowly pushed the door open, stepping into the room.

Gruca hovered over Dani, his back to Mitch. She leaned slightly and caught his eye. As Gruca turned to look over his shoulder, he drew the Browning. Dani then kicked her legs violently, breaking one leg free and striking Gruca's hip. He buckled and whirled around at her, firing off two quick shots. Mitch had raised his pistol, firing just as Gruca twirled back the other way. Gruca recoiled as the bullet struck him, falling back onto a nearby side chair. Rushing over to Dani, Mitch stopped cold at the sight of blood on her face. Meanwhile, Gruca had steadied himself, quickly lowering his head and pushing off the chair, he tackled Mitch, throwing him to the floor.

As they struggled, Willy burst into the room, shouting, "Chief, what's...?" He stopped at the sight of Mitch pinned to the floor face down, Gruca's arm around his neck in a chokehold. Mitch was using both hands, trying to loosen Gruca's grip. As Willy jerked up his gun to fire, Gruca quickly rolled Mitch over in front of him, still holding the pistol. Three more shots exploded in quick succession. Willy clutched his throat and fell to his knees, then sprawled to the floor, blood flowing from his open mouth.

Mitch struggled to pry Gruca's arm away. He rolled back over on top of him, striking at him with his elbow. One blow landed with a crunch, and Gruca's grip released. As Mitch tried to rise, Gruca swung at him with his .22, cutting into his scalp. Momentarily stunned, Mitch clutched at the wound. Gruca pushed up to his knees, slamming his pistol grip into the side of his opponent's head. Mitch groaned and dropped to the floor, limp.

Gruca stood up, wobbling. He peered down at Mitch lying prone beneath him, then aimed and fired two shots point-blank. Dani was still breathing, despite the blood oozing out of her upper chest. He aimed and fired again. Her head recoiled, then drooped onto the bed pillow. Seeing that Willy was sprawled unmoving on the floor, a pool of blood rapidly spreading beneath him, Gruca reached into his coat pocket, pulled out his keys, then strolled out of the room.

CHAPTER 76

"Mitch! Mitch! Wake up man!" Mitch could barely hear the words, as if they came from a great distance. He felt like he was spinning around in a dryer; his head was throbbing. The face in front of him slowly emerged, and he blinked his eyes to see Dave Bartlett kneeling over him. Shaking his head vigorously, he felt a sharp pain behind his left ear, then another pain in his side.

"Dave, what the...?" He said groggily, slowly looking around the room. They were alone.

"Where's Dani? And Willy? Are they okay?"

"They're in an ambulance, on their way to the hospital. It left a short while ago. They're both alive. We'll know more once they're examined."

"I should go..." Mitch rolled to get up but slumped dizzily.

Bartlett steadied him. "Whoa, boy! Take it easy. There's nothing you can do for them at this point. But tell me, what the hell happened here?"

"Gruca is what happened. He had Dani tied up, and he was going to kill her. Willy and I barged in and spoiled his party. I think I got him, though."

Bartlett looked across the room toward the door. "Well, judging from the blood trail, it didn't stop him. He was gone when I got here. I just found the three of you, and then I called for an ambulance."

"How did you come to...?"

Dave spoke over him. "Let's just say you're a lucky SOB that I don't take *no* for an answer." He propped Mitch as he sat up. "After our little discussion in the parking lot, I just couldn't let it go. I called the station on my way back. They tracked down Willy, and he told me what you were up to. I turned around and headed here, arriving just a bit too late."

"Good thing all around. But why am I still here?"

"The medics checked you over. They patched your side and said it would be alright for me to stay with you until another ambulance arrives. Should be just a few minutes...the weather's slowing them down. The wound in your side just cut through your spare tire."

"I don't have a spare tire!" Mitch grumbled, looking at the blood on his hand after rubbing his side.

Bartlett smirked. "At least you've still got a sense of humor. You've also got a cut and a good knot on your head but likely no concussion. Fact is I found you stretched out on your back. You must have passed out after you got whacked. Looks like he also shot you in the chest—twice—but the bullets lodged in your coat. What the hell is it lined with?"

"Kevlar. Old Army habit. I put it on just before we came up here."

"Good thing you did. You're all lucky Gruca was only using a .22, and none of you were hit in a place that would be fatal. Except for…" Bartlett caught himself too late.

"Except for what, Dave?"

"I'm sorry, Mitch. I didn't want to say anything. Dani took a shot to the head. She's in critical condition."

Mitch stared at the floor in silence, his head in his hand, praying that it wouldn't happen again. Then he forced himself to concentrate. "What time is it?"

Bartlett looked at his watch. "It's coming up on 9:40."

"What about Gruca? What's being done about him?"

"State police are on it. Bill Ryerson's got an APB out. But not much is going to happen in this blizzard. It's been snowing like crazy out there."

"I've got to get out there, Dave. He's getting away, and he's got a solid head start." Mitch pushed himself up to his feet, wobbling as he stood. His chest felt like he had been hit with a bat where the bullets hit the vest.

"You're in no condition to go anywhere right now, Mitch. Plus, we don't even know where he's headed. He could have gone in any number of directions."

"Any idea what he's driving?"

"Assuming you both drove squad cars up here, it's either yours or Willy's. There's a Ford Fusion in the garage, but I'm guessing that's stolen."

Just then CSI agent Chuck McNulty walked into the bedroom. "Hey, Mitch. You doin' okay?"

"Been better, but I'm okay, Chuck. Thanks."

"Well, it looks like your guy did some more damage, just a little while ago."

"Gordon Gruca?"

"Appears to be. Just came in over the scanner on my

way here. Sounds like he spun off the road up north of Kalkaska, and a state trooper stopped to check on him. Anyway, he really messed up that trooper. He didn't kill him, but he put him in ICU and took his car."

"Now we know what he's driving, and we know he's gone north. He's probably on 131, and he'll have to swing east sooner or later to get over to I-75." Mitch paused in contemplation. "If he keeps going in that direction, I'll bet he's headed for the bridge."

"No way!" Bartlett exclaimed. "Only a maniac would try crossing that bridge in a snowstorm, especially with the wind that's kicking up out there now."

"True. But that's what we're dealing with, a maniac. A very clever maniac. I bet he's counting on us dismissing the bridge as an option."

"Why is that?" said Dave.

"We'd never expect that he would try to cross the bridge in a blizzard. So, that's exactly what he'll try to do." He smacked Bartlett's shoulder. "Come on, let's go catch us a maniac."

CHAPTER 77

Bill Ryerson stood in the small study in his home, listening to Mitch Quinn over the phone as he and Dave Bartlett headed north to rendezvous with Ryerson's troopers. Mitch insisted that Gordon Gruca was going to try to cross one of the largest suspension bridges in the Western hemisphere in the middle of a nighttime blizzard. Mitch had called earlier to report the altercation at Atwood's, and Ryerson dispatched troopers to set up roadblocks on all of the east-west connectors from U.S. 131 to I-75.

"Mitch, I thought this guy is supposed to be a real genius? Heading for the bridge is about the dumbest thing anyone could do on a night like tonight. Wouldn't the smart thing be to hide out somewhere and start up again early tomorrow?"

"Maybe so. But Gruca has managed to outfox everyone by doing the unexpected, and my gut tells me that is exactly what he's going to do now. I wouldn't have your guys out in the middle of a snowstorm like this if I didn't feel pretty damned sure I'm right."

"I owe you one or two from way back, Mitch, so I'll keep my guys out there a while longer. But if we don't have anything in the next couple hours, I'm going to hang it up until morning. I've notified local police north of the bridge, so they'll be on the lookout at the other end. On this side there are only three main roads directly accessing I-75, leading to the bridge from the south and west, and he has got to come in from that direction. He can't make it there on any county roads in this weather. I've also got four of my men guarding the bridge itself, so if he's planning on crossing, he'll have to go through our blocks. I just can't imagine he'll try it, though."

"Thanks, Bill. Much appreciated." Mitch hung up and glanced over at Bartlett. "He's got a hell of a head start on us but getting stuck off the road and his run-in with that trooper had to slow him down. Regardless, we'll really have to press."

"Hopefully, those troopers will have him in custody by the time we get there," said Bartlett.

CHAPTER 78

G ruca had stopped on the roadside a few miles from the bridge, contemplating his next moves. The snowfall had become sporadic, but when he saw the police flashers ahead, he turned around and left the highway to weigh his options. The bullet wound in his shoulder was throbbing. He had applied ointment and gauze from the first-aid kit in the trooper's car, temporarily stopping the bleeding, and he hoped to cross the bridge before having to dress the wound again.

Because of unanticipated delays, it had taken much longer to get here than he had planned. The fact that they were waiting for him meant one of those he had left at Atwood's must have survived. But they would be looking for a police cruiser. Someone driving a late model Chevy pickup, which he had taken from its owner as he was closing his bar in a small town to the south, shouldn't be suspicious. Nonetheless, if he was going to be able to access the bridge, he would have to come up with a believable story as to why he was out in this blizzard.

Gruca thought about how he would deal with the officers manning the vehicles, then get across the bridge before help could arrive. Concluding they would not just let him cross, he decided to take them head-on, pretending to be a local resident headed home. He tapped the ten-shot Browning .22 resting in his shoulder holster. Then he pulled out the Glock 17 he had taken from the trooper, laying it on the passenger seat. He had been delighted to find it had a fully loaded, high-capacity magazine. An even bigger surprise was the AR-15 rifle he found in the trunk when he was looking for the first aid kit, not to mention all the extra magazines. It now lay within easy reach, butt propped against the console.

After twenty minutes of cogitation, he pressed the accelerator and drove back onto the main highway leading to the bridge. As he drew nearer, he saw that the tall lamp-posts lining both sides of the traffic lanes on the bridge were all turned off, leaving only the city area illuminated. There were four cars parked in front of both the entrance and exit lanes. He noted one trooper in the first car and two in the second, all talking to one another through their open windows. Pulling in front of the closest vehicle, he waved, hoping to lure the cop out into the street. The officer responded by waving him on, but Gruca stayed put. After ignoring a second animated arm wave, Gruca watched as the officer got out and abruptly plodded toward him as he rolled down his window.

"Sir, you'll have to move along. The bridge is closed due to the storm."

Gruca quickly scanned the area around the vehicles.

The two closest were in a "V" formation, pointing away from the bridge's on-ramp. The other two were slightly behind him and unmanned. He quickly considered options for how to get past the cops themselves: whether to take them out now or try to get a running start and drive around. Behind them he could now see all the traffic lanes were also blocked by large sawbucks, which would inhibit his escape. If he got out to move the bucks, the three policemen would surely try to stop him. Even if he managed to get past them, they would give chase, and he wasn't sure what the traction would be like driving over the bridge. Nor did he know what was waiting for him on the other side. If he left these three alive, they could warn anyone waiting at the other end. Then he would be trapped.

He smiled gratuitously at the impatient trooper. "Oh, I wondered why all the lights were out. I'm not planning to cross…just headed home. I was just over at a friend's house for the game. But I'm curious though, do you typically have this many police cars out just for the bridge closing due to a snowstorm?"

The cop hesitated. "Well, no sir. There was some trouble downstate. Fact is, we're looking for a fugitive who's pretty dangerous. He's supposed to be headed this way, so you'd better get on home now."

"Okay, officer. Thank you." He watched as the trooper started to return to his car. He then stopped, turned around, and took a step back toward the truck. "By the way, who won?"

"Won?"

"The game you were watching. Who won?"

Gruca had no idea who had even been playing, but the question made up his mind for him. In a split second, he grabbed the Glock, propped the barrel on the windowsill, and opened fire. Almost the entire burst of shots hit the officer point-blank, and his body flew back onto the road. Gruca reached over, grabbed the AR-15, threw open his door and stood behind it as the other two policemen began to move. Again, steadying the gun on the open window, he fired into the closest car first, immediately killing the second policeman. He then swiveled the barrel at the third, who was climbing out of his car as he drew his weapon. Gruca emptied the magazine, and the man dropped lifeless.

Gruca hurriedly began to clear the bodies so he could back one of the cars out of the way. He placed them in the trunks of the two cars, looking around in the process for any activity. He was relieved to see the streets remained deserted and quiet. As he got behind the wheel of one of the patrol cars, he noticed a distant beam of light barely visible through the now-thick curtain of falling snow. Gunning the car into reverse, he backed it quickly into the far outgoing lane, jerked to a stop, and ran over to take down one of the sawbucks. He failed to see another trooper approaching from down the street.

CHAPTER 79

M itch had slowed to a crawl, barely able to see two car lengths ahead as millions of tiny snow-bullets shot directly at his windshield. "Shit Dave, I can't see anything but white. Keep your eyes peeled on the side of the road and tell me if you see I'm going off." For the past half hour, they had taken advantage of a break in the storm, making great time, and he knew they were getting close to the bridge. If he stayed on the highway, they would run right into it.

"I think I see the lights of the town up there, Mitch." Bartlett squinted to make out the yellowish glow ahead of them.

Suddenly the snowflakes quit their assault, and the big bridge emerged into view. As they drew closer, they could see a parked pickup truck in front of a number of police cars, all but one of which had their lights flashing. Bursts of light flared alternately from behind one of the patrol cars on the left and a man crouching by a stand of trees far to the right. Mitch lowered his window, letting in the sounds of intermittent popping. "Those are gunshots! Who's shooting at who? Can you tell?"

Bartlett opened his door and stepped out to get a better look. Just then the glass in the window beside him exploded, and he lunged back inside, both legs hanging out below the door. He looked up at Mitch, whose head was ducked down behind the steering wheel. "Where'd that come from?" Dave demanded.

Mitch peered carefully over the dashboard. "I'm pretty sure it came from the direction of the patrol cars."

"The cops are shooting at us? We're in a police car, for Christ's sake."

"I can't see whoever is behind those cars, but I'm pretty sure that's a state trooper over on the right, by those trees." Another burst of bullets shattered the front window just above Mitch's head. "Close your door, Dave! I'm moving us over to the guy I think is on our side."

Bartlett drew his legs up inside and huddled as low as he could, knees in the footwell as he pulled the door shut with a *thud*. Mitch stepped hard on the accelerator, and they fishtailed across the street in front of the parked cars, sliding to a stop a half block past the trooper's position. "Stay in the car," Mitch said, breathing heavily. "I'm gonna go see if I can help."

As he opened the driver's side door, the rear window shattered apart, the car's frame rattling with thunks as bullets hit the trunk and rear bumper. Dave threw the other door open. "The hell if I'm staying in here. I'm coming with you!" The two of them ran crouching along the street to join the officer, who stared cautiously back at Mitch.

"I'm Mitch Quinn, chief of police in Lakeview

Village. I've been working with Captain Ryerson to get that guy shooting at us. What's your name?"

"Trooper Delaney. Paul Delaney."

"Are you alone here?"

"I wasn't alone before. There were four of us on a stakeout. I went up the street to take a leak, and when I came back, I saw that guy over there wearing a trooper's coat. At first, I thought he was one of the guys I was with, but when I yelled out at him, he started shooting at me. Then you guys got here. I have no idea where my friends are."

Mitch looked over at him. "I expect the answer's not good. The man shooting at us is Gordon Gruca. We'll need help. Is anyone else available nearby?"

"Only the bunch o' troopers at the other end of the bridge, but that's almost five miles from here."

"They'll have to do. Can you call them now, tell them to come over as quickly as they can? And alert them to be ready for Gruca. Meanwhile, I'll try to get into a better position. Give me some cover when I move." He turned to Bartlett. "Dave, this time stay put. No need to give Gruca another target." Mitch then crawled through the snow toward a large stone monument at the street corner, the trooper simultaneously opening fire and reaching for his phone.

Gruca had quickly reloaded magazines, pondering his next move. He had seen two men exit the police car which just arrived, meaning bad odds if he stayed where he was. If he went for the truck, he would be in the open, giving them a clear shot at him. The front tires on the patrol car providing cover had been shot flat during the exchange. Judging by the cops' position, it appeared the other car with lights flashing was partially blocked from their view. Making up his mind, he ran for it, hopped inside, and drove around the sawbuck onto the bridge.

Mitch stood up, looking after Gruca, then yelled back at the trooper, "He's making a run for it on the bridge. I'm after him. Get those guys going on the other end!" Delaney was already on the line, yelling at the officers to approach from both sets of traffic lanes and to stop the police vehicle coming from the opposite direction.

Hoping to find keys inside, Mitch jumped behind the wheel of the truck. He was relieved when he saw them hanging in the ignition and immediately took off after Gruca. As he sped up over the steel grating roadway, he could barely see the cruiser lights flashing ahead as a blinding curtain of snow suddenly fell across his view. He could tell that Gruca had also slowed down, continuing gradually over the bridge.

His cell rang. When he pulled it out, Bartlett's number lit up on the screen.

"What's going on out there, Mitch?"

"I'm about a mile or so out, I'm guessing. Visibility isn't for shit. I can barely see those flashers in the distance, but it's hard to ... damn it!"

"What's wrong, Mitch?"

"The flashers went out, and I can't see a thing. Only white everywhere in front of me. I'm slowed to a crawl. Any word on those other troopers?"

"Delaney's been on and off his cell with them since you left. They took off right away, so it can't be too long until they run into Gruca."

"I'm on the same side of the roadway as him, and the divider is too big for him to drive over. If he tries to turn around, he'll run right into me, so we've got him. There's nowhere else for him to go... wait a minute."

"What is it?"

"It's Gruca's car. It's stopped not far ahead of me."

"Watch it, Mitch. He could just be waiting for you."

Mitch slid the truck to a stop, headlights illuminating the parked vehicle looming in front of him. Getting out, he waded forward through the drifting snow piles, crouching low with his pistol drawn. As he drew closer, he spotted footprints and a slight blood trail leading away from the open driver's door into the darkness. Unsnapping his flashlight from his belt, he followed the tracks across the divider into the opposite lanes. Mitch blinked hard against the waves of flurries, wiping his eyes with his sleeve. His field of vision switched from white to black with the gusting wind.

Suddenly the white curtain lifted, and a silhouette appeared just ahead. Mitch pointed his beam at the figure perched on the guard rail, facing the lake. Gruca turned his head slowly back to Mitch, and the two men stared at each other, motionless.

Mitch broke the silence. "There's no place to go, Gruca. Get off that rail and put your hands up where I can see them." The wind gusting forced him to yell.

Gruca returned a sardonic smile. "You must be lucky Quinn. I thought for sure I'd seen the last of you."

"You underestimated me."

"It won't happen again."

"You can bet your ass it won't. Now get down off the railing."

Gruca didn't move. "Tell me, did your lady love make it? Must have, otherwise you'd have shot me already."

Quinn ground his teeth together, finger pressing on the trigger. "Dani's alive. So is Willy. Now, if you don't do what I say, I will shoot you, and it's a long fall to the lake."

Gruca laughed loudly, but it was barely audible in the howling wind. "I'm afraid I can't do that. You see, I have another matter I must attend to."

"Whatever. Just get down from the railing, with your hands up."

"This is just a farewell, Quinn." Gruca shouted. "We'll meet again." With that, he jerked away.

A white curtain snapped shut just as Mitch fired. When the blowing snow cleared, Gruca had disappeared. Rushing to the railing, Mitch peered over into a black void.

He twisted at the muffled sound of sirens, the flashers of state police cars slowly appearing as they approached from the other side. Within moments the lights from two cars gleamed through the blowing snow, and he heard the shouts of troopers. "Who's out there? Come over here with your hands in the air!"

"I'm the Lakeview Village police chief, Mitch Quinn."

"We'll believe that when we see you. Like I said, come over here with your hands up."

Mitch did as he was told, identifying himself to the four troopers facing him.

"I'm the officer in charge, Deputy Mike Malloy." He stooped down and pointed his light closer to the ground. "Looks like you hit him, Chief Quinn. That's blood."

"Mm, hum," Mitch grunted in response.

"Where'd he go?"

"Over here." Mitch turned, and the group followed

him back to the bridge rail. Their flashlight beams high-lighted more blood spots, showing brilliant red against the snow.

Malloy peered over the edge. "Well, sure looks like that's the end of him, Chief. There's no place to go but down from here."

"We should get a boat out and search for him," said Mitch.

"Not in this storm, Chief. We wouldn't find him anyway, not even his body. From here, that's almost a two-hundred-foot drop, almost twenty stories. Even if the fall didn't kill him, the water will. It's got to be about fifty degrees now. He wouldn't make it to shore swimming. Hell, the current in the straits down there would make it impossible for an Olympian. He's a goner for sure."

They all started trudging back to their cars.

"His body will eventually turn up on shore some-where. They always do."

"Always?"

"Yep. Suicides mostly. Maybe a dozen people have used the bridge. They all wash up sooner or later. He will too . . . maybe not until spring, though."

Malloy turned and disappeared into the veil of snow, his voice trailing after him. "You can talk to Captain Ryerson about it in the morning. I'm going home to bed, Chief. Good doin' business with ya."

EPILOGUE

May 2010. Early morning.

*M*itch stood deep in thought in the pine-paneled kitchen
of his small fishing cabin. Dani was sleeping in the
single bedroom; they had been staying there the past few
weeks while she recovered. She had been shot three times,
two bullets hitting her upper chest and shoulder, one bullet
shattering her cheekbone. The surgeon said that, had
Gruca's aim been ever so slightly higher, the result would
have been fatal. Hospitalized for weeks afterward, Dani
then rehabbed in a nearby nursing facility. Mitch visited
her regularly and invited her to stay at the cabin once she
was released. It didn't take much coaxing. He had promised to take care of her, and he kept his word, taking a
leave of absence.

Gordon Gruca's body was not recovered, despite an
exhaustive search. The police working the case up near
the bridge finally gave up, again assuring Mitch that the
body would eventually wash ashore. This didn't prevent

him from wondering if Gruca had somehow managed to escape. He kept telling himself the odds were against it, but he appreciated the monster was incredibly resourceful.

Willy had survived, but he had been shot in the throat, the bullet cutting through his larynx, severely damaging his vocal cords. Unable to speak much at first, he retired from the Lakeview police force. Mitch appealed to the county circuit court, and they hired Willy as a process server and part-time courtroom bailiff.

The election season was gaining momentum. Mitch had followed Rob Patterson's campaign for governor, his victory seeming all but inevitable since the Democrats couldn't come up with another candidate nearly as appealing as Lawrence Atwood. Meanwhile, Dave Bartlett was back at his job, busily preparing for another run at keeping his own position as county prosecutor. Mitch himself remained as the Lakeview chief of police, receiving commendations from both the Lakeview Village board and the local Rotary Club for his efforts in tracking down the serial killer Gordon Gruca.

The faint murmur of his name being called broke his concentration. He followed the sound through the living room, then stepped into the open doorway to the bedroom where Dani was stretching awake. Beaming, he asked teasingly, "Yes, madam? How can I be of service?"

"I was just checking to make sure you were still here, Chief Quinn," Dani replied in a Southern drawl. "As for being of service, we'll see about that later. But for now, a cup of coffee will do."

Mitch sat down on the edge of the bed and took her hands, responding in his best John Wayne imitation,

"Whatever you'd like, little lady." Then he leaned over and kissed her softly on the lips. She looked up at him, reaching her arms around his neck.

"Is all the bad finally over, Mitch?"

He smiled back, still kidding. "No worries, little lady. The Duke has saved the day."

Taking his face in her hands, she pulled him closer. "I'm serious. Please tell me everything's all right now."

Mitch laid his fingers on her forehead and gently brushed her hair back. "Yes, Dani. It's all over. Now we heal—together."

"I just wish we could be sure. You know ... that he's gone, forever."

"Tell you what ... I haven't talked with Bill Ryerson in a while. I'll call him and check in. Maybe they've found Gruca's body."

He kissed her and stood up. "But first, let's get that cup of coffee you asked for. This little inn has the best around."

Mitch grabbed his phone from the coffee table as he passed through the living room, shouting over his shoulder, "I think we should take a longer walk in the woods today, Dani. It would be good for you. We can go over to the inland lake. It's pretty cloudy now, but I think the sun's coming out."

She snuggled down into the bedcovers and yelled after him, "Why, Chief Quinn, I think you're just looking for a way to wear down my resistance."

As he entered the kitchen, he punched in Ryerson's number from his contact list. When the dispatcher said the captain was in a meeting, Mitch asked for the number *of the St. Ignace police station. Moments later, Deputy Malloy was on the line.*

"Hello, Chief Quinn?"

"Yes, it's me. I was calling just to see if you've located Gruca's body yet."

"Nope, nothing yet. Sorry Chief. I'll make sure to call you right away if anything turns up."

"Thanks. I appreciate it." He started to hang up, but hesitated. "There's no way he could have made it, is there Malloy? I mean, he couldn't possibly have gotten to shore alive, right?"

"I can't see how, Chief. That's at least a two-mile swim to the closest shore."

"And there is no other way down, is there? It's the road or the water ... that's it?"

"That's it. The only other way off is up."

Mitch grinned.

"That is, I suppose you could ..." Malloy's voice trailed off.

"Could what?"

"Well, there's substructure underneath the top level of the bridge. There are beams below, both horizontal and vertical, which support the upper bridge. But it's got to be at least twenty feet or so, probably more, from one level to the next."

"I don't get it. What are you saying?"

"Oh, I suppose, if the conditions were right. I mean, if the weather was decent, it's conceivable someone could make his way over the rail, shimmy down one of the vertical beams to the horizontal beams below and, well, they go all the way to shore. Almost like a walkway. But I don't

see how it could have been done that night, what with the ice and snow on the bridge. No sir."

"You're saying it would have been impossible?"

"I guess you could say anything's possible. But I just do not think there's any way Gruca got out alive. Trust me, chief. His body will wash up some day."

Mitch thanked Malloy, hung up, and started preparing a fresh pot of coffee. Leaning back against the counter as it brewed, he pondered Malloy's description of the bridge, committing himself to do a search for pictures on his laptop. When the coffee maker signaled ready, he turned to grab cups from a standing rack on the countertop. Looking out the window above the sink as he began to pour, he could barely see the lake through the surrounding trees. The light snow from the night before was melting as the sun began peeking through the breaking cloud cover.

Something caught his eye as he scanned the woods. He leaned forward and squinted, trying to focus on a spot about fifty feet from the corner of the cabin. His eyes widened, and he jolted upright, spilling the contents of his cup onto the counter. Sitting out among the pines nibbling leaves was a large white rabbit. Mitch stood frozen as the coffee cup slipped from his fingers and shattered on the floor. Whispering to no one, he said, "It's not over, Dani ..."

THE BEGINNING

ACKNOWLEDGMENTS

I owe a sincere debt of gratitude to many individuals who volunteered their valuable time and experience in assisting me in my efforts. Foremost among them is Andrew Voelker, a bright and talented author, the first to read my initial manuscript, who encouraged me every step of the way with positive suggestions for improvement. To Terry Dillon, an exceptional criminal trial lawyer, who schooled me on the fine points of the interplay between law enforcement and the criminal justice system. To Scott Devon, a gifted and incredibly imaginative writer, who motivated me by his example. To Lisa Smith, for listening and introducing me to the little-known and fascinating realm of rabbit breeding. To Dawn Orr and Eric Bazzett for their critical technical assistance during development. Especially to the entire team at Mission Point Press, led by Doug Weaver, each one of whom offered essential expertise in publishing this work. And most of all to my wife, Carol, who persuaded me to write, put up with me when I did, sustained me when I waivered and endured my many frustrations as I brought this initial novel to a finish.

ABOUT THE AUTHOR

A recovering trial lawyer, certified arbitrator, mediator and law professor, Lincoln Cooper lives in Southwest Michigan with his wife, who persuaded him to write after years of temptation. His infrequently indulged passions include boating, skiing, traveling, golfing and reading, punctuated with an excellent scotch, good friends and family, stimulating conversation, and a magnificent Lake Michigan sunset.

CPSIA information can be obtained
at www.ICGtesting.com
Printed in the USA
FSHW010004061221
86713FS